W9-ACU-271

"The pacing is steady and the action plentiful, while the plot is full of twists and the passion . . . is hot and electrifying."　　　　　　—*RT Book Reviews* (4 stars)

"Absorbing and edgy . . . an enthralling read."
　　　　　　—Lara Adrian, *New York Times* bestselling
　　　　　　author of *A Touch of Midnight*

"Grabs you by the heartstrings from the first page. . . . [The] complexity of emotion is what makes Laura Wright's books so engrossing."
　　　　　　—Sizzling Hot Book Reviews

"If you haven't experienced this series yet, you are totally missing out."　　　　　—Literal Addiction

"Enough twists that leave one anxious for the next in the series."　　　　　　—Night Owl Reviews

"Laura Wright has done it again and totally blew me away."　　　　　　—Book Monster Reviews

"Very sexy."　　　　　　　　　　—Dear Author . . .

"A sweep-off-your-feet romance."
　　　　　　—Leontine's Book Realm

"A must read."　　—The Romance Readers Connection

"Deeply satisfying."　　　　—*Sacramento Book Review*

"Certain to make it onto your list of favorite books and will leave you thirsty for more."
　　　　　　—Romance Reviews Today

"Page-turning tension and blistering sensuality."
　　　　　　—*Publishers Weekly* (starred review)

Also by Laura Wright

The Cavanaugh Brothers Series

Branded

Mark of the Vampire Series

Eternal Hunger
Eternal Kiss
Eternal Blood
(A Penguin Special)
Eternal Captive
Eternal Beast
Eternal Beauty
(A Penguin Special)
Eternal Demon
Eternal Sin

BROKEN

THE CAVANAUGH BROTHERS

Laura Wright

A SIGNET ECLIPSE BOOK

SIGNET ECLIPSE
Published by the Penguin Group
Penguin Group (USA) LLC, 375 Hudson Street,
New York, New York 10014

USA | Canada | UK | Ireland | Australia | New Zealand | India | South Africa | China
penguin.com
A Penguin Random House Company

First published by Signet Eclipse, an imprint of New American Library,
a division of Penguin Group (USA) LLC

First Printing, October 2014

ISBN 978-0-451-46499-6

Printed in the United States of America
10 9 8 7 6 5 4 3 2 1

PUBLISHER'S NOTE
This is a work of fiction. Names, characters, places, and incidents either are the
product of the author's imagination or are used fictitiously, and any resemblance
to actual persons, living or dead, business establishments, events, or locales is
entirely coincidental.

To Isa. My sweet, horse-loving girl.

BROKEN

Diary of Cassandra Cavanaugh

May 2, 2002

Dear Diary,

I saw Sweet again today. This time, it was outside the diner and we only got to talk for a second or two because he had to go somewhere. But it was enough for him to ask me to meet him later out by Carl Shurebot's old place. I CAN'T WAIT! I've never felt so excited about anything in my whole life. He's just so cute. So DIFFERENT. He doesn't look like the other boys around here, with their mud-caked boots and Wrangler jeans. Sweet looks like one of those surfer guys on TV. And every time he smiles at me, my cheeks feel hot.

I asked him why I hadn't seen him around River Black before. Everybody knows everybody in this town. But he didn't answer me. He had to go. But I'll ask him tonight. That, and what his real name is.

Maybe it's something like Tristan or Brad or Dillon.

Ahhhhh! What if he doesn't want to tell me? He seems to like me calling him Sweet, just like I like him calling me Tarts. (Note to self: Go by the dime store today and get some of our favorite candy for tonight!) I guess I could ask my brothers, see who's new in school. But then they'd start asking me questions, and I REALLY don't want them in my business. They'll ruin everything. They'll say he's too old for me, and they'll tell Mom and Dad.

I don't think he's too old for me. He can't be more than eighteen, and I'm almost fourteen. It's perfect. He's perfect. I still haven't said anything to Mac about him.

Is that bad?

I'll report back later,
Cass

One

"Lemon's the clear winner, right?"

Before Sheridan could answer, Mackenzie Byrd shoved another forkful of cake into her mouth. This time, rich, creamy chocolate assaulted her tongue. *Very nice.* But frankly, you couldn't go all that wrong when it came to chocolate. Unless, of course, it was covering up grasshoppers or scorpions or whatever the crazy insect-eating population was pairing with their cocoa these days.

She swallowed, licked her lips, and then reached for her napkin—which had been folded into a lovely bird of paradise by the owner, Albert Lee, and set next to her plate as soon as she'd taken a seat.

Mac stared expectantly across the white wicker table at her. "So? What do you think? Raspberry, lemon, or chocolate?"

Sheridan noted the look of panic on the forewoman's face, and wondered once again how she'd been roped into cake tasting with her boss's fiancée. Oh, that's right. She'd been strolling down the street—her first time strolling, mind you, but it had felt like the right thing to do in the small town—when a hand had suddenly shot out of Hot Buns Bakery, curled around her arm, and yanked her inside the oh-so-precious pink-and-white establishment.

"Well?" Mac pressed good-naturedly, pushing the brim of her Stetson back off her forehead. "Thoughts? I need them. Normally I have them. But today, for some reason, it's just blank upstairs."

A smile touched Sheridan's lips. She really liked Mackenzie Byrd. The dark-haired, blue-eyed, ever-grinning forewoman of the Triple C Ranch was funny and smart and took no shit from anyone— male or female—which was an attribute Sheridan wholeheartedly admired. In fact, in another life, where Sheridan didn't work for the man she worked for, she and Mac might've been friends. But she did work for Deacon, and friendship wasn't something she allowed herself to invest in. Either with time or her emotions. She'd grown up, maybe even hardened, watching her mother invest so deeply in her father's happiness and career only to be destroyed when he'd walked out on them. Determined to never risk her heart, she'd looked at all relationships as a distraction to her schooling, her work, and her goals. Sometimes it got lonely.

But Sheridan would always choose loneliness over destruction.

"They're all excellent," she offered in a professional tone.

Mac groaned and held her fork above her head, the tines stained with bits of frosting. "I know. But which one is the best?"

Chocolate, chocolate, chocolate. "That's really for you to decide, Miss Byrd."

Dropping back in her chair, Mac's eyes narrowed. "Sheridan, seriously, you can't call me that. We've talked about this."

The small smile that had touched Sheridan's lips a moment ago expanded into a full-fledged grin. She couldn't help it. She liked this woman. "You and Mr. Cavanaugh are engaged. I am his employee. In my very corporate world, there's no fraternizing with the boss's family. Or those who are soon to be family."

"Oh Lord have mercy," Mac said with an eye roll.

"And forgive me for saying so, Miss Byrd," Sheridan continued, "but isn't this something you should be doing with Mr. Cavanaugh?"

"As you very well know, Deacon's in Dallas for the next couple of days. This needs to get done." A slight wickedness flashed in her blue eyes. "And as his right hand, his most trusted employee—"

"Oh dear."

Mac laughed. "Come on, you know what he likes."

"As do you, I'm sure."

"He's abandoned me in my time of need, Sheridan," Mac said dramatically. "This wedding is less than three weeks away, and things like cake and flowers and food need to be decided on. Am I supposed to make all the decisions alone?"

"I believe some women would find that a blessing, Miss Byrd." *I know I would.* "Total control of the remote, so to speak."

Mac snorted. "I'm not that kind of woman, Sheridan. Now, if we're having beef for the fancy dinner, that I can pick out and drive right on over to the butcher." She paused for a moment as Hot Buns's head baker sidled up to their table and set a sizable piece of coconut cake between them.

"Wow, Natalie," Mac exclaimed, taking in the layers and the fluffy white coconut. "This looks amazing. I'll never decide."

"Maybe you should call off the wedding, then?" Natalie replied softly.

Both Mac and Sheridan glanced up at the dark-eyed woman, who was somewhere around Mac's age.

"I'm sorry; what did you say?" Mac asked, confused.

Natalie looked sheepish. Her eyes pinned to the table, she ran her hand through her short blond hair, which was cut in a cute pixie style. "I'm kidding. Of course." She swallowed tightly, then turned around and walked back toward the kitchen.

Sheridan stared after her. "Strange woman."

"Yep. Even back when we were in school," Mac remarked. "But she makes a mean doughnut. And a killer pumpkin-spice cupcake. And, of course, regular cake. She's a bakery genius."

Turning to face the forewoman once again, Sheridan laughed. "Well, then, she's excused. Geniuses are exempt from normality. You know . . . she could help you with your wedding plans. A school friend might be just the thing."

"Natalie isn't a friend," Mac clarified. "Wasn't back when we were in school either."

"Okay. Then maybe someone from the Triple C . . ."

"My closest friend is Blue." Sobering, she released a heavy sigh. "And he's run away from home."

"Right." While she didn't know the details of the newest Cavanaugh brother's exit to parts unknown, Sheridan knew enough to be sympathetic. "I'm sorry about that. I know you two are very close."

Mac's eyes went kitten-wide. "Don't say you're sorry. Say you'll be my wingman."

The woman was relentless. "Miss Byrd—"

"Mac," she corrected.

"You're really stubborn, you know that?"

She snorted. "Hell yes, I know. Part of my charm." She wiggled her eyebrows. "And this no-fraternizing-with-the-boss's-relatives business ain't gonna work anyway."

"Oh?" Sheridan said, her gaze flickering traitorously toward the coconut cake. She loved coconut cake. Made a pretty decent one herself. Maybe strange-genius Natalie could teach her a thing or two. "Why's that?"

"Well, James won't like you calling him *Mr.* Cavanaugh when he's kissing on you now, will he?"

Heat slammed into Sheridan's cheeks, and the entire bakery seemed to shrink around her. "Wh-what?"

Dipping her fork into the coconut cake, Mac's grin widened. "Oh, come on, Sheri."

Sheri? And . . . *James*? KISSING ON HER? What the hell was happening? This town and several of its residents were getting to her, making her appear soft. Making her forget why she had come to River Black. Work. For her boss, Deacon Cavanaugh. To further her career. Not to forge friendships or get caught up in dramas, imaginings, or, for God's sake, wedding plans!

Sitting up just a little bit straighter, Sheridan said in her most controlled voice, "I'm here to work, Miss Byrd. I'm not dating anyone. Especially not James. Er"—she cleared her throat—"Mr. Cavanaugh."

To be fair, she had noticed James Cavanaugh. Frankly, one would have to be blind not to. The man was decidedly handsome and rugged. He worked with horses, for heaven's sake, and knew his Shakespeare. That was a serious quadruple threat. But professionalism demanded that noticing was as far as it went. No dating. No kissing.

As she studied Sheridan, Mac slid another forkful of coconut cake into her mouth. "So, what you're saying is, he hasn't asked you out?"

Good Lord. *Grant me patience.* "I'm not saying anything," Sheridan answered quickly and with the slightest hitch of irritation. "And of course he hasn't asked me out."

But instead of picking up on the frustration, Mac looked utterly perplexed. "Really? I mean, how is that possible? I swear, whenever you're around, the guy can't keep his eyes off you, or his tongue inside his mouth."

"That's not true," Sheridan said tightly. But she couldn't stop the foolish and juvenile voice inside her that was already wondering if it were. Lord, if Deacon were to ever think she was interested in his brother, her position could be jeopardized. And she'd worked way too hard to endanger her career—not to mention her heart—over a rugged horse-whispering man with a pretty face.

A *very* pretty face, her inner voice persisted.

Sheridan mentally rolled her eyes at herself.

Thankfully, something caught Mac's attention out the window and she turned away. "Well, well," she said in a near-purr. "Speak of the devil."

Sheridan followed her line of vision and promptly forgot her middle name. *What was it? Dorie? Donna?*

"Holy cripes," Mac said, shaking her head.

"He's got one of the mustangs out. Is he nuts? Riding that stallion down Main Street like he was a tame little pony driving to Sunday service."

Sheridan's pulse jumped and her skin tightened around her muscles. *Delilah? Danielle? Oh, that was it. Sheridan Danielle.* Her eyes widened. A man was riding down the street atop a very rebellious-looking black-and-white horse. No. Not a man. A cowboy. No. Not a cowboy. The *hottest* cowboy she'd ever seen in her life. Probably the hottest cowboy in existence. Dressed in jeans and a black thermal, pieces of his brown hair peeking out from under a black Stetson, James Cavanaugh kept strict command over the snorting, frustrated animal beneath him. Not by being big and loud and cruel, but with that quiet, confident strength he always seemed to possess. Quiet confidence. It was one of the things about him that intrigued her—and one of the things that would remain a tightly held secret from the woman seated across from her, if she wanted to keep her job secure and the probing questions to a minimum.

"Looks like he's in the process of breaking that stallion," Mac observed, chin lifted, eyes narrowed. "I've heard about his work, but I've never seen him in action. Quite a sight, eh, Sheri?"

Sheridan was just about to tackle the "Sheri" issue when James Cavanaugh turned to look in the direction of the bakery and caught her staring at him out the picture window. As heat infused every cell of her body, Sheridan held his gaze. For a heartbeat, or maybe two, she forgot everything else around her. Including that pesky truth about her work and her employer. All she saw was James Cavanaugh's gorgeous blue eyes. They were probing, hypnotizing. And suddenly, completely without her permission, her hand lifted and she gave him a small wave. Which he acknowledged with a clipped nod, then turned back to the mustang and continued down the street.

Unnerved, Sheridan blinked and the world came back into focus. What was that? she wondered, turning to face Mackenzie once again, her cheeks flaming and her breathing uneven. What had just happened? And god, what had she done? The wave . . . the staring . . .

"That was a beautiful animal," she managed to push out from her dry throat. Then she quickly clarified, "the mustang."

Amusement glittered in Mac's eyes. "They're his passion—that's for sure."

Passion. It wasn't a word Sheridan wanted her mind to associate with James Cavanaugh. Too late, mocked the foolish and juvenile voice inside her.

"So, is that why he's staying in River Black?" she asked. "To care for them?"

Mac shrugged. "There's a lot of reasons, I'm sure. Dealing with Everett's will. The wedding. And there might be some new information about Cass's passing."

The sudden yet soft heat in Mac's voice gave Sheridan something solid to focus on. Cass was not only Deacon's and James's sister, but she had been Mac's best friend. Sympathy rolled over the lingering unease James Cavanaugh had ignited within Sheridan.

"But I 'spect with the mustangs on Triple C land, James'll be here for quite a while. I hope so anyway." Mac's eyes connected with Sheridan's again and they were ripe with more questions. "For everyone's sake."

Sheridan eased back her chair, placed her napkin on the table, and got to her feet. She tried not to think about how unsteady her legs felt or why that would be. She'd allowed way too much today. Discussing Deacon's brother, the staring, the waving . . . "I should get back to the office."

Mac picked up her fork again and started in on the last few bites of coconut cake. "Which one are you in today?"

"Town. But I'll be heading out to the ranch in the afternoon."

"Oh. Maybe I'll see you there." She shrugged. "I want to take another look at the spot we may use for the ceremony."

"I'm sure whatever you decide will be lovely, Miss Byrd."

Sheridan turned to go, but Mac grabbed her hand. "Hey."

Preparing to be scolded once again for the formality, Sheridan turned back.

Mac was chewing her lip. She looked sheepish. "Look, I'm sorry. I know you're here to work. Deacon's your boss and you don't want any problems with that. I'm being a pushy jackass."

Sheridan gave the woman an easy, but decidedly professional smile. "It's no problem. And, Miss Byrd, I'm here for whatever you need." She slipped her hand out of Mac's grasp and turned and headed for the door. But halfway there, she paused and glanced back. Professionalism was one thing, but truth in bakery goods was another. "I think the coconut cake would be the perfect choice."

Mac looked surprised, and she called back, "But you didn't even try it."

Sheridan nodded at the empty plate in front of the forewoman. "'This above all: To thine own self, be true.'"

Ah, Shakespeare, she mused as she exited Hot Buns Bakery and started down the street. He always knew the perfect thing to say.

James slid off the mustang's back and gave the young creature a few strokes down his warm neck. Bringing a nearly wild animal into town wasn't the best idea he'd ever come up with, but Comet—that's what he was calling the stallion for now—needed to be looked at. And after all the mini bombs Dr. Grace Hunter had been dropping lately regarding her father, the ex-sheriff of River Black, and what he did or didn't know about Cass's killer, James wanted another chance to see if he could get any more information out of her.

As he moved his hand down the stallion's withers and back, Comet eyed him suspiciously. *You using me, cowboy?* he seemed to be asking. *Because I'm sound. Nothing but a little scratch. What d'you say we head back through town toward home, see if that pretty redhead with the sexy gray eyes is still in the bakery? Get us a slice of carrot cake or somethin'.*

James frowned. None of what had just come ticker-taping through his mind was from the stallion or his cautious gaze. That was all him. And unfortunately, it was not the first time he'd been having thoughts like those. Ever since he'd come upon Sheridan O'Neil in the rain a few weeks back, stranded on the side of the road near the Triple C, her beautiful wary eyes, that smart mouth—hell, that spectacular ass—had been assaulting his mind fast and furious. They were the kinds of thoughts that normally made him antsy, made him get out the duffel, pack up his duds, and head to one of the many hang-your-hat spots he'd purchased over the past five years or so.

But this time he didn't have the luxury of a quick and painless departure. There were too many glass balls in the air here in River Black. Someone needed to stand beneath 'em. Catch them before they fell and shattered and did some permanent damage. So the unwise attraction to his brother's citified employee? Hell, he'd be ignoring that. Because women, in his experience, were even more fragile than glass balls. And his track record for catching the fallen ones was dismal at best.

"Mr. Cavanaugh?" Dr. Grace Hunter emerged from the small veterinary clinic and started down the path toward him. She was a pretty thing. Small, lots of curves, thick dark hair. Cole's type all the way. Probably why his little brother's voice changed to a wolf's growl whenever he talked about her. She came to stand in front of Comet, her green eyes so guarded James wondered if he'd lost the battle before the war had even begun. Not that he gave a damn. She was going to talk—tell him something. She couldn't avoid the Cavanaugh brothers forever. Not after dangling a goddamn carrot in front of their starving faces, then yanking it away.

"Morning, Doc," he said.

Her gaze shifted to the stallion. "Something wrong with your horse?"

"Matter of fact. And since you couldn't come out to the ranch, I thought I'd come to you."

"Right," she said quickly. "Sorry about that. I'm just really swamped at the moment."

He took a gander at the empty parking lot. "Yeah, I see that."

She ignored him. "So, a flesh wound on his hindquarters, you say?" She headed around back to check things out.

"I did the best I could to treat it, but it didn't seem to heal, and then it started to look infected."

She gave Comet, who was uneasy at best, a gentle pat on the croup, then ran her hand down his thigh. "Probably something still inside the wound." She took out her bag and riffled through it. "I'm going to clean it up first, and then we'll see what we got."

James watched her work, watched as she used Comet as a protective barrier between herself and him. Anything to discourage a real conversation between them. She had to know that wouldn't work. That, hell, he wasn't giving up that easily. When he did manage to get a ten-second glimpse of her, he found himself impressed by her manner and skills. He'd been gone from River Black for a long time—long enough for a few new businesses, like RB Animal Care, to open up. But he'd heard about the young vet's skill and nature. And true to telling, she had a calm, gentle way about her, yet was unwilling to take any bullshit from the animal she was treating. Damn fine recipe for a good country doc.

After a minute or two, she held up a pair of silver tweezers, a thin strip of brown pinched between the tips. "Looks like we got a wood splinter. From a fence, no doubt. I'm going to put some topical on the wound, but I'm also going to prescribe antibiotics."

"Sounds good," James said, rubbing Comet's neck. "Then after maybe we can talk."

She didn't answer him.

"Dr. Hunter—" James began.

"There's nothing to talk about, Mr. Cavanaugh," she answered abruptly, her focus remaining on the horse's hindquarters. "I told you and your brothers. Several times, in fact. What I said in the Bull's Eye, what I thought I heard from my daddy, it was a mistake."

Yeah, she'd been saying that for days. Every time he or Deac or Cole tried to get her to talk. She'd made a mistake. Her daddy wasn't right in the mind. Dementia had set in. What horseshit. None of them believed her. Well, they didn't want to believe her. Because with just a couple of words—*Diary existed. My father has it*—she'd brought on something all three of them had lost a long time ago.

Hope.

It took supreme effort in that moment to tamp down the frustration simmering inside James. This woman didn't understand the magnitude of that word—what she'd started—what she couldn't undo. No matter what she said now, or tried to get them to believe, in their minds her father might very well hold the key to a twelve-year-old mystery. To the truth—the hell of his sister's murder, and every damn day afterward.

His gut tightened. All that time not knowing what had happened to Cass. Or *who* had happened to Cass. His sister had lay dead and alone, with no comfort and no justice. That would not stand. James and his brothers owed the truth to the sister they had all failed. But with the way the vet was playing this, he knew that to get that truth, he and Deacon and Cole had to go easy: Break down the real reason she was backpedaling on that declaration she'd made at the Bull's Eye.

He summoned his calmest voice. "If you'd just let one of us speak with your father—"

"No," she said tightly. She stood up, her bag in hand, her eyes lifting to connect with his. "My father's ill. His mind's not his own anymore. He's highly medicated."

James bit back the urge to snarl, *And my sister is dead.* "We wouldn't push him, Doc. You could be there to make sure. We just want to ask him about what he said to you—"

"He didn't know what he was saying," she interrupted caustically. "He doesn't even remember saying it."

"What about the diary? Have you even looked for it?"

"I looked in all his belongings. There's no diary," she insisted, her tone as tense as her body language. "It was just ramblings. Something he'd wanted to find, no doubt, and hadn't."

James ground his molars. Clearly, the woman in

front of him was trying to protect her father and backing her into a corner wasn't going to make her tell him the truth. It would just make her dig her heels in further. For now, he'd leave it. He and Deac and Cole would have to find another way to get the information they needed.

"Well, thank you for patching him up, Doc," James said in a careful voice. "Better be on my way."

Grace looked momentarily startled, as if the last thing she expected was for him to drop the subject. Then relief and professional distance settled over her features. "I'll get that prescription."

He watched her walk up the path, then disappear inside the clinic. Was it possible? Could it actually be possible that Sheriff Hunter was just a sick old man with wild ravings about a past he couldn't remember, a past that didn't exist? Hell, he didn't know. But he was going to find out. Because discovering and revealing the truth about Cass's disappearance and her killer was the only way the Cavanaugh brothers could honor the sister they loved.

The sister they had failed to protect.

Two

"That's not going to be acceptable, Mr. Palmer."
Sheridan stood on the porch steps of her boss's
new ranch property with her back to the late-
afternoon sun and her eyes on the contractor she
was ever having issues with. "Your quote in-
cluded all materials for the work."

The man, who looked to be in his midfifties,
tipped his hat back and regarded her with an almost parental glare of frustration. "Things change
when you work over a long period of time, honey."

Honey. So, we're going to play that game, are we?
"That's not my problem, Mr. Palmer," she said.
She may not have been wearing one of her power
suits, but her don't-try-to-screw-me-over attitude
transcended both attire and office building.

"Prices for materials aren't fixed," the man continued.

"Of course they're not," Sheridan agreed. "Which

is something you should've factored into the estimate."

He chuckled softly. "You're new to these parts. We do things a little different 'round here."

"Is that right?"

"Yup."

"And if I decide not to accept that excuse?"

His shoulders lifted and lowered in a carefree shrug. "Then maybe we can't get the work done on time, sweetheart."

Sheridan stepped down so she was face-to-face with the man. If there was one thing she had grown accustomed to and knew how to handle, it was a certain brand of men in business. The ones with the disease her aging, single, working mother had called Bastard-Male-Itis. The one, during her second year of business school, Sheridan had renamed Underestimate Me, Assholery in honor of a particularly douchey econ professor.

"You could walk away from this project, Mr. Palmer," she stated evenly. "Refuse to honor your agreement with Mr. Cavanaugh. But understand if you do so, you'll be hit with a lawsuit so devastatingly fierce and impossible to fight, it will not only bankrupt you, it will bury your entire family in debt."

He blanched, but his eyes flared with anger.

"Wait. I'm not done," she continued coolly. "Or you can choose to stick around and finish the job you signed on to do in a timely and cost-effective manner."

His expression pinched, he looked her over. "Well, aren't you somethin'?"

"I need your answer, Mr. Palmer." She eyed him sharply. "But if you do choose to stick around, know this—and I'm only going to say it once—my name isn't sweetheart, honey, baby, or sugar. It's Ms. O'Neil."

Palmer's jaw flicked with tension.

Mom would be proud, Sheridan thought, her eyes pinned to the man before her. As a salesgirl at Sears for twenty-two years, the other Ms. O'Neil had never been called anything but Georgia.

"Do we understand each other, Mr. Palmer?" she pressed.

Before he could answer, someone called out from the driveway below, "There a problem here?"

The male voice brought Sheridan's head around and her heart plummeting into her belly. James Cavanaugh and his massive black horse were parked about fifteen feet away, at the end of the stepping stones leading up to the porch. How hadn't she heard him ride up? Moments ago, she'd been verbally kicking ass; now she couldn't seem to find her voice. That was not like her. She did not melt in front of men. Ever. Well, not exactly ever. There had been a little melting when she'd ridden on his horse with him a couple weeks ago, and in his car with him. And then there was the crazy window wave at the bakery today . . . Oh Lord, he looked so intense, so gorgeous, so imposing on top of that stallion. But truly it was his eyes, those twin pools of probing, hungry ocean water that really turned her knees to melted butter.

She sounded crazy. Crazy and slightly infatuated. She was going to have to watch that. Only disappointment and pain came with unsteady limbs.

"No problem," the contractor said, though his tone hinted otherwise. He pulled off his hat and wiped his brow with his shirt sleeve.

"Mr. Palmer and I were just coming to an understanding," Sheridan said, clearing her throat. "One I'm assuming we won't have to repeat again."

James walked his horse to the very edge of the stone path, his gaze shifting to the man beside her. "That right, Caleb?"

Caleb? *Dammit.* So, they knew each other. She supposed that wasn't a surprise considering how small the town was. Odds were then that James was probably going to take the older man's side in their dispute. Or at least smooth Palmer's ruffled feathers. Long-held relationships, nepotism, they trumped most any issue in business. And around here—with the Stetson-wearing boys' club—she guessed it was probably even more so.

Caleb pushed out a breath, then uttered, "Ms. O'Neil and I have an understanding."

"I hope it's that she's your boss and you're her employee," James said, his tone surprisingly serious.

That made Sheridan's eyebrows lift. And maybe her chest tighten a little too. No boys' club. Or maybe there was and James Cavanaugh, Esq., just wasn't a member. She liked that. And she liked that he'd remained on his horse and let her handle her business.

Wanting to keep things civil and productive, she turned back to the contractor and stuck out her hand. "I'll see you tomorrow, Mr. Palmer. Bright and early."

"Sure thing," Caleb ground out. Then after giving her hand one irritated pump, he stormed past James and headed for his truck. Yes, he was going to be trouble.

"I see why you're Deacon's right hand," James said as he dismounted, and the contractor's truck sped off in a cloud of dust behind him. After tying up the stallion, he climbed the steps and came to stand beside her on the porch. He touched the brim of his hat. "Ms. O'Neil."

"Mr. Cavanaugh." Tendrils of heat skittered down her back. "Lately, it seems, I'm both of Deacon's hands."

His brows drew together. "Really?"

Okay, that hadn't come out right. She stared at

him. Up close, the man's eyes were shockingly beautiful. Like the sunlit water in Hawaii or Bali. "You know, the business side of things, and then helping his bride-to-be with wedding plans."

"Oh, right," James said with sudden understanding. He scrubbed a hand over his square jaw, which carried a night's worth of stubble. "I saw you at the bakery earlier."

Perfect. "Yes, you did."

"You waved at me."

Double perfect. "Possibly."

He grinned. "So what'd y'all choose?"

Food. Much better topic of discussion. "I suggested she go with the coconut cake, but who knows which way the wind blows? Sweets are a very personal decision. Now, if it were my wedding, I'd be all over a Reese's Peanut Butter cake." Could she talk any faster? God . . . And was that sweat trickling down her back?

"Your wedding?" Those eyebrows drew together once again.

"I just meant—"

"Are you engaged, Miss O'Neil?"

Sheridan laughed, but it came out sounding like a choke. In fact, it probably was a choke. "No. God, no. No."

He leaned back against the railing, regarding her, and crossed his arms over his chest. His very broad, very muscular chest. "That's a pretty passionate answer. You against marriage or something?"

"Of course not!"

"Because if you think it's a sham institution, maybe you shouldn't be helping out a couple who's gettin' hitched."

"Okay, you're really misunderstanding me here," she said quickly, thankful for the breeze picking up around them. She looked him over. The casual stance, the relaxed expression, the amused, ocean eyes. "What's this all about?"

"What?" he asked innocently.

"Your obsession with my feelings on marriage."

His face broke into a wide grin. "No obsession. Just curious about you, Miss O'Neil. That's all."

Oh. Right. That's all. He was curious about her.

Was that her heart fluttering around inside her chest, butterfly-style? Good God, did Deacon have to have such a swoon-worthy brother?

"You know," he continued casually, "you mentioned the Reese's wedding cake, and I just thought there might be someone cutting into the cake with you."

"There's not." Sheridan was pretty sure her answer was spoken at the speed of sound.

"Okay."

"I mean, I think the idea of having a partner you can trust with your heart, who's your friend as well as your lover . . ." She cleared her throat.

Why was she continuing to speak? What was wrong with her? "It's a nice, romantic idea. But I don't know if I really believe it's possible."

He nodded, his expression turning serious all of a sudden. "I agree. I'm never getting married."

His words—his statement—had Sheridan's eyes widening, her chest tightening, and her mind clearing of all that crazy-girl fog. *Wow.* She knew what had formed her opinions on marriage, and relationships in general, but she was very curious about what had formed his. Not to mention strangely disappointed. But James Cavanaugh's romantic future—or his past, for that matter—wasn't her business. Couldn't be. And she needed to keep reminding herself of that when he was around.

"So," she began, forcing a professional tone. "You obviously came all the way out here for a reason, and I'm guessing it wasn't to debate the merits and/or pitfalls of romantic and committed relationships."

Amusement returned to his gaze. "You're something else, Sheridan."

The way he said her name . . . it was like being given only one lick of an ice-cream cone on a very hot day. Deliciously irritating and a giant tease. *Not your business, Sheridan.* "Is there something you need, Mr. Cavanaugh?"

"Do you know when Deacon's expected back?" he asked, his eyes still holding her captive.

Deacon. Well, now that made sense. Of course he was here to see his brother. Not to banter about inappropriate subjects like marriage, or demonstrate how blue his eyes could get in the light of the ebbing sun. "Tomorrow night, I believe. But he has a meeting with investors, so that one day could be stretched into two."

"Shouldn't you be with him?" James asked.

"Excuse me?"

"Well," he began with a casual shrug and a grin. "Doesn't he need both his right and his left hand?"

Did he know that when he smiled his entire face lit up? Probably not. And she wasn't about to tell him either. "I think he needs me here to straighten out greedy contractors who think they can slip and slide when a mere filly's in charge."

He checked over his shoulder, took in the spot where Mr. Palmer had made a hasty departure a few minutes ago and turned back. "That what I came up on?"

She nodded. "Sometimes country boys underestimate strong women."

He laughed, took off his hat, ran his hand through his tousled and possibly sweaty hair. "Oh, I think that applies to all boys." Then he put it back on and captured her with those devastating eyes once again. "And even more so if the filly in question happens to be breathtakingly beautiful."

For a moment, Sheridan wondered if she'd

heard what she'd thought she heard. Or if maybe that foolish and juvenile side of her brain had taken over and was tossing out heart stoppers. And then James Cavanaugh added another whopper to the mix and she was toast.

"Maybe what you need to be dealing with is a man, Miss O'Neil."

It was truly unfortunate how warm she felt inside her red skinny jeans and tailored white blouse. And it had nothing whatsoever to do with the blazing sun poised overhead. She swallowed, her throat dry. She needed to find some water. With ice. Maybe a bucket of it to throw over her head. And she needed to get away from the gorgeous cowboy. Like maybe permanently.

Avoidance was key.

"Well, I'd better get," he said, as if he'd just read her mind. Or seen the sweat droplets glistening near her hairline. He pushed away from the porch steps.

"Of course," she acknowledged. "Back to your horses."

"Well, they ain't mine exactly, but . . .yeah. I'm trying to find them different lodgings."

"Oh," she exclaimed softly. "You don't want them at the Triple C?" She remembered how angry he'd been when Mac had brought those BLM horses onto the property. All the brothers had been at odds about what to do with the place. But since Deacon had given up his quest to destroy his father's ranch, Sheridan had assumed that maybe James had given up his anger and come to accept that the wild mustangs were home for good.

"They need someone around who knows what they're doing, how to handle 'em," he told her as he descended the porch steps.

Sheridan's brows slammed together in confusion. Someone who knew what they were doing? Well, that was most certainly him. So what was the issue? "Are you planning on not being around to care for them?" she called after him. It was surprising how the thought of him leaving River Black anytime soon made her chest ping.

Yes, avoidance, Sheridan! Learn it, know it.

He untied his horse, then stuck a foot in the stirrup and easily swung up into the saddle. "I'll be here for the wedding. But after that, who knows?"

Who knows? That was pretty much her future plans with regards to the small Texas town as well. Her gaze moved over him in a lazy, yet problematically possessive way. All that lean, tanned muscle and quiet, capable talent. Those raw blue eyes that searched hers, and that mouth that turned up at the corners in an irresistible smile before saying her name. He was the stuff of fantasies, and she needed to do everything she could to keep herself away from him and focus on her work. Because fantasies were trouble. For suckers. They got you hurt and broke and sidetracked and miserable.

She hugged her files closer. "I'll be sure to let Mr. Cavanaugh know you came by when he returns. Or when he calls, if you'd like."

Under the brim of his black Stetson, James's eyes shuttered, no doubt noticing the suddenly cool professionalism threading her tone. But he didn't acknowledge it. Just gave her a polite "Appreciate that, Sheridan" before turning around and leading his horse down the drive.

"Beautiful sight," Sam remarked as the mustangs thundered past, heading for the creek bed half a mile off.

"They are that," James agreed, his eyes on the stallion out front—the paint who had won his place as the sole alpha among the mares. "But we need to find them a different ranch to roam."

The old cowboy tossed him a curious look. "Why is that now, boy? They got all they need here. Water and vegetation. Why don't you put those thoughts away for the time bein'. Deacon's not selling his share of the Triple C; Blue ain't back from wherever the hell he's gone off to."

"But he will be back. And when he does, he'll have a say in what happens here." Their father, Everett Cavanaugh, had passed on a few weeks ago, leaving a mess of trouble in his wake. Not the least of which was a will that named a Cavanaugh brother they'd never known they'd had. Blue Perez. Blue Cavanaugh. Hell, the man hadn't known either. Now Blue was strapped with his share of the Triple C, and judging by his up and leaving town after Everett's funeral, he didn't seem to want anything to do with it. Or his new brothers. 'Course that could be because Deac, James, and Cole had pretty much treated the man like shit when they'd first found out.

"Blue might want to sell the C when he gets back." James pulled off his hat and wiped his brow. "I don't want the horses gettin' used to something they may have to quit. And in a hurry."

"They're animals," Sam said, as if that explained everything.

"Doesn't matter. They feel the loss same as we do."

The old man shook his head. "I don't understand you, boy."

James sniffed. Wasn't the first time he'd heard that. "The longer they're livin' here, the more attached they become, to the air, to the land—"

"To you," Sam finished.

Turning his horse around, James kicked the stallion into an easy walk. Sam moved in beside him. "Look, I can't stay here indefinitely," James told him. "It's not where I belong. I got work. My own life."

"Don't be tellin me you're gonna do that TV show."

A Horse Whisperer in Hollywood. James frowned. That's what they wanted to call it. Sounded like something that'd get him laughed right out of Texas. Honestly, he hadn't even considered it until recently. Besides the bullshit title, he wasn't all that comfortable in front of a camera, in the limelight. . . . But lately, well, he'd started to think maybe it could be an interesting change of pace.

"That Hollywood woman doesn't give up easily," James said as they headed for the north pasture, and hopefully to the mare who needed her wound checked and another hit of antibiotics. "She thinks it'd be a big hit." He laughed. "I dunno about that. But the offer keeps going up every time I turn her down."

"You don't need the money," Sam pointed out.

He tossed the man a wry grin. "Everyone needs the money."

"Why are you really considering this? Something you never did before? Or had any kind of interest in? A job whisperin' to fancy, celebrity horseflesh." He snorted. "What do they got to be mopin' about anyway? A job that takes you away from River Black right now, and for God knows how long." Under shaded eyes, the cowboy studied James. "Or is that the answer right there?"

James turned away from him. "Don't go analyzing me, old man."

Sam chuckled. "Oh, shoot. Nothing else fun 'round here to do. Except for waiting on Deac and Mac's wedding, the rest of life at the Triple C is damn stagnant. Depressin' even. Though she's cookin' up a storm, Elena sulks and pines. Blue took off without telling anybody where he was headed or if he's coming back, including his mama. And Cole's in and out, training and fighting—coming back here with black and blues and reds all over his face." He shot James a worried look. "And I hear you all been sniffin' around the vet about Cass's end."

Pain smacked James in the chest and his lip curled. "I ain't talking about that."

"With me, you mean. Your daddy's closest friend."

James stilled. He hadn't really thought of it, but maybe Sam was right. Maybe James didn't want Everett's memory anywhere near what he and Deac and James were trying to do, trying to uncover. Maybe he was afraid that even from the grave the man would taint things—crush their spirit, their hope.

When he didn't reply, Sam just shrugged. "Fine. Just be careful. Sometimes when we look too closely at something, we find things we never wanted to see."

"Like the truth?" James spit out.

"Truth's a rectangle, boy. Many sides to it."

Behind them, the sound of hooves thundering against the ground rent the air. Both Sam and James halted their horses and turned. About five hundred yards away, two mares, who had probably broken from the herd he and Sam had just passed, were coming their way, picking up speed with every inch they covered. Without a word, James kicked his horse and raced to a nearby tree. When he pulled up and jumped down, Sam was right there beside him. He thrust his bridle into the man's hand and took off.

"What the hell you doin', boy?" Sam demanded as James headed back on foot to where they'd just come from—right into the line of equine fire.

He didn't answer the old man. Didn't even think about him. Didn't think about anything but the mares and his own body. He stopped directly in their path and brought his hands up, real gentle, palms out. He softened his gaze, slowed his heart, and with every breath he expelled, he called to the mustangs as they approached.

"Whoa. Whoa, easy," he cooed. "There we are."

At first, they didn't seem to take notice or care. They were too fired up, coming quick and hard, dust flying everywhere. But as James continued, as he walked slowly toward them, asking them to stay easy and go gentle, they downgraded into a canter, then a trot. Eyes wild, heads tossing, they pulled up short before him. One stopped a few feet away, nostrils flaring, but the other came right up to him and nuzzled into his side.

James closed his eyes, let his body, his breath, his pulse return to normal. The energy that rushed from the mares into him was making him light-headed, but he held his ground. It was his way. Their way too. How they communicated together.

Somewhere, far off, he heard Sam call out, "Holy buckets of shit," but James was too far in the zone to reply. The sweet, wild girl continued to push her soft, warm face against him, and before long, he had his arms around her neck, stroking her. Christ, he would do right by her—her and her brothers and sisters. He understood how they worked, what they needed to feel safe and secure. He *would* do right by them. While he stayed, thinking about the TV show and waiting for Deac's wedding, he would find them a permanent master and advocate—find them land they could truly call home. And while he did that, he would push the vet for answers. Go around her if he had to. Find that diary and get to the goddamned truth so he maybe—just maybe—could finally forgive himself and move the hell on.

A certain gray-eyed woman flashed into his brain. She was in there far too much lately. Swimming around in rainwater, mooning over Reese's Peanut Butter anything, and making James question the oath he'd made to himself after he'd left college, after Tori had been attacked—shit, after he'd failed to protect her. There was no disputing the fact that he found Sheridan O'Neil attractive. Hell, more than attractive. But he wasn't going there. Couldn't. She wasn't a one-night-stand, let's-just-have-some-fun-and-walk-away kind of gal. No matter what she claimed regarding relationships and marriage, she had picket fences and promises, diamond rings and auburn-haired kids written all over her. And that was never happening for him. Not for a broken loner who didn't deserve love, and could protect females only if they happened to be of the equine variety.

Stepping away from the mares, he shooed them in the direction of their herd. For a moment, they didn't move. Their eyes remained on him, watchful, curious, infinitely soulful. Then James made a clicking sound with his tongue, and they turned and took off into the coming sunset.

Three

"You're distracted tonight," Matty called out from the corner of the ring. "Which means the likelihood of brain damage just went up fifty percent."

"Bullshit." Cole barreled forward, sending his fists first into his sparring partner's gut, then into the man's jaw.

Saliva fanned the air to his right, but Cole barely noticed. He was filled with something, up to his neck in it. Rage? Insanity? It was like those days before he became a UFC fighter. Those days on the street, just surviving—grabbing his high, not from any kind of drug, but from imagining the face of Cass's killer in every shithead that tried to mess with him.

"Fuck!"

Before he could get another shot off, he was grabbed by the waistband of his shorts and yanked backward.

"What the hell?" he growled.

"You're fighting like you're on the blacktop and it's recess," Matty whispered in his ear. Not angry. Never angry. So damn calm it was irritating.

Eyes narrowed on his bruised opponent, sweat dripping down his face as he danced back and forth in the center of the ring, Cole shot back, "That's a good thing."

The trainer reached for him again and whirled him around sharply. Dark eyes narrowed, all that calm from a moment ago gone. "Only when the battle's being fought underground. You don't do that anymore, remember?"

Cole was so worked up, it took everything inside of him to keep his gloves down and away from his trainer's face.

"For what we're going after here," Matty continued as if Cole's hyped-up and highly aggressive attitude was something he'd witnessed a million times before, "you need to have focus and clarity and strategy—"

Fuck that. "I have heart," Cole fired back.

"Christ." The man looked away, eyed Cole's sparring partner, whose lip was starting to swell. "Take ten, Reg," he said, then turned his eyes back on Cole. "Now. Want to tell me what's going on?"

Still dancing, fists twitching inside his gloves, he uttered a terse, "Nothin'."

Matty shook his head. "Nope. Try again." His chin dropped. "And remember I've known you for a while now. Seen you keyed up, seen you pissed, seen you with heart, passion, all of that. This is something else."

Cole shook his head to get the sweat on his face and neck a flyin'. "It's just some shit back home, okay? It's fine. Being worked out."

Matty took a deep breath. "This have to do with your dad's passing?"

"No."

"Then what?"

Cole answered with a growl of irritation. What was making him manic—exploding inside him—was raw and overwhelming. He didn't know what to make of it, how to explain it. Where to begin. He hadn't given a shit about the Triple C or its future since he'd left home at seventeen. Hell, maybe not even then. Then that night at the Bull's Eye happened. And the vet had brought up Cass and the diary. Now, all Cole could think about, dream about, was that day his twin sister had been taken, and the motherfucking nightmare that followed. How he'd felt ravaged and guilty. How his mama had looked at him—or couldn't look at him. Shit . . . just last night Cass had come to him in his dreams. Begging him to find her. Come to her.

He inhaled deep, shook the images out of his head, and stopped dancing. "Listen, I'm going back end of the week." His eyes lifted to meet Matty's. "I'll be there for a couple of days. I'll get my shit worked out, come back and do what I need to do."

The man studied him for a second or two, trying to decide if he believed what Cole was selling. Then his expression changed to one of concern. "I hope so. You can go into that fight with passion and drive, and, hell, even anger. But you can't go in without focus and skill and a shitload of training. You'll get murdered."

Cole flinched. His trainer had no idea what he'd just said. He knew a few things about Cole's past, but nothing substantial. He didn't know about what had happened to Cass or anything that had happened to him afterward. It was something he didn't share with anyone. Not because he was embarrassed, or because he wanted to keep his private life private. No. He kept it to himself—inside his guts and his mind—because the shame and guilt drove his rage. It had made him an unbeatable fighter.

It made him win.

And winning was what he had. All he had.

"Let's go," he ground out. His game face back in place, he shook the cobwebs out of his brain and started dancing again. "Let's do this."

"You sure you're ready?" Matty asked him.

"Absolutely."

Maybe not for the truth about what had happened to Cass, he thought, as Reg climbed back into the ring. But he was ready for a fight. Hell, he was always ready for a fight.

*   *   *

Starvation had officially set in. It was ten thirty a.m., and Sheridan was running on fumes. 'Course that's what one got when she forgot to eat dinner the night before. She'd just been so focused on going over the budget for the ranch construction. Though things were looking good on the surface, something wasn't right, wasn't adding up, and by three a.m. she still hadn't discovered what it was. Of course, she would. She wanted to have all her ducks in a row by the time Deacon returned from Dallas.

The bell over the door jangled as she entered Marabelle's. It was pretty late on a weekday for the diner to be packed, but it was. With no tables free, she headed for the counter, which was completely vacant on one side. Her stomach grumbled and she laughed at herself as she sat down on one of the red stools and reached for a menu. When she was hungry like this, no scrambled eggs and a side of toast would do. She needed big portions. Starch and carbs and butter and syrup.

"Can I help you, honey?"

Sheridan looked up and gave the older woman with the striking orange hair and heavily tanned skin a broad grin. "Yes, please. I'll have the blueberry pancakes, a side of bacon, a side of hashbrowns, tomato slices with capers if you have them, and—"

"A Reese's Peanut Butter milkshake," someone cut in behind her.

The waitress's eyes lifted, then warmed, a reaction that Sheridan completely understood. She'd warmed many a time looking into those ocean-blue eyes.

"We don't have that, James Cavanaugh, and you know it," the woman scolded. Though it came out sounding more like a coo. She eyed Sheridan again. "Sorry, hon. Might wanna try the ice cream shop for somethin' like that. We do have a cookies-and-cream shake if that'll please."

"No, thank you," Sheridan said, trying to calm her racing heart. But it was difficult with six feet, two inches and one hundred and ninety pounds of lean muscle standing right behind her. "I'll have tomato juice."

The woman winked. "Coming right up."

Before Sheridan could turn to look at the man standing behind her, he appeared at her side.

James Cavanaugh leaned against the counter in a way that was both casual and sexy. Damn him. "So, who you got joining you this fine morning?"

"No one," Sheridan said, confused and slightly flustered. Why would he think someone was joining her? He who hadn't shaved yet today. She tipped her head to the side. Boy, that night's growth of beard really set off his lips. Made them look fuller and . . .

"You sure about that?" he asked, cutting into her inane thoughts.

"What do you mean?" *Stop looking at his lips, Sheridan.*

"It's just that I heard your order and . . ." He trailed off, lifted one chestnut eyebrow.

Heat slammed into her cheeks, and she bolted back to reality. She knew exactly what he was insinuating. *Jerk. Hot and sexy jerk.* She lifted her chin and gave him her most imperious glare. "For your information, sir, I missed dinner last night. I'm very hungry."

He just stared at her, his eyes glittering with amusement.

"And," she continued, "pointing out that my order sounds as if it's for two people is rude and unbecoming a gentleman."

His lips twitched. "Who said I was a gentleman?"

She rolled her eyes with impatience, but inside her belly things were a'tingling. "No one. I just assumed."

"Well, you know what they say about assuming things, Miss O'Neil."

"That it's the surest way to make an accurate judgment call on someone or something?" she fired back.

Both brows went up this time. Then he started to laugh. It was a rare sound, and its husky quality drowned out all the other voices in the diner and coiled around Sheridan like a blanket. Or a snake.

"You gonna ask me to sit down?" he said after a moment.

Him beside her. His eyes holding her captive. Oh hell, that sounded good. *No. That sounded bad. Very, very bad.* "Why? So you can insult me further? Maybe while I'm consuming a haystack of pancakes and an entire side of pork?"

He laughed again. "Come on, Sheridan. I was just playin' with you."

"Sure. So much fun."

"Frankly, I'm glad you're tuckin' in." His eyes moved lazily down her body. "You could use a little meat on your bones."

Heat flickered through her. Heat hadn't flickered through her in a long time. It was disturbing. "My bones?" she repeated tightly.

"Don't get me wrong . . ." His mouth curved up at the corners. "You look damn fine coming and going, but I'm bettin' I could carry you soaking wet and fully clothed all the way from here to Dallas."

He'd looked at her coming and going? Good Lord. "Well, aren't you sweet?" she managed to utter.

"Obviously not sweet enough to get me an invitation to sit down."

A smile broke on her face, and she shook her head. She gestured to the empty stool beside her. "Hey, it's a free country—and a free counter. But I'm sure you're waiting for someone, so—"

"I am," he said.

It was pretty spectacular that in a mere moment, her good humor and all that tingly heat that had been running around inside her died a quick death. Granted, none of it should've been in there in the first place. After all, he was her boss's brother and, therefore, off-limits in the romance department. But the fact that he was meeting someone bothered her all the same.

"But they're not here yet," he said just as the waitress set a plate of blueberry pancakes the size of a life preserver down in front of her. James whistled softly through his teeth. "Lookin' good, Stevie."

The waitress batted her long fake eyelashes at him. "The pancakes or me?" she shot back with a wry grin.

He leaned into the counter. "Shoot, woman. Those flapjacks can't hold a candle to you."

Sheridan could practically hear the woman swoon. Or maybe that was her. She needed to eat. Blueberries were good for mental acuity and sharp reasoning, right?

"You've grown into quite the charmer, James Cavanaugh," Stevie said, reaching back to take a plate of bacon from the cook. "That what Hollywood does to a cowboy?"

"Wouldn't know."

Hollywood? Sheridan thought. What did that mean? Was his work with horses taking him to California? Away from River Black? *And if it is?*

Not your business. Heck, she wasn't going to be staying in town all that much longer either.

Stevie snorted, then looked at Sheridan and said, "Juice and potatoes'll be up in a jiff, hon," before moving on to another customer.

Boldy, proudly, Sheridan picked up the cute little glass syrup dispenser and poured the warm, pale brown topping all over her pancakes, then cut them up into bite-sized pieces. Her stomach growled in anticipation. She felt James move in closer, watching her.

She stared at her plate. "You're drooling, Mr. Cavanaugh."

"Am not," he said, his gorgeous face way too close to hers now. "But you could offer me a bite."

Liquid heat filled the emptiness in her belly. Seriously, the guy was too much. And clearly her insides thought so as well. Those blisteringly hot insides that were right now urging her to pierce a triangle of pancake with her fork and hold it out for him, maybe watch as his mouth closed around it.

She swallowed thickly.

But her brain—her stupid, party pooper of a brain—warned her against it. Deacon's brother. Your work. Your future.

The bell over the front door jangled again. Sheridan turned just in time to see a petite woman dressed in dark green scrubs and sneakers enter. It was the town veterinarian. Grace something.

Sheridan hadn't formally met her, but she did know that the woman's father was somehow connected with the disappearance of Cass Cavanaugh, and that Deacon, James, and Cole were all trying to get information out of her. So far, it looked as though they weren't getting anything.

Once the woman was inside, her gaze floated over the crowded diner. She waved at someone in the corner and smiled. But when she spotted James at the counter, that smile evaporated and she visibly recoiled. For several seconds, she just stared at him. Then she turned around and left.

Sheridan ventured a glance at James. His jaw was tight with tension, but the rest of him was very much in control.

"Wow," she said, turning back to her plate. "That was cold."

"What do you mean?" James asked her.

She stabbed at her pancakes. "Your date. She took one look at you and walked out. That's got to sting."

"That isn't who I'm meeting."

Her lips twitched with humor and she looked up at him. "Really?" She wasn't sure why, but she was glad to see that some of the tension had eased from his strong, oh-so-handsomely-stubbled jaw.

He shook his head, his eyes glittering with sudden heat. "You playin' with me, O'Neil?"

"I never joke about dating," Sheridan said in all honesty. "That's serious business."

"Well, it's a good thing I don't date, then." He gave her a wry grin and pushed away from the counter. "Better go before someone steals my table."

Sheridan just stared at him. He didn't date? Curiosity swirled inside of her. He wasn't ever getting married and he didn't date. He was like her. She'd never met anyone who was like her in that way. And she wanted to know why. What had bought on that decision.

"Enjoy those flapjacks, Miss O'Neil. Eat every bite." His brows descended a fraction. "Can't have you blowing away, back to Dallas. Not just yet anyway."

As he walked off, tall, lean, and masculine in the extreme, Sheridan forced herself to turn back to her meal. The pancakes, bacon, tomatoes—all of it untouched. A strange mixture of heat and anxiety stirred low in her belly, and her breathing felt uneven and forced. What the hell was wrong with her? He was just a good-looking guy. She'd known plenty of them. She needed to get herself together and stop the mooning and the swooning—curb the palpitations.

She picked up a piece of bacon and held it to her lips. Her stomach was clearly beyond empty, growling up a damn storm, and yet she didn't feel hungry anymore.

At least not for the breakfast laid out on the counter before her.

Four

"He says you can come out and take a look, but he doesn't think the place'll suit. And frankly, neither do I."

James put his fork down on his empty plate. "Why's that?"

The foreman of the Bronco Barn Ranch finished off his coffee, then answered. "Only ten thousand acres, James. With that many mustangs—"

"It's enough," James cut in.

"Barely."

"He agreed, Micky—"

"To let you come take a gander. Convince him it's possible and not a gigantic pain in the ass." He motioned for Stevie to come over. "Look, he knows he owes your daddy a big debt. This could be a right solid way to repay it. If—and that's a big if—there's room."

Normally, James wouldn't have been interested

in his father's personal relationships and debts, but this one he'd take if he could get it.

"How far you out again?" he asked.

"Hour or so," Micky told him. He thanked Stevie for the coffee refill, then turned back to James. "Depending on how fast you drive or what's clogging up the roads."

Movement up at the counter caught James's attention. Sheridan was looking at her bill, confused. His gut tightened as she leaned over the counter to talk to Stevie. Damn, the way those jeans stretched over her legs and backside. He'd been right about her being something to see coming and going. When the older woman told her that her bill had already been taken care of, she turned instantly to look at James. Her cheeks were flushed all pink and pretty, and he had the strangest urge to vault over the tables and pull her into his arms. Then those gray eyes left him for the foreman across the table. For a few seconds, she seemed to be deciding what to do—if she should come over or not. Then she turned back to James, gave him quick smile, and headed for the door.

Something popped inside of James. Not that he'd expected her to come over, but he'd wanted her to. Wanted to see her up close again, hear her voice. He liked their sharp back-and-forth, liked teasing her, seeing her eyes flash with heat when he did. Maybe it was a bad idea, for him and for her, but he couldn't help himself.

As the bell over the front door jangled and she disappeared outside, James pushed his chair back. "Thanks for meeting me, Micky," he told the foreman. "I'm going out to check on things."

The man paused, steaming coffee cup to his lips. "Right now?"

"Right now."

James dropped a bunch of bills on the table, gave the man a quick handshake, then followed Sheridan out the door. She had a small head start, but it didn't take him long to catch sight of her auburn hair and citified style. Black boots on her feet, tight, classy denim covering her toned legs and sensational butt, and a fitted, dark gray tank top that showed off her tiny waist and tanned arms. She was crossing the street a block and a half away. He eyed his truck. It was parked right outside the diner. Maybe it wasn't the best of ideas, considering who her boss was. He didn't want to make trouble for her. And yet, even so, he was inside the cab, gunning the engine and pulling away from the curb before she made it another block.

Traffic was pretty light, and when he caught up to her, he slowed to a crawl. "Heading back to work?" he called out.

Her head came around so fast he was worried she might get whiplash.

"Oh, hi," she said, her expression a mix of surprise and curiosity. "I'm actually going out to the ranch."

He patted the side of his truck. "Let me give you a lift."

She smiled, but it didn't reach her eyes. "That's okay. Thanks, though. And thanks for breakfast." She gave him a wave, then turned and continued down the street.

His gut tightened, and he tapped the gas, followed her. "Why not?" he called.

This time she kept walking. "I'm working off my breakfast, if you must know."

He chuckled. "I thought we talked about that, Miss O'Neil. You don't need to work a damn thing off that body."

Her cheeks flushed pink and she picked up her pace.

"Come on now," he coaxed. "You tryin' to avoid me or something?"

"Why would I do that, Mr. Cavanaugh?"

Mr. Cavanaugh, huh? He sighed. "Maybe because it's the smart thing to do."

As if his words had struck some kind of nerve, she stopped and turned to face him.

James hit the brakes. Someone honked behind him, then went around him with a pissed-off screech. James didn't turn to give the driver a wave of apology for his asshole move. His attention was on the woman walking up to his window. She was stunning, sexy, her hair swirling around her shoulders and face in waves of red and gold and brown.

His fingers curled around the steering wheel as he waited for her to give him a cool dressing down. But it never came. Instead, her gray eyes studied his blue ones for a moment; then she asked, "Are you even headed out that way?"

"As a matter of fact I am," he said with a grin.

He thrust the truck into park and got out. He went around to the passenger side and opened the door for her. For a few seconds, she stayed where she was, mulling things over, chewing at her bottom lip. The slightly sensual action caused a small fire to erupt within James's chest, but he didn't say a word.

Finally, she came around the truck and gave him a cautious smile. "All right," she said. "Truth is, that car of mine is giving me fits. I think it's the alternator or the oil pan area." Slipping inside the truck, she looked up at him and laughed. "I'm thinking my air filter needs to be replaced. And I should check my transmission fluid. Just haven't had the time."

James stared down at her. "You know about cars?"

"Little bit. In college I had the hardest time falling asleep at night. Only thing that helped was reading my owners' manuals. Car, fridge, television, toaster . . . that kind of thing."

He closed her door and went around to the driver's side. Beautiful, intelligent, hardworking, knew her Shakespeare . . . He didn't think it was possible for Sheridan O'Neil to get any sexier. But she just had.

He belted up and put the truck into gear. "So," he said pulling away from the curb. "You could fix my fridge?"

That brought on a bright, almost wicked smile. "Possibly. If it was something like a blown fuse or a tripped circuit breaker."

Damn. . . . James stifled a groan as they left the small town behind and hit the interstate.

"But I feel like I am most gifted in the toaster arena," she added, her hair blowing in the breeze that was rushing through her open window.

"I don't have a toaster," he said. *But I'll sure as hell be buying one tomorrow.*

Her hair was blowing in the breeze, swirling around her face, and he had this intense and worrisome desire to reach over and run his fingers through those auburn strands. Hell, run them up until he cupped her skull, eased her face his way, took his eyes off the road for a second to steal a kiss.

His eyes caught and held on the exit to Redemption Ranch. It was about a quarter mile off. Miss Sheridan O'Neil had work to do. For her boss. *Your brother, asshole.* Seriously, he didn't want to screw anything up for her. But something was happening to him when she was around. He felt different, lighter. Able to catch his breath. It made him both nervous and hungry for more. And instead of slowing down and taking the off-ramp when it came up a second later, he pressed down on the gas pedal with his boot.

Sheridan noticed right away. She looked back over her shoulder at the exit, then turned to face him. "Wait," she said, her expression confused. "That was where we get off."

"I know." He was a damn fool.

"Well, then maybe we should turn around and go back?"

James kept his eyes on the road and his boot on the gas. "That work of yours . . ."

"Yes?"

"Is it pressin'?"

"Pressing?" She paused, no doubt thinking. He wanted to tell her not to. That thinking got in the way of people being impulsive. And goddamn, he really wanted her to be impulsive today. With him.

"Not terribly pressing, I guess," she said at last.

His glanced over at her. She was looking at him, those gray eyes warm, hair swirling around her face, and something in his chest pinged.

She shrugged, her smooth, tanned shoulders lifting and lowering. "I worked until pretty late last night, so I'm caught up."

"Good." *Real good.* He turned back to face the road and tried to suppress the gleeful grin that wanted to emerge.

"So, where are we going?" she asked.

He didn't answer. But his grin widened.

"Oh dear," she said. "Do I need to take out my cell phone and call nine-one-one, Mr. Cavanaugh? Report an abduction?"

"Nope."

"And why's that?"

He turned to look at her again. "No reception around here."

Her soft, pink lips curved into a smile. "Come on, I don't like surprises."

"Seriously?"

She nodded.

"Everybody likes surprises, Sheridan."

"Not me." She took a deep breath, then blew it out. "When I was eight my mom threw me a surprise party."

"Surprise parties are fun."

"Not this one. Picture it: fifteen screaming eight-year-olds jumping out from closets and bathrooms and behind couches in the near darkness. I had a panic attack and spent the night in the hospital."

"No way."

"Way." She gave him a serious look. "So. Not a fan of the surprise."

He laughed and turned back to the road. "All right. We're going to see a piece of ranch land for the mustangs."

"Oh." That one word was doused in curiosity. "Okay. And you want me to come along because . . ."

"Come on, woman," he grumbled.

"I'm just trying to ascertain my role in this endeavor."

"Your role?" he repeated. Shoot. He turned to look at her. "Are you really going to make me say it?"

She blinked innocently back at him. "I think so."

"Fine," he ground out, facing the road again, his hands fisting around the steering wheel. "I want you to come with me because I like you. There. I said it."

He waited, just for a second to see if he'd get the "Oh" again. When she didn't say anything at all, he ventured a glance at her. She was staring straight ahead at the highway, chewing her bottom lip. It was sexy and annoying at the same time. What was she thinking? That he was an idiot? Inappropriate? Well, she'd be right.

"But I'll turn around and take you back to Deac's place if you'd rather not," he said, hating every word as it exited his mouth.

"Yes," she said at last, her tone tight and professional. "Please. Take me back."

James's gut rolled over. He turned to look at her. "You kiddin' me?"

A sudden and shockingly wicked smile broke on her face and she started to laugh. "Yes."

James just stared at her. "Sheridan, you're something else."

"I hope that's a compliment, Mr. Cavanaugh."

"Oh, it is."

Grinning, she turned back to the road. "So, how far is it to the ranch?"

"Well, now, that all depends," he said, taking in the three paint horses walking a white fence line to his left.

"On what?"

"If you like it fast or slow."

He felt her turn to look at him. Felt her eyes bore into his skull. And it was his turn to laugh. "I'm talking about speed, Miss O'Neil. In my truck, to our destination."

"Well in that case," she said, facing forward again. "I like it fast, please."

Sheridan loved the city. Both living and working there. She adored its skyscrapers, its Starbucks on every corner, and all the sensational clothing shops and restaurants within walking distance of her small but modern condo. But the more she lived and worked in River Black, the more that love she had for city life diminished. There was something to be said for the country roads she traveled down, the clean air and open sky she was exposed to, and the townspeople whom she was just getting to know, but who always seemed genuinely pleased to see her. All of it made her feel . . . calm. And truly, with her drive and ambition and blind need to prove herself, she hadn't felt calm since grade school.

That said, there was one thing about River Black

that didn't make her feel calm. Quite the opposite, in fact. And he was standing right beside her near the fading red barn at Bronco Barn Ranch. He wore brown boots that were worn and scuffed, dark blue jeans that showed the world what riding horses on a regular basis did to a man's thighs, and a white T-shirt that was pulled tight across his broad chest. But it was his eyes that truly made Sheridan's heart weaken. They could go from expressive to amused to serious to tough to sensual in seconds. It was those ocean-blue pools that had made her forget who she was and who she worked for and agree to this jaunt without any real hesitation.

"You two from the Triple C?" someone called out.

Sheridan lifted her gaze. A cowboy was walking out of the barn, heading their way, leading two silvery white horses with deep-set black eyes and thin faces.

"That's right," James answered in a friendly manner, pushing away from the fence they were leaning on. "Micky call you?"

"Yup."

"How'd you know there were going to be two of us?"

"Didn't. Figured you might want a guide. But I see you brought along some company." The cowboy handed the reins over to James. "They're sisters. Love being together, and'll stick close. Names

Brigitte and Bardot. Watch 'em 'round the wild-flowers though. They love 'em. Will do just about anything to get to em."

"Appreciate that," James said. "Can I pony one of 'em?"

"You bet. Either one'll work. But Bridget likes to lead mostly." He jerked his head in the direction of the corral at their back. "Lead rope's hanging on the post there."

Sheridan had been so taken with her surroundings and the beautiful animals: Brigitte and Bardot—so cute!—that she hadn't really been listening or using her brain. Her skin bristled with nervousness. James wasn't here to just walk around the place on foot—safely on the ground. Or drive a truck or tractor or whatever they used to get around great spans of ranch land.

"I suggest going up to the rise 'bout a mile west," the cowboy said. His eyes flickered toward Sheridan, and the nonriding outfit she was sporting. "Take it at a walk, I think."

James turned to Sheridan and winked. "That's the plan."

The nervousness inside Sheridan bloomed into a full-fledged panic. She didn't ride, and heights scared the shit out of her.

"I'll be here when you get back," the cowboy said before walking off toward the barn.

As soon as he was gone, Sheridan turned on James and ground out, "Riding?"

"I need to see the land, Sheridan."

She gestured to the ten thousand acres of rolling hills that stretched out in green waves and was dotted with wildflowers and pods of grazing cows. "There it is."

He chuckled. "I need to see if there's really room for them. And it's not always about acreage. I need to see how the land is laid out, where the water is, how the fence line's maintained."

That absolutely made sense. He should see it. "I understand," she began in a more professional tone. "While you survey, I'll hang out here and wait for you."

She saw how much that idea appealed to him by the insta-frown he tossed her way.

"Hang out?" he repeated, his brows coming together. "I'm not leaving you here. I want you to come with me." He gestured to the horses. "Look at those pretty girls. They can't help but treat us right."

Sheridan looked from one saddled horse to the other. They were stunning, amazing creatures. She shook her head. "Pass."

James came toward her, all soft concern and gorgeous cowboy. "What's got you so scared? These mares are gentle. And we won't be doing anything but a walk. I swear it."

Her eyes fell to her boots. They weren't the riding kind, just pretty. "It's not the horse, it's the height."

"You're afraid of heights?"

"I've been known to be, yes."

"But you rode with me before. Couple weeks ago. On Triple C land. I remember it very clearly."

"That was an emergency situation."

She felt his hand under her chin, and then he was lifting her face and her eyes to his. They were deep blue and filled with lighthearted warmth. "You're going to enjoy it. Trust me."

Her heart stuttered and everything south of her belly button warmed. "I barely know you."

He grinned, released her chin so he could take her hand. Back in Dallas, in the Cavanaugh Towers, every hand she shook was smooth, even the men's. Now, against her palm, she felt calluses and strength, pure rugged masculinity that stated very clearly that the man doing the holding wasn't getting manicures or lotioning up after his shower every night. This man worked with animals and rope, with his hands, pushed his body to the limit, and didn't give a lick about hydration or grooming. It was intoxicating and potentially addictive.

"Besides," he said, leading her over to the mare. "If you're going to be hanging out with me, Ms. O'Neil, horses are part of the package."

"Hanging out with you?" she said, the air inside her lungs vanishing. "So we're buddies now?"

He turned to look at her, those blue eyes vivid under a dusty black Stetson. He could seriously make a girl melt with just that look alone. It wasn't fair.

He held out the stirrup. "Put your boot in here, buddy."

Her heart was beating furiously inside her chest. For so many reasons. What did she do? Run? Fake a hamstring injury? There were about three things she was actually afraid of—and dammit, two of them centered on heights. But she had the feeling that if she refused, James wouldn't go either. Then it would be her fault if they didn't see the ranch land. Oh, those potentially homeless mustangs . . .

Dammit again. With a quick prayer for her safe return and the hope that there would be no symptoms of vertigo, she muttered a terse, "Fine," and slipped her foot into the stirrup. She was about to pull herself up when she felt James's hands around her hips. In one smooth movement, he lifted her up and placed her in the saddle. Totally breathless, her hips humming with a tingling sensation, she grabbed hold of the horn.

James crossed his arms over his very impressive chest and stared up at her. "You need more pancakes, Sheridan. That was like lifting a butterfly. I was scared I'd rip a wing."

No doubt he was saying that to lighten the mood and calm her fears. Which, she had to admit, was kind of sweet—even though it wasn't working.

Her knuckles white as she gripped the horn, she glared down at him. "I'm rolling my eyes right now, in case you can't see me through that mist of bullshit."

He pretended to look hurt. "No bull. I'm serious. You're a skinny thing." He scrubbed a hand over his jaw. "Not everywhere of course. Not where a woman ought to have some extra, if you don't mind me sayin' so."

Oh my God. She blushed terribly. Her cheeks, and maybe other more intimate places too. He was talking about her chest, right?

"I might need to take you out for a meal or two," he continued. "Make sure you're getting enough food."

The horse shifted beneath Sheridan and she inhaled sharply. "That's totally unnecessary. I eat plenty—as you saw. I just have a fast metabolism. No need to meet me at the diner—"

"Doesn't have to be the diner," he interrupted, attaching a rope from his horse to hers. "We could go to the Bull's Eye. May not look it, but they have some pretty decent grub."

"Be careful, Mr. Cavanaugh," she said as he jumped up and settled himself on the horse she believed was called Brigitte.

He tipped his hat back an inch. "Of what, Miss O'Neil?"

"You're getting awfully close to this sounding like a date."

He kicked Brigitte and set her in a circle. Bardot followed.

"And you and I . . . we don't do dates," she continued, taking one hand off the horn so she could grasp the reins.

"I say we just call it a friendly meetin'."

"Meetin'?" she said, using his inflection.

He smiled, shrugged. "I like you."

He said the words as if they explained everything. When in truth, they only incited more questions and confusion. As he led the way past the barn and out into the pasture, Sheridan tried to calm her beating heart. Not because she was afraid of the horse beneath her—in fact, the easy walk felt okay, nice even, and in time, she knew she would relax—but because of what he'd said. Twice now, in fact. He liked her. And if she was being honest with herself, she liked him too. Which sounded like a recipe for disaster. She worked for his brother and was here only for a short time. She didn't do this. Get involved. Especially now. Her career was just getting started, and the last thing she was ever going to allow was for romance to derail her future.

"Lookie there," he called out, knocking his chin in the direction of a manmade lake in the distance. "Some decent water. Could handle cattle and the horses. That's good news."

"Are you sure you want to do this?" she asked him as they passed through a set of gates.

"Everything'll be all right, Sheridan," he said, glancing over his shoulder. "You look comfortable, and I really need to see the place with my own eyes."

"No," she corrected quickly. She was actually feeling okay. "I mean, transfer the mustangs to a different ranch? Do you really think whoever ends up with the Triple C in the end would kick them out or treat them badly?"

He didn't answer right away. But when he did, it was after a weighty breath. "I don't know. But I can't take that chance."

"If I remember correctly, you weren't the one who brought them to the Triple C in the first place," she said as they started up a hill. "They're really not your responsibility."

"Doesn't matter."

" 'Course it does."

"Lean back in the saddle a little as we go down," he instructed. "Horses and their welfare are my life, Sheridan."

Her curiosity forced her to push him a little. "How long have you felt like that? Since you were a child?"

"Nope. Sometime around college."

He wasn't giving much away, and she couldn't help but wonder why. She also couldn't help the many questions that kept rolling off her tongue. "And that's why you started working with the horses?"

"Yup."

"When did you notice that things were going past caring for them?"

He didn't answer. He was looking around, taking in the verdant valley below. It stretched on forever. Or it felt that way.

"That you had a special gift?" she added.

"Shit," he said tightly. "I don't have a special gift."

"I just mean—"

"I'll say this," he began, turning to look at her. "Then I'll be done with it, if you don't mind."

She nodded, her breath catching inside her chest. He'd turned serious. Storms on a sunny day.

"Horses saved me from a very dark time in my life. I will always return that kindness."

His words settled into Sheridan's chest with a beauty and a pain that was startling. Lord, she wanted to ask him more. She wanted to know what that dark time involved. Was he talking about Cass or something else? Some*one* else? But he'd been pretty clear that he was done sharing.

"Oh!" she exclaimed as her horse suddenly lurched forward, losing its footing.

James brought Brigitte to a quick stop and was off the horse in seconds, heading for her sister. His hands moved over Bardot's neck as he whispered something so soft and soothing, it worked on both the horse and on Sheridan.

Her heart squeezed. There was nothing she

wanted more in that moment than to just keep watching him with the animal. He was almost part of the landscape, of the air the horse was breathing. Like he was malleable. A strange idea, she knew, but it was how she saw him in that moment.

"You all right?" He was staring up at her now.

"Fine," she assured him.

"Come here." He helped her down, then ran his gaze over her, checking.

"I promise," she assured him. "I'm okay. Good, actually. I was enjoying myself."

He smiled. "Nice to hear."

He turned back to her horse. "Let's see about you, girl," he said. "What you got yourself into."

Under the heat of the midday sun and cloudless sky, surrounded by the sweet-smelling earth and grass, Sheridan watched this focused, gentle, and highly mysterious man check each of Bardot's legs and hooves. When he got to the front right foot he cursed.

"What's wrong?" she asked. Her own height phobia aside, she liked the beautiful, sweet horse, and she hoped whatever was wrong was nothing serious—or, God forbid, something she'd done.

"She picked up a rock in her foot," he said. "Got a stone bruise."

"Will she be okay?"

"Oh, sure. But we need to get her back, and you

can't be riding her." He released the horse's hoof and turned to look at her. "I'll take you with me on Brigitte."

Sheridan's cheeks flushed immediately, and she nearly rolled her eyes at herself. What. The. Hell. Seriously. The very put-together, strong-willed, professional-at-all-times Sheridan O'Neil of Dallas, Texas, and the Cavanaugh Group didn't seem to exist when this man was around. Under the ocean-blue gaze of one James Cavanaugh, she was Sheridan, the blushing, uber-smiling, knee-weakened female. It was super irritating. Not to mention dangerous. She'd seen it firsthand. A smitten woman was not a thoughtful, rational, successful woman. She was a broken heart waiting to happen.

"We already have the lead line," James said, cutting into her thoughts. "So we can pony Bardot here back." He motioned for Sheridan to come to him. "Let's get you on Brigitte. Not to worry. Everything will be fine."

She believed him. With the horse, she believed him.

She went to him, put her boot in the stirrup right away. "I'm not nervous anymore."

Grinning, he lifted her up, waited until she swung her leg over. "You're enjoying yourself?"

She smiled down at him and nodded. "I feel bad about what happened to Bardot, but yes."

"I'm enjoying myself too." He swung up in

front of her, and without him prompting her to do so, she wrapped her arms around his middle. He smelled so good. Like leather and soap.

"It's been a long time," he said, kicking Brigitte into an easy walk.

Diary of Cassandra Cavanaugh

May 2, 2002

Dear Diary,

Tonight was the best night of my life. And the worst. I snuck out of the house after dinner. Mama was watching something on TV, and I don't know where Daddy was off to. Deac and James and Cole were down by the creek like always.

Carl Shurebot's old place was kinda creepy. At least when I first got there. But what do you know? Sweet had brought in some candles and some cake from Marabelle's, and we ate it and talked. Well, I guess I talked and he listened. He's a good listener. Doesn't think I'm a silly thing like my brothers do. I told him all about my family and Mac and life at the Triple C.

He didn't say much about how long he'd been in River Black or how long he planned on staying. But he did tell me that he was visiting, and that the people he was living with were strange.

We're going to meet up again tomorrow night, if'n I can sneak off again. I hope he'll tell me more.

Off to bed. Can't wait to dream,

Cass

P.S. Maybe you're wondering if anything romantic happened. I can only say that now I know what a boy's lips feel like. Warm and a little wet. I think I like it. I know I like him.

Five

Redemption Ranch was going to be one helluva homestead when it was completed, James thought as he walked Sheridan up the porch steps to the front door. Deacon clearly knew how to showcase the views and vistas of River Black, while still maintaining a homey warmth. Though James wasn't going to be settling here anytime soon, it was nice to know a Cavanaugh would still have a place in River Black. No matter what memories might want to drive them out.

"Sun's going down," James said, watching her put the key in the lock.

"That's what happens when you keep a girl out past her work time," Sheridan answered good-naturedly. "She's gotta make it up after hours."

He leaned against the side of the house. "Sorry 'bout that."

She turned and gave him a wicked smile. "No you're not."

"All right, I'm not." She could smile at him like that all day long. And maybe a few hours at night too. "I enjoyed being with you today. Truth is, I haven't had much fun lately. Hell, can't remember the last time I smiled so much."

Her eyes warmed, and her smile deepened. "I'm glad."

"Dealing with my father's estate, and Deacon wanting to bulldoze the Triple C to the ground, it's been complicated at best. I haven't felt a moment's peace since I got here. In fact, all I wanted to do was get things wrapped up so I could leave. But today, riding out on a fresh property, you squeezing the breath out of me—"

"Hey!" she said, laughing.

He grinned. "It felt good." He studied her. "You're damn fine company, Sheridan O'Neil."

She inclined her head. "Thanks. Back atcha."

He shrugged. "We should do it again sometime."

"Yeah." Her gaze faltered. "I'm happy to help. Let me know when you plan to visit another ranch."

"Doesn't have to be a ranch visit."

She chewed her lip for a second or two, then said, "We'll see."

We'll see? He didn't like that answer one little

bit. Or how the smile had evaporated from her eyes. "That sounds like a no."

She shook her head. "I work for your brother."

"Right."

"And I love my job."

"Well, that's a good thing."

She gave him a look of extreme impatience. "Come on, I know you understand what I'm saying."

"You can't think Deacon would fire you if we . . . hung out together. If we were . . ." He paused, cleared his throat. "Friends."

"Having a hard time getting that word out?" she observed, the lightness and humor back in her gaze.

"Not at all." He dropped his chin and lifted his brows. "Friend."

Her gaze shifted to the coming sunset. "Look, I don't believe Mr. Cavanaugh would take issue with us being friends, if that's truly what it was. But, come on—"

James didn't let her finish. He stuck his hand out. "Then it's settled. Friends."

She stared at his hand.

"I ain't gonna bite, Sheridan," he said. He'd meant it as a joke, but when her eyes lifted to meet his, he saw a struggle there.

"You wanna stop hanging out with me?" he asked gently.

"No, but—"

"I don't want to stop hanging out with you." He shrugged. "We both know where we stand. Both know neither one of us is staying here permanent. No expectations. Just fun."

"Just fun?" she asked. "'Words are easy like the wind,'" she said.

Heat slashed through him. Quoting Shakespeare from those lips . . . "What can I say, Miss O'Neil? 'I do desire we be better strangers.'"

Her eyes brightened and for a moment he thought she might return his quote with another. Maybe something about rejection of the heart. But instead, she started to laugh.

"All right, Mr. Cavanaugh." She slipped her hand in his and pumped it a couple of times. "Friends it is."

Her skin was warm, soft, and her hand fit against his palm so perfectly it made his damn idiot brain conjure up other ways she would fit perfectly against him.

"How long you plan on staying tonight?" he asked, keeping her hand in his, wondering stupidly if "friends" kissed each other good night or not.

He guessed *not*.

"Maybe ten, eleven," she said, her voice slightly breathless. "I need to run the numbers again. I still think Mr. Palmer's records are incorrect."

That made him pause. "You think Caleb's cheatin' Deacon?"

"I don't know. But something's not right."

James didn't like that idea one little bit. River Black folk didn't cheat one another. He didn't know Caleb Palmer all that well, just that the man was River Black's main contractor, and had a wife and a grown daughter. But from what he knew about Sheridan O'Neil, if she thought there was a potential issue, there probably was. Maybe he'd pay Caleb a little visit on his own.

His eyes found hers again. "How 'bout I come back and get you, take you home."

"No." She eased her hand from his, reminding him that he'd been holding on to her all that time.

"You don't have a car here, Sheridan."

"Mr. Cavanaugh instructed me to use the truck in the garage anytime I needed it."

James snorted. "That's a pretty big piece of machinery."

"And?" she said, humor and pride crossing her gaze.

"Just sayin', when you're used to those standard commuting cars from the big city, a truck like that can be a bit of a challenge."

"It's a good thing I like a challenge then. I can handle it. You know my relationship to motor vehicles. Well, to their manuals anyway." Her lips twitched, and in that moment, there was nothing James wanted more than to reach for her, take her in his arms and capture her mouth under his—taste that goddamn perfectly wicked smile. But the sound of one of those challenging trucks he'd just been talking about was hauling ass up Deacon's driveway that very minute. It yanked his brain, and all those other parts that were growing fond of Miss O'Neil, back to reality.

Leaving the open doorway of the house and heading for the edge of the porch steps, Sheridan shaded her eyes as she tried to see who was coming. "I think that's Mackenzie Byrd."

"What does she want?" James muttered, coming up behind her.

Sheridan glanced over her shoulder, eyed him in an almost playful way. "That sounded hostile. You don't like your brother's fiancée?"

"I like her fine," he grumbled. "Hell, I've known her since I was in diapers."

"Now there's an image."

"I was damn cute in diapers, Miss O'Neil," he growled good-naturedly.

"I don't doubt it."

He knocked his chin in the direction of the truck coming around the curve of driveway. "She just has bad timing, that's all."

"Oh, thank God," Mac called from the open window as she hit the brakes, causing dirt to spit and splatter onto the stone walkway. Within seconds, she was out and rushing up the front steps to Sheridan. "I've been trying to call you for hours."

"I hear the cell service out here is sketchy,"

Sheridan said, pressing her elbow into James's gut. "Right, Mr. Cavanaugh?"

"Yup," James agreed, wishing she'd press the rest of herself back into him while she was at it. "You're going to have to do something about that when you move in, Mac."

"Great," the woman grumbled. "One more thing to add to my to-do list."

"Everything okay?" Sheridan asked her.

Mac opened her mouth to reply, then promptly shut it. She looked from Sheridan to James, then back again. Her eyes narrowed. "Were you two off somewhere together?"

"No," Sheridan said quickly. Then amended, "Well, not really *off* together. We were looking . . . well, James—Mr. Cavanaugh—wanted to see some property, and he asked me along."

Trying to suppress a grin, James just stared at her profile. Brilliant, efficient Sheridan O'Neil was flustered. And all because of him. Or explaining him to Mac. What did that mean? That maybe she was more than just mildly attracted to him? And if so, wasn't that a problem to fix, not something he should be feeling all pleased about? After all, they'd just agreed to be friends. Shook on it and everything.

"So, Miss Byrd," Sheridan began, adopting that impenetrable professional smile of hers, "Something I can do for you?"

Once again, Mac looked from one to the other.

She seemed to be on the fence. Keep pressing about what the two of them were off doing and why—or go straight for the reason she'd come over. Oddly, she didn't pick either one.

"So . . . what do I gotta do, Sheri?" she asked, pressing her hand to her heart.

Sheridan looked genuinely confused. Probably because she'd just been called Sheri. Was that a nickname James didn't know about?

"I'm sorry?" Sheridan asked her.

"To get you to call me Mac?"

"Oh." Sheridan's face relaxed, and a smile the size of Texas broke out on her face. "Let's see. Maybe not call me Sheri?"

For a moment, Mac looked confused. Then she burst out laughing. "Done."

Sheridan laughed too. "So, what's going on? Everything okay?"

Quickly sobering, Mac turned and tossed James a gigantic *get lost* look. He found it irritating as hell, but he knew better than to piss off Mac. Besides, when women wanted their time together, you gave it to them. No discussion. No questions asked.

"Well, ladies," he said. "I'm going to head out." He turned to Sheridan and touched the brim of his hat. "Thank you for the help today, Ms. O'Neil."

Her cheeks flushed. "Of course." Then she added, "That's what friends do."

A growl hovered in his throat as he acknowledged Mac with a nod and headed for his truck.

Yep, that had been his suggestion. His word. *Friends*. Not because he really wanted to be her buddy, her pal, but because he didn't think she'd feel comfortable hanging around with him if she knew just how attracted he was to her. How much he wanted to see her again.

And damn, he wanted to see her again. Be around her. At least, until the inevitable happened. Until they both finished with River Black and moved on, moved back to their real lives.

No ass had the right to look that good in plain old dark blue denim, Sheridan mused as she stared after him.

"I believe someone's got the hots for someone," Mac said behind her.

Sheridan whirled around and overreacted. "I do not have the hots for him!"

It was an overreaction that Mac, to her credit, took in stride. She gave Sheridan an understanding smile. "I actually meant James. But come to think of it, you're looking pretty blushy too."

"Blushy?" Sheridan repeated, her hands going to her face.

"I know it doesn't sound like a real word. But it is. My friend Cass used to say it about me. Whenever I was around her brother." She grinned. "Still applies. Just sayin'."

"It's a warm night," Sheridan pointed out, even though the sun hadn't really even set yet.

Mac nodded. "And it was a hot day."

"Yes, exactly," Sheridan agreed, then realized where the woman was headed—or hell, where she'd landed—and started laughing. "Oh my God, I know. But I don't want to talk about it. I can't. In fact, I'm hoping it goes away. All things blushy." She sounded like a moron, and yet she asked, "You know?"

Mac nodded sagely. "I understand. But if you do ever want to talk about it. Say, if the blushy continues or . . . worsens—"

"Oh my God."

"I'm around."

Sheridan heaved a sigh. "I appreciate that." And she did. Though she knew she could never take Mackenzie up on the offer. Not if she wanted to continue to work at the Cavanaugh Group. Lord, just the thought of Deacon seeing her like this—hearing her all flustered and . . . female . . .

She blinked and forced her face into a mask of composure. "Now, what's got you rushing over here?"

As if she had just then remembered why she'd made the trek out to Redemption Ranch, Mac blanched. "I need your help."

It didn't take the deduction skills of Sherlock Holmes to know what was wrong. "Wedding?"

Mac nodded. Where a moment ago, she'd been this strong, confident ranch forewoman who knew everything about love and romance and obscure words like *blushy*. Now she was reduced to a puddle of insecurity.

"Cake?" Sheridan asked.

"I picked the coconut."

"Good choice."

"What I need help with is so much bigger than cake." She took off her hat and tossed it to the ground. "Dress."

Sheridan suppressed a smile. But it wasn't easy. The woman looked positively freaked out. "Okay, the first thing to do is not panic. Do you have any ideas? Magazines to look at? Is there a shop in town you could visit, or maybe you have an appointment in Dallas to see a designer?"

"Deacon hired someone to come here," she said, her voice reed thin. "He knew I wouldn't take the time out to go shopping for a dress, so he's sending them to me."

This fact looked to be the worst thing imaginable to Mac. "When?" Sheridan asked.

"Tomorrow."

"That's soon. And good."

The bride-to-be grimaced. "I need to be moving cattle tomorrow." At just the mention of her work, she leaned down, scooped up her hat, and placed it back on her head.

"You're going to need to take a couple hours off," Sheridan said. "Maybe around lunchtime?"

Soft puppy-dog eyes implored her. "Will you be there with me? Give me your honest opinion about what looks good and what looks like something a ballerina would wear?"

"I don't know," Sheridan began tentatively.

"Please."

"I'm no expert in fashion."

"Trust me, you're a thousand times more stylish than I could ever hope to be."

Sheridan hesitated. Mackenzie Byrd was her boss's fiancée, and that fact should make her eager—or at least obligated—to help the woman out. But the friendlier she became with Mac, the more anxious she felt. Like she wasn't just extending herself to her boss's soon-to-be wife. She was starting to form a bond. A potential friendship.

Her eyes moved over the woman's desperate expression. How did one say no to that? "Okay," she said, caving. "Sure. What time?"

Mac burst out with a massive sigh of relief. "Oh, thank you, thank you. Lunch was a great idea. One o'clock work for you? At the Triple C. Up at the main house."

"I'll be there," Sheridan assured her, then added for good measure, "Mac."

The smile she received in return was brilliant and genuine and made her heart hurt a little. In all her years during school and then work, she never allowed herself to even contemplate what might be missing in her life. It wasn't productive. She didn't want the distraction . . . or the course in vulnerability. But ever since she'd been in River Black, things had changed. People were coming into her life, refusing to stay on the perimeter. And Sheridan wasn't altogether sure anymore if she wanted them to.

Six

James had tried like hell to sleep. Done everything he could think of except take a bath. He'd heard they were soothing or something. But he didn't do baths. Not even when he was a kid. He and Deac and Cole had all refused the hot-water-and-bubbles routine, opting instead for the cold, clear water of the creek. But riding out and jumping in wasn't going to scrub a certain filly from his mind tonight.

Sheridan.

He couldn't stop thinking about her. Worrying about her. If she was still at Redemption or if she'd gone back to her hotel. Sure, she was capable with what was under the hood of Deac's truck, but what about driving it? Had she been able to handle that monster? Shit, could she even get it out of the garage?

As he drove down Redemption's dusty drive,

he knew he was about to find out. He also knew that coming here was a mistake. The kind he'd been pretty successful in steering clear of. For good reason. He was no woman's protector. He'd come to terms with that long ago. And yet, as he climbed out of his truck, headed up the porch steps, and found the front door open, a rogue desire to find her and make sure she was okay barreled through him.

Except for one dimmed lamp in the entryway, the rest of the first floor was dark. *What was she doing? Door open, lights off?* Sure, this was the country and all, but that didn't mean shit didn't happen from time to time.

He hauled ass up the stairs, where harsh yellow light was blazing down the hall. His gut tight, he followed it all the way until he came to an open door.

Damn woman, he thought as leaned back against the doorframe of what was going to be Deacon's office space. On the long metal desk, two computers, an iPad, and a laptop were on, though all were in sleep mode. Paperwork was spread in a fan shape on one side, while notebooks, pens, and coffee were littered on the other. And in the middle of it all? Sheridan, fast asleep.

James felt equal parts softness and pissed off. She'd fallen asleep in a remote house, door unlocked, all alone.

He pushed away from the door and walked

into the room. She needed to get back to the hotel and rest, and he was going to make sure she got there.

"Sheridan?" he said in a soft voice. When she didn't respond, he placed a hand on her back. "Sheridan? Honey, you need to wake up."

She stirred, then made a sound that was almost a moan. Keeping his hand on her back, James watched her eyelids flutter and her lips purse. Damn, she was beautiful. Her auburn hair falling loose across her smooth, pale cheek.

"Sheridan," he said again a little more forcefully.

This time her eyes opened. She blinked, then suddenly she focused on him. "Oh my God," she squealed as she sat up. "You scared me to death."

He backed up a foot. "I'm sorry."

"James?" she asked as if her sleepy brain was still trying to wake up and make sense of her surroundings. She glanced around, no doubt reminding herself where she was and why. "What are you doing here?"

"It's late, Sheridan." Didn't really answer her question, but it was all he was giving her.

"What time is it?"

"One thirty."

"In the morning?" she cried. She turned around and looked at the paperwork spread on the desk. "Oh my God."

"You fell asleep in an unlocked house far from

anything and anyone," he scolded. "You think that's good decision-making?"

She turned to look at him, her gray eyes wide and her hair wild around her face and shoulders. Was this how she looked in bed after sex? he wondered. Tousled and sexy, lips pink and plump?

"Maybe not," she said.

"Most definitely not," he corrected, his tone harsher than he meant it to be. "This is a small town, sure, but that doesn't mean there aren't bad people about."

"I just got into something, and was reading . . . I—"

"That's no excuse," he cut in.

She turned back to face him with a look of bewilderment. "Okay, why are you getting so pissed? I didn't do it on purpose. It was a mistake."

Sometimes mistakes get people killed.

The words were right there on this tongue. He knew they'd come out sounding bitter and angry and uncompromising, and he wasn't prepared to explain why. Just like he wasn't prepared to go into detail about why he hadn't been able to sleep, why he'd driven all the way out to Redemption to check on her. She knew he liked her, and that was excuse enough.

"You should head home," he said, tamping down his ferocity. "Find your pillow instead of the top of a desk."

Still confused, she stood up, stretched her back a little. "I will."

He tried not to stare at the way her breasts and tight, round backside pushed out with the effort. "Listen, Sheridan, you driving that monster truck back to the hotel doesn't sit right with me. I'm going to take you myself."

"James," she began, but he interrupted her.

"That's what friends do, right? Help each other out?"

Her cheeks stained a pretty pink as she stared at him, unsure.

He gestured toward the door. "Come on. Let's get you home. Deacon would never forgive me if I left here without you."

Of all the things he'd said since he'd gotten there, this one seemed to make sense to her, or at the very least gave her a plausible excuse to agree.

"All right," she said, turning toward the desk. "Let me just get my stuff together."

The ride back to town was a quiet one, windows down, air rushing into the cab. But James didn't mind. He didn't need chitchat. He was just glad she hadn't fought him about taking her home. He was pretty sure that if she had—if she'd insisted on staying at Redemption to work—he would've camped out on the floor downstairs.

He glanced her way. She'd pulled her hair back

into a loose knot at her neck, but a few pieces had managed to get free and were flapping around in the breeze. His fingers itched as they wrapped the steering wheel, curious to know how those strands would feel against his skin.

Christ, this was bad. He'd gone right past desire and interest to something far more worrisome. Something he hadn't felt in years. Something he hadn't allowed himself to feel. He liked Sheridan O'Neil. Wanted to get to know her better. See what made her tick, see her heart.

See her naked . . .

When they pulled up in front of the hotel, Sheridan didn't wait for him to come around and open her door. She seemed bone tired as she gave him a quick thank-you, then got out and started for the front door of River Black's modest hotel. Maybe he should've, but James didn't give it a second thought when he parked the truck illegally and followed her. Or when he came up beside her and placed a hand protectively on her lower back.

Sheridan didn't protest, didn't say a word. At least, not until they were on the second floor, at her door and she had her key in the lock. Then all of a sudden she sighed heavily, yanked the key back, and turned around to face him.

"Okay," she said, letting her head fall back against the wood. "What's going on?"

He shrugged. "Just walking you to your door."

"Simple as that, huh?"

"What? You don't have gentlemen in the big city, Sheridan?"

Her gray eyes narrowed. Not in anger, but in frustration. "Why did you come out to Redemption in the middle of the night? That goes way beyond gentleman—"

"I told you we're friends."

"We both know this isn't a friendship. Not in the traditional sense of the word anyway." She took a deep breath. "I'm not good at pretending, James. I'm normally a very straight shooter. I tell it like it is. And I don't get involved with anything that's a lie or a charade. But because you're Deacon's brother, and because I'm Deacon's assistant, and"—she chewed her lip—"because I'm obviously attracted and captivated by you, I allowed myself to play along with the friendship game." She lifted her chin and stated resolutely, "But I can't keep doing that. And I'm asking you to stop as well."

There were very few times in James's life when he'd felt rattled, like his insides weren't connected anymore, like they wanted to escape the bonds of his skin. But as he gazed down into the beautiful, weary, impassioned face of Sheridan O'Neil, he felt completely and totally unhinged.

"Stop pretending this is a friendship?" he said through gritted teeth. "Or stop pretending I'm not attracted to you?"

"Both," she whispered.

"Or stop pretending that every time I see you I want to kiss you."

She looked down both sides of the hallway, then back again. "That would probably be good too."

He leaned in, placed his palms on the wood, one on either side of her head. "Well, then, if I do that, I'm going to need to stop pretending that your smart, sexy, passionate ways . . ." He dropped his head and cursed, then lifted his eyes to hers once again. "Don't make me yearn and think, make me wonder, make me crazy with a need I didn't even know existed inside me anymore."

Her lips parted, and she stared up at him with huge, stunned eyes. "James, don't do this," she begged, breathing heavily.

Hell, woman, he thought. I wish I could stop it. Stop myself. Stop running my mouth. Stop wanting yours. "And that when I'm looking into your eyes or sitting next to you in my truck or hearing your voice, I'm wishing you were mine."

He was a fool. He knew that. People didn't say shit like that after knowing someone for only a few weeks. And *he* should never be saying it. But being this close, staring down into those beautiful, sexy eyes, he couldn't seem to hold on to his usual brand of resistance. The past felt far away, not weighing heavily on his shoulders.

He couldn't resist. Her, himself. It was the middle of the night, and maybe his madness wouldn't count tomorrow.

He dropped his head and brushed his lips over hers. Just once. Easy and slow so he could get a taste of her. But one taste was all it took to ignite the need that had been building inside him ever since he'd found her on the rain-soaked road outside the Triple C. It was like pouring gasoline on a lit match. And he wasn't the only one feeling it. As his mouth captured hers, Sheridan groaned and slipped her arms around his neck. It was all the encouragement he needed, and he kissed her hungrily. She was so warm, her lips so soft. What the hell was he going to do when it was over? When this incredible taste, this moment, was taken from him? Would he be able to just go on, to pretend like it hadn't happened—that he didn't continue to want her in this almost desperate way?

His hands went to her hips, and his thumbs pushed through the loops on the waistband of her jeans. He tugged her to him with a grunt of male possessiveness, then growled as he felt how perfectly she fit against him. Her belly against his fly, her thigh between his legs, her breasts locked tight to his ribs.

She tasted like night, like waking up and finding your woman burrowed deep into your chest—like the promise of warm sex under cool sheets. For several amazing, wonderfully drugged moments, all there was—the only sounds that could be heard in that hallway at two a.m.—were hungry, frustrated, needful groans and sighs as James continued to kiss her, tug her closer, bite at her lower lip, then lap at the indentation with his tongue.

But then it ended. As perfect moments—mindless moments—do. Sheridan's arms dropped from his neck and she pulled away.

James's body instantly protested. "What is it, honey?" he inquired softly.

She wasn't looking at him as she shook her head almost imperceptibly.

"Hey." He cupped her chin gently, lifted it so their eyes met. "Remember what you said. Straight shooter. Always telling it like it is."

She blinked, slowly, sadly.

"Tell me," he coaxed.

Her eyes searched his; then she seemed to deflate. "I'm scared."

It was the last thing James had expected her to say, and the worst thing she could've said to him. He released her instantly and stepped back, his gut tight and his heart slamming against his ribs.

Sheridan sagged against the door, breathing heavily, her nipples pressing tight against her tank top, her lips a deep pink and swollen from his kiss.

Scared.

Christ. His brows knit together, and nausea rose up to claim him. The last thing he ever, *ever*, wanted was for a woman to feel scared around him.

Shoving a hand through his hair, he tried to get the words out. "I'm sorry. Shit. I'm real sorry, Sheridan."

"It's okay."

"No," he said with blatant and quick ferocity. "It's not. Ever. You're right. I'm an ass, and this is a mistake. I'm so sorry I pushed you." He gave her a quick nod, then turned to head down the hall. "It won't happen again," he growled.

"James, wait," she called after him. "Please, I didn't mean . . ."

But he was already through the door to the stairwell and on his way down to the lobby, to his truck—to his way back home. Or at least to where he was hanging his hat until he could get his stupid ass out of River Black for good.

Jogging sucked.

Especially when you were uncoordinated and hadn't slept more than two hours the night before because you were amped up from the best kiss you'd ever had, and worried that the man who'd given it to you didn't understand why you'd felt fear afterward.

Hellooo . . . Complicated Girl Feelings 101?!?

But there was something about punishing one's body that killed the freaked-out-and-feeling-sorry-for-yourself blues. Everything had to be given over to breathing right and trying not to puke.

As the sun contemplated rising in the gray sky to her left, Sheridan pushed herself onward. Town was a mere half mile away. Easy peasy. She could definitely make it. Then again, who knew? With little sleep and no breakfast, things could get ugly. She could collapse in the very center of Main Street and curl up in a sweaty, shaking ball yards away from her hotel. If that did happen, hopefully there wouldn't be too many people witnessing it. After all, it was barely dawn. Who was up that early who wasn't . . . you know, out working their land?

"Hey, there," a voice called from behind her, nearly making her stumble.

Trying to keep her pace steady, she glanced over her shoulder. Wearing only a pair of running shorts and sneakers, his chest bare and his tattoos blazing, Cole Cavanaugh easily caught up to her, then slowed to match her pace. He was the more fearsome of the Cavanaugh brothers, with his nearly shaved white-blond hair, sleeves of ink, and the twelve-pack, or whatever the number was for the most waves of abdominal muscles a person could have.

"I didn't know you ran, Sheridan," he said, his black eyes warm and interested, his breathing completely unlabored.

"I don't," she managed to get out before she coughed.

He looked appropriately concerned. "You all right?"

"Fine. Just my lungs."

"What's wrong with them?"

"They deflated a mile or so back."

He laughed. It was a nice sound. Reminded her of his brother. As if she needed any reminding.

"They're on the side of the road with my rapidly beating heart," she added with a grin.

"You're funny."

Her feet were really starting to ache and she groaned without embarrassment. She desperately wanted to stop and walk the rest of the way. Hey. There was absolutely nothing wrong with walking. Best exercise there was. Of course, collapsing *outside* of town might be a bad idea. . . . Who knew when someone would come along to collect her body.

"I'm heading back to town," Cole said, interrupting her insanity. "You?"

"That's the plan," she uttered through gritted teeth. Cole looked unfazed by the exercise. Maybe he could strap her to his back. Or carry her fireman-style. No, that wouldn't be embarrassing at all. *Hey, look: Isn't that Deacon Cavanaugh's assistant riding on his brother's back like a monkey?*

"How's Deacon's ranch?" Cole asked. "Nearly finished?"

Sheridan kind of wanted to slug him for his near-tranquil breathing. But she didn't want to do anything that might cause him to not help her if she needed it. And besides, slugging took energy and will. She had neither.

"We're getting there," she managed to say. "There've been a few contractor issues, but other than that we're on schedule."

"Better be, right? Isn't that where Deac and Mac are doing the deed?"

She laughed, or tried to. It came out sounding like a wheeze. "The ceremony will be outside, but yes."

He shook his head. "Can't believe Deacon's getting hitched."

"Why's that?" After working with the man for years, she'd thought the same thing, but she was curious about his brother's position.

Cole shrugged his powerful, inked-up shoulders as they hit the outskirts of town. "I don't know. It isn't because he doesn't deserve it or that I thought he was going to be a three-piece-suit of a bachelor for the rest of his life. Just makes me feel like we're all outgrowing our bindings, our pasts."

Sheridan wanted to know more, wanted to hear what his bindings were, maybe what James's were. But she was starting to hurt in more places than just her feet. Her legs, her ass, and maybe her chest. Just as she was thinking about stopping, or lying down in the street for a quick nap—or just to get some air back in her lungs—she nearly collided with someone who was crossing the street. As she tried to sidestep, she felt Cole's hands on her, jerking her back.

"Oops," a woman called out, doing a bit of her own stumbling. She righted herself quickly and looked at each of them in turn. "Sorry about that."

"You weren't looking where you were going," Cole scolded in a voice completely unlike the one he'd used with Sheridan only a few moments ago.

The town veterinarian, Grace Hunter, ignored him and focused on Sheridan. "Again, I'm sorry. I was distracted."

"And I was desperate for a reason to stop," Sheridan said, leaning over and putting her hands on her legs. "So, bless you."

The woman laughed.

"Lesson number one in running, Sheridan," Cole said, his tone remaining ice-cold. "It's important to keep your eyes open and your guard up so you can see a problem coming."

Sheridan glanced up just in time to see two pink patches warm Grace's cheeks. "I need to get to the clinic." She gave Sheridan a tight-lipped smile and continued on her way.

The anger's flowing freely around here, Sheridan thought, unfolding her body so she was mostly standing straight again. Holding her side, she started walking in the direction of her hotel. Instead of getting back to his running, Cole did the same.

"Please don't feel obligated to walk with me," she said. "Especially at this snail's pace. I'm sure I'll get back to my hotel. It might be around dinnertime, but I'll get there."

He laughed, his eyes now clear of the bitterness from a moment ago.

"I'm sorry about that, Mr. Cavanaugh," Sheridan began. "I know this situation with Dr. Hunter and her father has got to be difficult."

"Cole," he said. "Please. I'm so far from a Mr. Cavanaugh it's laughable."

She smiled up at him through her pain and nodded. "All right."

"I know you were at the Bull's Eye when she came to the table, talking about her daddy, claiming he had a diary that could name my sister's killer. But did Deacon or James tell you how she ain't talking about it anymore? How she won't let us see the man? How she tells us it was just his rattled, sick mind, his medication that made him claim those things?" His jaw tightened.

Sheridan's pulse quickened again, and it wasn't because of the run. "I didn't know all of that, no."

He looked at her, brow lifted. "What would you do?"

"I'm sorry?"

"I mean, how would you handle something like that—someone like that. A person who you're sure knows more than she's saying? Someone who's covering up the truth to protect a man who might just hold the key to an unsolved murder?" He swallowed hard. "To a truth you were never sure you wanted to hear, but now can't get out of your mind for anything?"

Honestly, she couldn't imagine. The pain of losing a sibling had to be devastating, but not knowing what happened to her or who took her life? That had to be hell on earth.

She treaded carefully. She was still a little surprised that he'd shared so much with her. After all, they were basically strangers. Then again, she wanted to help.

"Have you talked with Dr. Hunter?" she asked as they headed up Main.

"Deacon and James have. They got nowhere."

"But not you?"

He eyed her. "I'm what some might refer to as a 'loose cannon,' Sheridan. Deac and James, they have control over their tempers. I know my limits, and what'll push me over them." He dropped his chin. "Outside of the ring anyway."

Yes, she'd heard something about his history

with fighting. Underground mostly, and for huge purses. But she believed he was training for some kind of mainstream fight these days.

"I think you might surprise yourself," she told him. "Especially if you're vulnerable."

His lip curled just a hair. "How do you mean?"

"Tell her about your sister. Tell her some of your best memories. Make it personal."

"Why?"

"All everyone's focused on is the crime." She shrugged. "Maybe someone needs to focus on Cass."

For a moment, it looked as though he might combust—from grief, anger . . . she wasn't sure. But after a moment or two, he sighed out a curse and uttered, "I'll think about it."

When they reached the sidewalk in front of her hotel, Sheridan turned to him. "This is me. Thanks for the company."

He nodded, gave her a tight smile. "Thanks for the advice." He glanced down the street. "I think I'm going to go again."

"Another run?" she exclaimed. She said it so loudly and sounded so shocked, he laughed.

"Yeah."

"How long was your first one?"

"Only ten miles."

Her brows lifted, and just that tiny movement made her muscles ache. "Impressive. And kind of insane."

Cole gave her an absolutely wicked grin. "That's me. Insane and impressive."

Sheridan broke into a trickle of unabashed laughter. That is, until she heard a male voice rumble with irritation behind her, "Up early, and getting sweaty with my little brother, Miss O'Neil?"

Seven

James understood that the jealousy rushing through his blood was complete bullshit and yet he couldn't stop himself. He just didn't like anyone making Sheridan laugh. Even his little brother.

"You're up early, James," Cole pointed out.

"Grabbing some coffee," he explained, his voice tight with tension. "Elena wasn't around when I stopped by the house." He turned from Cole to Sheridan. She looked hot, sweaty, tired, and sexy. She was wearing tight black exercise pants and a navy blue jogging bra. She was definitely a lean woman; he hadn't been kidding about that. But in that outfit, you could see plain and simple how ample her assets were. His hands twitched. Cole could see her too.

"You two workout buddies now?" he asked, sounding exactly like what he was—a jealous jackass.

Clearly Sheridan thought so too because not only did she ignore his question, but she looked behind her at the door to the hotel.

"Excuse me," she said, giving him a tight smile. "I have a busy day." She waved at Cole. "Good luck with the run."

Feeling like a damn lech, James watched her walk away, his body reacting to every stride in those tight black pants. The woman had the sexiest ass on the planet. A fact he knew he'd never be able to expunge from his memory.

"Maybe you need to do something about that, J."

Cole's words brought James's head around. He blinked a couple times to refocus. "About what?"

"The drool running down your chin," Cole said, deadpan.

Instinctively, James brought his hand to his mouth, then when he realized he was being played, dropped it and narrowed his eyes on his little brother. "What are you doing here?"

Cole laughed. "In River Black or in like a metaphysical sense?"

"Why are you with Sheridan?" James clarified with irritation.

"Ahhh," Cole said. Then shrugged. "We went running together."

James's heart dropped like a stone. "What?"

"Jeez." Cole laughed. "Take it easy. I was kidding. We met up on the road."

"Like that?" James asked, knocking his chin in the direction of Cole's chest.

Glancing down, the man asked, "You mean without my shirt?"

"Not everybody needs to see your ink, Cole," James ground out.

"Maybe not," he agreed. "But they want to." Once again he started laughing. "Look, brother. We just jogged and talked. That's it."

"She say anything about me?"

"Nope." Cole looked at him oddly, maybe like he thought James was losing it. And hell, maybe he was.

He didn't know if that made him relieved or pissed off. It should be the former.

"You know you could just ask her out," Cole suggested.

He pretended not to understand. "Who?"

Cole ignored him. "It's pretty simple. You like her and she likes you. God knows why she does. I know you have those eyes and all the horse-whisperer mystery shit going on, but you acted like a real jerk back there."

He lifted one eyebrow. "Horse-whisperer mystery? Really?"

Cole shrugged. "I'm just guessing that's why a chick might be into you."

"And it's not simple, by the way. She's Deacon's assistant."

"So what?"

James waited for a couple people to walk by before he responded. "You're only saying that because you have no boundaries."

"Very true." Cole bent down to tie his shoelace. "And you know, maybe you're right about her being on Deac's payroll and that's inappropriate and everything. But just because you can't have her, and that pisses you off, doesn't give you an excuse to be a dick to her."

"I wasn't a dick."

He stood up again. "Okay, sunshine. I got to go."

Christ, had he been a dick? He hadn't wanted to come across that way. Maybe aloof or cool. Something that kept distance between them.

Cole was just about to bolt when he stopped. "Hey, I forgot to tell you, we ran into the vet. Like literally. She and Sheridan nearly gave each other matching concussions."

The puzzling and frustrating Dr. Hunter. James had left her half a dozen messages in the past two days. All of which had been ignored. So while Deacon was pulling up the ex-sheriff's financial records from his office in Dallas, James was searching the Internet for all care facilities within a hundred-mile radius. So far, he'd found six. None of which housed a Peter Hunter. "Did she say anything?"

Cole shook his head. "But your girl was trying to convince me I should take a turn talking to her."

"Sheridan's not my girl."

"Would you have a problem if I made her my girl?" Cole asked, deadpan.

Heat rushed into James's chest, and his head was suddenly filled with buzzing. "Are you trying to piss me off, little brother?"

"Yes, I think so." A giant grin broke out on the fighter's face. He wiggled his eyebrows at James.

"Idiot." James gave him a reluctant smile, then jerked his head in the direction of the street. "Get out of here."

Without another word, James turned and headed for Marabelle's, leaving his brother and the man's diabolical laughter behind.

"Okay, one last time and just to be clear," Sheridan warned, "I'm no fashionista."

"Not required," Mac called out from behind the closed bathroom door that was attached to the large master suite inside the Triple C's main house. "You do have nice taste though. And I'm pretty certain that if I look hideous, you'll tell me." She opened the door a crack and stuck her head out. "Right?"

Sheridan grinned at the woman who had a nervous smile and two or three dirt streaks from working cattle earlier on her face. "Absolutely."

"Okay, then," Mac said on a dramatic exhale. "Here goes." She opened the door completely and revealed both herself and the Triple C's housekeeper—and temporary dresser—Elena, who was standing behind her looking wistful and misty-eyed. "This is number one."

Seated on a leather chair near an unlit fireplace, Sheridan took in the woman who was walking toward her. Her thick brown hair was piled on top of her head in a loose bun, and her blue eyes were filled with hope and anxiety as she stopped in the center of the room, her back to the freestanding full-length mirror. The dress she had on was a brilliant white satin with intricate lace and beading. It seemed to cover nearly every inch of her, but when she turned around in a circle, a panel of nearly see-through lace displayed her tanned back to perfection. It was beautiful and elegant, and reminded Sheridan of something a member of the royal family would wear.

"So . . . ?" Mac said, turning back to regard Sheridan.

"Before I give you my opinion," Sheridan began, "let me ask you something. Can you see yourself walking down the aisle toward Mr. Cava—," she paused and checked herself. "Can you see yourself walking toward Deacon in this dress? Can you imagine dancing with him in this dress? Does it feel comfortable or confining? Does it feel like—"

"You hate it," Mac broke in with her singular brand of candor.

Sheridan laughed. "I don't hate it. I actually think it's beautiful. It's just not right for you."

Her blue eyes no longer anxious, but direct, Mac cocked one hip and regarded her. "Sheridan, honey, you don't have to ask me anything, all right? This is a yes-or-no proposition. Ugly or stunning. Love it or hate it."

"I was going for diplomatic and supportive," Sheridan called as Mac disappeared behind the door again.

"I don't need any of that horseshit," Mac called back.

Sheridan laughed again and shook her head. This was going to be a process. But clearly not a boring one. Boring wasn't possible when Mackenzie Byrd was around. It was one of the many reasons Sheridan liked the woman. She'd never met anyone who both told it like it was and allowed others to see her vulnerability. It was a striking and brave combination.

The next dress was infinitely better. It fit her perfectly, and was cut off the shoulder. With all the work she did on the ranch and all the time she spent outside, Mackenzie had a gorgeous tan and a killer body, and the white satin mermaid-style gown showed that off to perfection. But even so, when she paraded herself in front of Sheridan this time, the executive assistant gave it to her like she'd wanted—no punches pulled.

"Not it."

Mac beamed. "That's my girl." Then disappeared behind the door again.

The next two dresses were horrible. One was knee length and pale pink, which did not suit Mac's coloring at all, and the other fit well, but looked like lingerie. Sheridan even suggested Mac keep it for her wedding night. Which brought on a string of giggles so unlike the forewoman of the Triple C Ranch, Sheridan couldn't help but join in. Even made her wish she'd brought along a little champagne to celebrate the occasion.

Three more followed; two were decent, and one reminded Sheridan of the Black Swan. She was really starting to worry that they wouldn't find anything right when the door opened again and *it* walked through.

Moments like those can only be described as magical. Where Sheridan had been so sure of all the previous dresses—so sure they weren't right—as Mac walked toward her, her entire body flooded with warmth and happiness and uncomplicated knowing. Sheridan covered her mouth with her hand, and, without her permission, tears sprang to her eyes.

And Sheridan O'Neil did not do tears.

She swiped them away quickly. But not before Mac noticed, and hurried forward, looking panicked. "Oh my God, is it that bad? I thought it fit pretty well and so did Elena."

Sheridan shook her head. "It's perfect."

The words seemed to transform the woman,

ease her, thrill her. She clasped her hands together. "Really?"

"Elena?" Sheridan called past her. "This is it, isn't it?"

Elena was standing in the doorway, her blue eyes pinned to the stunningly beautiful, floor-length, white strapless dress with tulle and lace appliqué on both the bodice and hemline. "Deacon won't know what hit him, honey," she said. "I think you got your wedding duds."

Strange sensations washed over Sheridan as she watched Mac turn in slow circles in front of the mirror. And those unwelcome tears . . . Where had they come from? Yes, Mac looked beautiful and excited for her big day, but that wasn't what had brought on the waterworks.

Was it the idea of marriage? Or rather the belief that it wasn't an institution she would ever be entering into?

She searched her heart. Her father's choice to leave and her mother's struggle to put food on the table and a roof over their heads had certainly caused Sheridan to form many opinions and to resist trusting anyone with her heart. But her decision to never get married had always brought her comfort, not tears.

James Cavanaugh's movie-star handsome face entered her mind, those aqua eyes fringed by dark lashes lifting to pin her where she stood. Was it

him? This new presence in her life? This man who
told her outright that he liked her, kissed her like
he wanted to consume her, connected with horses
like it was the most spiritual act in the world?
Were her tears about him?

Or about the realization that, for the first time in
her life, she might want to wear a white dress for
someone?

"Sheridan?" Mac called, pulling her from her
thoughts.

She looked up. "Yes?"

Looking slightly sheepish, Mac walked over to
her again. She looked like an angel. A beautiful,
funny, tough, loving, country angel.

"Would you consider . . ." She paused, looked
away, then back again. "I know this is unusual,
but I don't have many friends who aren't cowboys
or ranchers."

"I'm sure that's not true," Sheridan said.

"What I mean is, I don't have many friends who
are women."

"Oh." It was something Sheridan understood
all too well, and could empathize with.

Mac stumbled on quickly. "I work so much, and
the people I work with are mostly men."

Sheridan nodded. "I understand. I actually
have the same problem."

Mac brightened, her eyes growing hopeful.
"Well, then, maybe you would consider it."

"Consider what?"

"Being my maid of honor?"

The room seemed to bow with the weight of that question. And the responsibility. It was so stunning, so unexpected. It didn't belong to her. She hardly knew this woman.

Taking Sheridan's silence as a sign to explain further, Mac continued. "I know you work for Deacon, but that just can't be the thing that stops us from being friends. I think it would be a real shame if it did, don't you?"

Sheridan sighed. "It's a very important job, Mac . . ."

The woman grinned and cocked her head to the side. "It would mean a lot to me."

"I've never been in a wedding. I wouldn't know what to do—"

"It's not all that much," she jumped in quickly. "I promise. You'll need a dress. So, a couple of fittings. And you can pick out your own. I'd just like it to be red. And there's a few odds and ends to see to, and the rehearsal dinner. It's usually hosted by the groom's parents, but they're not here so . . . The job is going to the maid of honor and the best man." She grimaced. "I guess that isn't a small number of things. You can say no."

Sheridan knew she could say no. That Mac would understand and all would be fine. But the woman's impassioned words about friendship had pierced her heart a few centimeters, and Sheridan didn't want to let her down. She gave Mac an amused shake of the head. "I'm not going to say no."

"You're not?" the woman squealed, then quickly composed herself. "Thank you, thank you."

Moving easily into professional mode, Sheridan took out her phone. "I suppose I should get started on a few of the main things. The dinner, mostly, since that's going to need some planning. Who's the best man?"

Mac glanced up, her blue eyes flashing like twin sapphires. "Someone both easy to work with and easy on the eyes."

Sheridan's brows slid together. "What do you mean?

A slow smile spread across the bride-to-be's face. "The best man is James Cavanaugh."

Eight

James sat on his naked ass in the river, letting the current move over and against him, healing his slightly sunburned skin and washing away all the grime and sweat of the day. It was something he and Deac and Cole had done when they were boys. Especially in the summertime. Back then, the river wasn't as deep as it was now. Maybe reached their knees, if that. And they'd had a hell of a time covering up their bits and pieces when they were sitting. But since no one really came out that way, except a stray cow, a few chattering squirrels, or other ranch varmints, they didn't think all that much about it. Later, after Cass was taken from that movie-theater bathroom, taken from all of them, it had been their solace and their escape when Mama would forget herself and allow her anger to drive her actions. James's hands fisted in the water. Sometimes she had hurt them with objects, sometimes with words. Most of the time, he'd wished she'd used a whip or a paddle, her hand or a wooden spoon. Anything but words. There was nothing that crushed a boy more than hearing his mama tell him he was a worthless coward for not having protected his sister.

Except maybe a father who looked the other way when she did.

Movement and the rustle of leaves echoed all around the riverbank. No doubt one of those ranch critters he'd just been thinking about, though that didn't stop him from running his gaze over the heavily treed area. Like he'd told Sheridan last night; this was a small town with lots of good country folk. But that didn't mean there weren't a few vipers slithering around.

When the sound came again, he knew he had company of the human variety. "Who's there?" he called out. "If you don't have four legs and a tail, I'd suggest you show yourself."

To his surprise, Sheridan stepped out from behind a tree about halfway between the river and the bunkhouse. She looked real pretty, kind of dressed up for a day mucking around. Her hair was piled on top of her head and she was wearing a black silk tank and tight jeans that were tucked into an expensive pair of boots. His chest tightened, and below the surface of the water, things were starting to get problematic. As in, he wasn't going to be standing up anytime soon.

She headed his way, but stopped by a large but-tonbush shrub when she got a look at where he was, and the clothes that were tossed into a pile on the bank.

"I knocked on your door," she called out to him. "You weren't there." She laughed at herself. "Prob-ably because you're here."

She seemed rattled, and he both loved and hated that he had that effect on her. "Something you need, Sheridan?"

Her eyes dipped from his face and traveled down his chest. "I was just helping Mac choose a dress for the wedding . . ."

"Oh, right," he said, wondering if she liked what she saw. He knew he did. With every move-ment she made, his mouth got drier, and shit worsened down south. Tight jeans and boots re-ally worked on her. "How'd that go?"

"Good. Great, actually." She covered another couple of feet, stopping beside the nearly buried rock that held his clothes. "She found the perfect thing. A gorgeous dress. She looked amazing. She's going to be a stunning bride. I can just see her, you know? Walking down the aisle, the sun setting all around her, the breeze off the lake . . ."

"I think I can see it too," he said with a thread of amusement. He never would've figured Sheri-dan O'Neil for someone who got all flustered over wedding duds.

Her eyes shot to his and she shrugged. "Got

carried away. All that lace and satin messes with your rational mind. Just FYI."

He grinned. Damn, she was adorable. "I'll try to remember that."

"Good. And I'm not positive, but I think tulle and tiaras might have the same effect."

"Oh, shit," he said completely deadpan.

Her eyes went wide and she stilled. "What?" She looked around for something, anything that could've caused his reaction.

He sighed dramatically. "I guess I'll have to stop wearing my tiaras."

For a moment, she just stared at him. Then she started laughing, and the sound drilled a hole in his chest, trying most ardently to get to his heart.

"Perfect," she said. "Very smart." She cleared her throat. "Anyway, I have a point in coming here. And it's not to talk about the mental effects of fabric choices or to sneak up on you when you're nak—" She cut herself off, her cheeks turning a lovely shade of pink.

Hell, James mused, if she continued like this he was going to have no choice but to rush out of the water and kiss her again. Hard-on, or not.

"You're Deacon's best man," she said finally.

"I am." If he asked her to come closer, right up to the water's edge, would she? And if she did, and if he pulled her into the river with him, would she be mad? Getting that silk shirt wet, those tight jeans even tighter? Or would she welcome his touch, him holding her?

"I'm Mac's maid of honor," she announced, tugging him from his thoughts.

His brows drifted up. "Is that right?"

"I know. It's crazy. We hardly know each other. It's just she doesn't have many friends who are girls."

He gestured to his face. "It's not surprise you think you're seeing here."

"No?"

He shook his head. "What you're seeing is relief. Being the best man is serious pressure. You don't want to add to it by having some crazy stranger take up the part of the maid of honor."

"I'm glad I could help," she said with humor.

"Now, now. It's not just that. There's happiness too. For Mac. She's a good egg. Like a sister to me and Cole. And you're right, she doesn't have a ton of female friends. It's nice for her to have someone like you by her side."

The humor in her gray eyes died away and in its place was a softness, a genuine warmth that made his insides crackle. "She told me that we host the rehearsal dinner the night before the wedding."

"With our parents gone, I suppose that's the best option," he said.

"Do you have any ideas?" she asked him.

"I . . ."

"For the dinner."

"Well . . ."

"It's coming up pretty quickly."

He gave her a sheepish grin. "You want the truth?"

"Always," she answered.

"I was planning on thinking about it the morning of."

"Thinking? The morning . . ." Her eyes bulged and her mouth dropped open. "You can't be serious?" She sounded as if his lack of enthusiasm was tantamount to kicking a puppy.

"Come on now," he chided. "It's just family and close friends going to that thing. We can take them anywhere. The Bull's Eye maybe."

"I see." She started chewing her lip.

Oh Lord. "You want to plan something, don't you?" he asked.

She nodded, then quickly amended, "But you don't have to do anything. I can take care of the whole event. I'm very good at this kind of thing."

"I bet you are." He lifted an eyebrow at her. "You already have an idea."

It was her turn to look sheepish. "Kind of."

Normally, in a situation like this one—and hell, if the maid of honor had been anyone else—James would've said, "Thank you very much, ma'am, and just tell me where to park my horse that night." But it was Sheridan and, God help him, that made him want to get involved.

"Turn around, Miss O'Neil," he commanded good-naturedly.

She looked offended. "I told you, you don't have to be involved. I'll take care of everything."

"Good God, woman. I'm not asking you to leave. Just to turn around so I can get out of the water and put my clothes on."

"Oh," she said, her entire demeanor changing. "Right. Turning around now." Then promptly gave him her back.

James stood up and trudged out of the water. "Listen, Sheridan, I want to apologize again for last night—"

"There's no need."

"There is," he insisted, heading over to the rock. He grabbed his jeans and yanked them on. "I was a jackass. I scared you—"

"Okay." She turned back around. Her eyes dropped immediately to his bare chest and her cheeks flamed. "Let's get something straight. You didn't scare me. I wasn't afraid of you."

His gut twisted. Just the words coming out of her mouth made him sick. "Sheridan . . ."

"I was afraid of me, James. That kiss . . ." She chewed her lip for a second and released a weighty breath. "Oh my God . . . It was magical. I've never felt that out of control. I wasn't thinking. I didn't want to think. And I was scared I'd do something . . ."

"What?" he asked, existing somewhere between wanting to know and knowing it was dangerous as hell to know.

"Life altering," she said finally. "You don't want to get into something serious or committed, and neither do I."

No matter how much truth her words held, James despised them. It almost would've been easier if she *had* been afraid of him. Now he knew she wanted him just as much as he wanted her. And like him, she was trying to tamp it down, bury it.

Where the hell did they go from here?

He walked up to where she was standing. "Come on, maid of honor."

"Where are we going?" she asked.

"My place." His chin dropped and he said in all seriousness, "To talk, plan this shindig." And to try to forget she'd just called their kiss magical.

Sheridan paced the living room floor of the bunkhouse as she listened to the sound of a shower running. James was in there. Naked once again. Water hitting those waves of abdominal muscles that she'd seen up close and personal down at the river. Not for the first time she wondered if Mac had known what her soon-to-be brother-in-law was doing when she'd suggested Sheridan go and find him to discuss their ideas for the rehearsal dinner. She couldn't have, right? Granted, Mac seemed keen on the whole matchmaking thing between Sheridan and James, but she wasn't keeping tabs on the guy's comings and goings.

Even with her eyes open and focused on the sizable living space and its furnishings, the image of James Cavanaugh in the river—and out of it— was burned on her retinas.

She stopped near the short hallway that led to the bathroom. Would it be irrational, inappropriate, and several other adjectives for her to go into the bathroom and offer up her shampooing services? He had such great hair. And sometimes, it was hard to reach the back of the scalp.

Groaning at her insanity, Sheridan headed for the couch. She sat in one corner and just let the breeze through the open windows soothe her. The fading sunlight too. It seemed every spot in River Black came armed with beauty in some form or another. She'd miss it when it was time to go.

She sighed a little wistfully. Just a couple more weeks and she'd be leaving River Black. After the wedding and the completion of construction on the house, she was pretty sure Deacon would want her back in the office in Dallas.

And hell, that was what she should be wanting too. She'd worked her ass off to get where she was. A crush on a cowboy was not going to derail her dreams and goals. No matter how amazing the cowboy happened to be. Giving up a solid future you could see and control for a romance . . . she'd seen how that ended.

Her phone buzzed, and she glanced down at the incoming text. Her mouth turned into a tight, thin line. That bastard was working her last nerve. She was pretty convinced that Caleb Palmer was buying inferior materials and pocketing the difference, but she hadn't found definitive proof yet. She would though, and then she'd have enough to fire him, and bring in a reputable contractor. Hopefully all before Deacon returned.

"Everything okay?"

Sheridan startled and looked up from her phone. Holy buckets of ice water, she thought as she took in the sight before her. Standing beside the couch, looking like something off the pages of *People* magazine or one of those other celebrity rag mags, was a freshly showered James Cavanaugh. His hair was still wet, darker looking and finger combed. His eyes appeared impossibly blue and— *heart, don't fail me now*—genuinely concerned about the way she had been staring at her phone. But it was the clothing he had on that had her mouth drying up quicker than a rain puddle in the desert. It was nothing fancy, just jeans and a white T-shirt. But it was how that T-shirt fit over his powerful chest, and how a few damp patches where the towel had missed made that T-shirt slightly see-through.

Licking her lips in case there was actual drool present, she put away her phone. "It's just Mr. Palmer. He's trying to get out of meeting with me."

"Why's that?"

Telling James about her suspicions felt unwise and premature. And something she should discuss with Deacon first. She attempted to be vague. "It's not uncommon for people to see what they can get away with when it comes to money. They push, and I'm required to push back."

That answer didn't seem to appease him. "I can have a word with him."

"Absolutely not," she said firmly. "This is my job."

"Just saying, if you need backup . . ."

"I appreciate that, but no, thank you."

"All right." His eyes moved over her face. "But it's a standing offer."

Her skin warmed and tightened under his gaze, and she replied with the dumbest question in the world. "How was your shower?"

To his credit, James didn't laugh or ask her to leave and never come back. Instead, he smiled. "Wet."

Her eyes widened and every inch of flesh below her navel erupted into flames.

"And hot," he continued, his tone even.

Her lips parted to accommodate her quicker breaths.

"And if I say it was also a little lonely, will that make you think less of me?" he asked, brow lifted.

"Not at all," she said weakly. Think less? Was he kidding? That was a thinking MORE kind of question if ever she'd heard one. "But isn't that the very nature of a shower?" she returned. "To wash yourself . . . alone?" Was she actually saying these words? Out loud?

"Not if you're doing it right," he said with a roguish grin.

Sheridan's heart stuttered. Why had she come here again? *To stare at his chest?* No. *Gaze into his eyes?* No. *Request a nonlonely shower of her own?* Absolutely not!

"Can I get you something to drink?" he asked her. "Water? Beer?"

"I'll take a beer." In fact, if it would tame her mood, maybe she'd have a few.

He headed for the kitchen. "Never would've pegged you for a beer-drinking girl," he called back.

"I am very versatile, Mr. Cavanaugh."

"I'm starting to learn that, Miss O'Neil." When he returned, he handed her a bottle, then dropped down on the leather couch opposite. "So, tell me your plan."

Hmmm, let's see. Drink my beer and try not to keep imagining you naked in the river, or the shower, or . . . here and now . . .

"For the rehearsal dinner," he continued, his eyes sparkling with amusement.

Kind of like he could read her mind. Or her expression.

"Right." She took a healthy swallow, then eased

back against the couch cushions. "I was thinking outside, under the moonlight, a few long wooden tables covered in flowers or greenery. A feast, family-style. Maybe a jazz quartet or something fun playing a ways off. Wine and beer," she lifted her bottle, "Lemonade and laughs. Elegant country."

"That's a lot of thinking for such a short amount of time," he said. "I like it."

A quick grin touched her lips. "Really?"

He nodded. "And where are you imagining these tables set up? Or the music playing? Redemption?"

The grin slipped. This was the part she was dreading, though she really wanted to put it on the table for discussion because she believed it would mean something to both Deacon and Mac. "I was actually thinking it could be here, at the Triple C."

James's easy mood changed in a heartbeat. A storm moved across his expression, and his lips hardened. "Absolutely not."

Nine

James hadn't meant to shut the idea down so quickly and so ruthlessly, but instinct was like that. It jumped to your defense before your rational mind got there. He leaned forward and tried to be as diplomatic as possible. "Thing is, I don't know if Deacon would be okay with it."

She nodded, and didn't look nearly as affronted as he thought she might be. In fact, it was almost as if she'd expected this response. "I'll ask him. When he returns."

"Let me save you the trouble, Sheridan. I know my brother." *And he'd feel the same way as I would.*

"I think it could be a good thing for everyone," she suggested.

"Do you?"

Once again, his tone was bordering on harsh, but it didn't seem to faze her. Clearly, she knew more than he realized about her boss's past. And

for a second, James wondered if she knew anything about his. Just the thought made his flesh
crawl.

"It just seems like this place has taken too much
control away from those who used to live here—
and hell, maybe the ones who still do." She took a
sip of her beer and shrugged. "Maybe it's time to
take that control back."

"Not sure how that's possible. Or if anyone
even wants to try." He appreciated her sentiment.
He knew it came from the heart. But even so, it
didn't make the idea any more attractive. "No
wedding celebration should be held in the steely
and constricting arms of pain."

She paused, regarded him with curious eyes.
"That's not Shakespeare."

"No, Ms. O'Neil. That's me." He pointed the
neck of his beer bottle Sheridan's way. "Let's
come up with an alternative. Maybe something
on the way out of town." He inhaled deeply.
"Now that would hold some good memories for
Deacon." He snorted. "For all of us."

Sheridan didn't say anything at first. Sipping her
beer, she studied him. Then finally, she asked,
"How old were you?"

"When?"

"When you left River Black?"

Ah, Christ. Were they really going here? "I dunno,"
he said. He took a healthy swallow. "Eighteen,
maybe."

Her brows drifted upward. "That's young."

"Trust me, I was plenty grown," he assured her.

"And did you know you wanted to work with horses?"

"No. That didn't come until later."

"So, what did you do?"

"Went to college." Leaving the C, River Black, his father behind—even his brothers—and walking into the university, he'd been like a kid in a candy store. Hungry, excited, ready to try just about anything. "After testing the waters a bit, I landed on English literature."

That brought about a stunned expression. Cowboy from a small ranching town in Texas going off to school to read and critique poetry and fiction and the lot. It was always a surprise to people.

"You have a degree in English literature?" she asked.

His jaw went tense. "No." He stood up and headed for the kitchen. "I didn't finish," he called back as he rummaged in the fridge. "I left before my senior year."

When he returned with two more beers, she asked him the inevitable question, "Why's that?"

He placed one down on the coffee table in front of her. "I realized it wasn't the place for someone like me."

"That's an odd thing to say. Someone like you? What does that mean? A country boy? An animal lover?"

James inhaled sharply. He'd reached that point when answers became an invitation to judge or resent or worse, pity. And he didn't want any of that from Sheridan. He didn't want her to know about the girlfriend who'd gone out one night without him and been attacked. Just like he didn't want her to know the depth of his guilt about not going to the bathroom when his little sister had asked him to. It was somehow okay that he knew his track record for failing the women in his life. But for her to know . . .

"Were the other students jerks?" she pressed. "Or was the school too big and you were used to something smaller?"

"You ask a lot of questions," James ground out.

She shrugged. "Is that wrong?"

"Maybe." Definitely.

"Just trying to get to know you. Remember?" She smiled gently.

"Not sure I see the point in that," he said sharply.

"Excuse me?"

"You're going back to Dallas, and I'm going somewhere else, right?"

She instantly recoiled, but managed to say, "That's the plan."

"All right then." He shrugged casually, but inside he was all firecrackers just lit and ready to explode. He felt defensive and exposed, and he just wanted to drop the whole goddamn thing and get back to wedding nonsense and party planning. He brought his beer up to his mouth and drained the second bottle. "I say we just make it easy on ourselves, and book the Bull's Eye. This wedding is about Deacon and Mac, not some quest to drive out the demons from our past. Because trust me when I say that's never going to happen. And even if it could, it's not your place to try."

He knew he sounded fierce, but he didn't realize just how fierce until the haze cleared and he saw her face. Her expression. Though she tried to hide it well, she looked hurt. No. It was more than hurt. She looked wounded. And he was responsible.

With grace, she set her half-empty beer down on the table, then stood. "Thanks for the drink."

"Sheridan?"

She was already headed for the door. "Good night, James."

James cursed. He was such an ass. But she'd pushed him too far. What was he supposed to do? Spill his guts? Tell her all that had happened? Tell her no matter what he was feeling for her, she deserved something more, something better? Tell her how she would never truly be safe with him? That he was cursed. And deserved to be.

And then what?

She'd walk away from you just like she was doing now.

Fuck.

He was up and rounding the couch. "Where you going, Sheridan?"

"I have a lot of work to do," she said, reaching for the door handle. "And honestly, when someone reacts like that to a person, it's usually a sign they don't want the person around."

Shit, if she only knew. How badly he wanted her around. How desperately he'd wanted to press her back to the couch and kiss her breathless, kiss her until she stopped asking question after question about a past that was too painful to discuss.

The door was halfway open by the time he got there. He didn't try to block her way. "Don't go. Please."

She didn't look at him, but her jaw was tight with tension.

"Sheridan?"

"Why stay?" she asked, her eyes pinned to the door.

"Because . . . damn . . ." He shook his head. Yeah, asshole? Why should she even consider staying here with you? After the way you talked to her. Unless you're gonna be honest. About the past, and how you feel about her.

She headed out the door and onto the porch.

Why couldn't he say it? What the hell was wrong with him that he could be so easily cruel, but he couldn't be even remotely vulnerable?

"You should stay," he said, coming to stand in

the doorway. "Because you make the air around me easier to breathe."

At the bottom of the stairs, she stopped.

"You should stay because you make me smile and laugh." He released a breath. "And I haven't done much of either for more years than I care to count. You should stay because I actually do want you to know me despite how hard I keep trying to stop that from happening. You should stay because I want to know you too. Want to make you smile. And then, of course, there's the thing about not wanting to take showers alone when you're around."

For a moment, James wondered if he'd crossed the line with that last bit. But then she turned around, and though her expression wasn't by any means light, it was open.

She exhaled heavily, then shook her head. "You said I was going back to Dallas and you were going somewhere—"

"I know. And I was an ass for saying it."

"But it's true. For both of us, it's true."

He broke from the doorway, headed across the porch and down the steps. When he reached her, he gently took her by the shoulders. When her eyes found his, he said, "Tell me what you want, Sheridan."

Pain and fear crossed her expression. "I don't know. I've lived for one thing most of my life. To protect myself against just this sort of situation."

"What situation is that?"

"Liking someone." She smiled softly, sadly. "Liking someone so much you can see losing your-self in them. Liking someone so much you *want* to lose yourself in them. Does that make sense?"

"Yes." Perfect, problematic, worrisome sense. " 'The wheel is come full circle.' "

The tension in her body eased somewhat and she gave him a small smile. *"King Lear."*

He nodded.

"You love the tragedies, Mr. Cavanaugh."

He shrugged. "I suppose because I am one, Miss O'Neil."

She reached up and touched his face. " 'Having nothing, nothing can he lose.' "

Her words made his gut ache and twist. Not because she knew her Shakespeare and that tied him in knots in a whole other way, but because they made absolute and tragic sense to him.

"I'm going to go," she said, though she didn't move away from him.

"Can I take you?"

She shook her head. "Thank you. But I got a ride."

"Mac?"

She laughed. "Me."

He wanted to talk her out of it, then talk her into letting him drive her over to Redemption. But he didn't want to push her any more tonight. He had to respect her space and her choices.

When she finally broke from him, he watched

her walk away into the coming sunset. Across the field and up toward the main house. He watched her until he couldn't see her anymore.

Another night of detective work. That was the best thing. No. That was the *only* thing that was going to keep her mind occupied and off James— off everything he'd said and she'd said back at the bunkhouse.

After she'd locked every door and window and turned all the downstairs lights to blazing (*there you go, James*) she'd texted Caleb Palmer, replying to his message with one of her own. Another request to meet in the morning to discuss finances. She hadn't given him any more information than that because she'd wanted him to show up. He'd written back that he'd come by around ten. So that gave her a full night to gather evidence, make sure she had everything prepared to confront him about the discrepancies in billing and materials.

Tucking her chair deeper into the desk, she took a sip of her smoothie and hit the keyboard of her laptop, pulling up the receipts for lumber, stone, bathroom fixtures, and molding. She'd thought about contacting Deacon first, but knew that he'd put her in charge for a reason. He believed she could handle things, and she wasn't about to prove him wrong.

She was just hitting PRINT when her cell rang. She pressed the speaker button. "Hello?"

"Are you working?" Mac's voice boomed into the quiet space. "You have your work voice on."

"I have a work voice?" Sheridan asked, smiling in spite of herself. "Is it intimidating?"

"Hello," Mac said in her most professional tone. "This is Sheridan O'Neil, and if you don't do your job properly, you will all be fired."

Sheridan snorted, grabbing paperwork from the printer's feeder. "I think you're confusing me with Donald Trump."

"Maybe. You two are so similar."

"Except I have a better comb-over."

Mac laughed. "Come on. Want to meet for a late dinner at Marabelle's? My treat. And it's lemon-meringue-pie night."

She stared at the phone. Boy, times had changed. Going out during work hours, or even after, had never held much appeal for her. Of course, that was before she had a—dare she say it—friend.

"I would love to," she said genuinely. "But I have to work. I have a meeting with the contractor in the morning and I need to prepare."

"Mr. Palmer?" Mac asked. "Everything okay?"

"Absolutely." She didn't want Mac to worry about the property with all she had on her plate. In fact, if Sheridan could manage it, she was hoping Mac wouldn't need to know anything about it. She'd make up some reason about the man not working out.

"All right," Mac said, disappointed. "Another time."

"Save me a piece of pie?"

Mac laughed. "I'll do my best. But I've seen hands scratched and fingers removed for trying to save a piece of that pie. You know Palmer's daughter Natalie makes it."

"The head baker from Hot Buns?" Sheridan asked, surprised.

"The very same. She pretty much supplies every business in town with their required sweets."

Interesting. Truth was Sheridan didn't know all that much about Mr. Palmer. And maybe with what she believed he was doing, she didn't really want to.

Speaking of which, she really needed to get back to work. She switched on her mock professional tone. "I must hang up now, Ms. Byrd, or resort to mass firings. Granted, there's no one here except me. But if I am forced to fire myself—I will."

Mac snorted. "Bye, crazy lady."

"Back atcha." Grinning, Sheridan hung up the phone. It was fun. Mac was fun. How had she gone twenty-five years without this kind of fun? She gathered up her printed copies of research and placed them in separate folders.

Maybe she could work an hour or so, then call Mac back and see if she'd already eaten. They could go to the Bull's Eye for a bit, and Sheridan could down some liquid courage and persuade Mac to spill the beans on James's past. Was it Cass's death that had closed him off to love? Or was there something more? She was desperate to know what had broken his spirit.

For the next thirty minutes, she worked furiously. Searching, printing, calling. Until she finally found what she was looking for, her smoking gun. A contact who had faxed her a statement regarding Mr. Palmer's order for both wood flooring and bathroom tiles. It was three times what the project required. Someone was skimming off the top or using the extra materials for another job.

She was about to grab her phone and dial Mac's number when she heard something outside the office. At first, fear licked at her insides, but then she wondered if maybe it was James, if he'd come to check on her, drive her home, like he had the night before. Maybe she was foolish to continue hanging out with him. Maybe she was signing up for a course in How to Live Out a Shakespearean Tragedy with River Black's Hottest Horse Whisperer. But she didn't care. She liked him. She felt good around him.

When he didn't come up, she got up and headed for the door. Maybe he was waiting in the living room—didn't want to bother her. But as she stepped out into the hallway, she remembered she'd locked all the doors. How could he possibly—

"Evening, sweetheart," Mr. Palmer drawled.

Sheridan's skin instantly prickled. There he was, down the hallway, less than ten feet away. Her gaze shifted past him. No one else. Just him. "Mr. Palmer?" she began cautiously. "What are you doing here?"

The man looked older in the dim light, and his eyes narrowed with every second that passed. "You had questions for me."

"Yes," she said, forcing her tone into one of confident control, not the anxiety she was truly feeling. "But we have a meeting scheduled for tomorrow—"

"I think we'll talk now," he interrupted caustically.

Inside every person is a warning bell. Sometimes you ignore it, tell yourself it's just your imagination. Other times, you listen to it. Both choices carry risks. But as Sheridan took in the man before her, she knew without a shadow of a doubt that he'd come there to hurt her. She didn't know if he'd guessed what their conversation was going to be about tomorrow or if he just wanted to harm her. But she didn't have time to figure it out.

"I can't talk now, unfortunately," she said, gingerly moving backward toward Deacon's office. If she could just get inside, there was a lock on the door. Of course Palmer might very well have the key. But while he was looking for it, she'd have a few precious seconds to slide whatever she could find in front of the door, then call 911.

"Mackenzie Byrd is coming over any minute to take me to dinner," she said lightly. "You know, she's asked me to be her maid of honor."

Palmer laughed. It was a dark, foreboding sound that burrowed inside her chest and tried to steal her breath. "I just saw Ms. Byrd eating at the diner not ten minutes ago." He cocked his head to one side. "I guess you've been stood up, honey."

Shit. Sheridan's heart started to pump wildly. *Back up. Get to the office.*

"I suppose I should be surprised at the dedication you've shown in trying to get me fired," he said, still not moving from his spot in the hallway. "Women can barely manage a checkbook, if you know what I mean. And yet you were able to dig up some very well hidden receipts." He grinned. "Oh, yes, I know."

She needed to run. She could make it.

"But then you're not just the average woman, are you?" One brow slowly lifted. "Sweetheart."

That final word was like a starter pistol firing. Sheridan turned and bolted for the open door of Deacon's office. Once inside, she slammed the door shut and went to lock it. But when she glanced down, thinking herself safe, she saw that the door wasn't closed at all. A black boot tip was wedged just inside it. She was about to slam herself against it when Caleb Palmer entered like a seething, hungry bull, his eyes immediately finding hers.

Her eyes darted past him. Could she get around him?

"Not a chance, sweetheart," he drawled.

Pulse racing, Sheridan turned and headed to the desk. *Please. Please.* Her hands fumbled with paperwork, searching for her cell phone. But she couldn't find it. Not before he grabbed her by the arms and hauled her against him, crushing her. He was shockingly strong, and for a second Sheridan wondered if he was on some kind of drug.

"A man's got to make a living, sweetheart," he said, his body weight driving her back against the wall. "You won't be taking that away from me."

"I don't know what you're talking about," she ground out, struggling, her eyes flickering around the room, looking for anything she could use as a weapon.

"After tonight you won't know much of anything," he threatened, his breath foul against her cheek.

Trembling, her eyes returned to his and she tried once more to be the asshole employer with a very true threat of her own. "If you don't let go of me right now and leave this house, Deacon Cavanaugh will take your life from you. You have no idea what he's capable of."

"And he has no idea what I'm capable of," he returned, then ran his nose up one side of her face. "Honey."

Sheridan turned to him and without thinking, spit in his face. Palmer cursed and jerked back just an inch, but it was enough for her to bring her knee up between his legs, crushing his balls.

He groaned, slumped slightly, but continued to hold her firmly. "Bitch," he ground out, rushing her, slamming her back against the wall.

Air rushed from Sheridan's lungs and spots dotted her vision. But even so, she refused to give in, give up. This piece of shit bastard was not going to fucking take her out. With every ounce of will and strength she had in her, she brought the heel of her boot down hard on his foot, then slammed her head into his nose.

The action made him release her, but it also blurred her vision terribly. She knew he was still in front of her and brought her knee up hard once again. With a groan of shocked pain, he went down on all fours.

Go, go, go!

Breathing heavily, she stumbled to the desk and spotted her phone, which was peeking out from under some paperwork. She grabbed it and ran from the room. And though pain surged through her and her vision was compromised, she refused to stop. Down the hall, down the stairs, through the living room, and out the front door. She didn't think of anything but escape until she was inside her car, windows and doors locked.

Then she stabbed in three numbers with her shaking hands.

"Nine-one-one. Please state your emergency."

"I've been attacked," she cried, tears streaming down her cheeks. "Please come. Redemption Ranch main house."

"Is the person who attacked you still there?" the man asked in a calm, highly trained voice.

"He's in the house," she whispered. Pain shot through her and her vision was narrowing. "It's Caleb Palmer. He tried to kill me."

It was all she could get out before the world went black and she collapsed onto the passenger-side seat of her Subaru.

Ten

Getting ten pills down a gentled horse's throat was near to impossible, and James wasn't even going to attempt to do that with a wild mustang.

After examining Comet's leg, checking to see if the wound was healing properly, James had thrust a syringe inside the stallion's mouth, pumped the medication in real quick, then held his jaw closed until he swallowed. By the time he did, James was drenched in sweat. Luckily, the stallion seemed healed enough to get out of the barn and back to his herd. It wasn't good for the wild ones to be away too long. Tomorrow morning, first thing, he'd take him out.

James started to gather up his things. He needed to get something to eat; then it was going to be a long night in front of the computer. More care facilities to search, sure, but he'd had another idea as he'd worked on Comet. In all the years since leaving River Black, he'd never allowed himself to read any of the newspaper articles or headlines from when Cass was taken. With no hope of finding answers, he'd just pushed the questions away, back into the place where he stored his pain.

But the vet had—like it or not—lit the fire of hope in their hearts.

Tonight he was going to read every last article; see if there was anything he and James and Deac could explore outside of the ex-sheriff. Maybe something about that Sweet character. None of them had remembered a new kid in school at the time. But someone around town had to have known him.

James was just giving Comet one last look-over when Sam came running into the barn.

"Shit, boy, there you are," he exclaimed.

"You out for an evening jog, Sam?" James joked, barely glancing up.

"To your bunkhouse and back."

"Why's that?"

"It's Deac's assistant . . ."

It wasn't the words that had James turning and rushing the stall door. It was Sam's tone. Heavy and scared. Add to that the anxious expression on the man's face, and every hair on James's body was standing straight on end.

"What happened?" he demanded. "Where is she?"

The old cowboy shook his head. "Caleb Palmer.

I've known that man for years. He worked on my sister's place. I see his daughter near every day at the bakery, and his wife's at the church more than the reverend himself! I can't believe it."

Black tangles of fear coursed through James. He vaulted over the stall and headed straight for the old man. "What the fuck happened, Sam? Talk to me."

The man's eyes filled with dismay. "Palmer attacked Miss O'Neil tonight, out at Redemption. Banged her up real bad, I hear."

Ice water froze his veins. "Where?"

"They took her to Green Valley Memorial."

James took off past him, was already running out the barn door when Sam called after him, "They're not letting anyone see her who ain't family."

His head buzzed and his heart slammed fiercely against his ribs. Sheridan had to be okay. Had to be.

He ran for his truck, hoping that he'd left his extra set of keys above the visor.

He'd never laid claim to her. He'd pushed her away. She wasn't his. This shouldn't have happened. He'd done everything he could to keep her safe—keep her away from himself, and that cursed, black cloud overhead. And yet she'd still gotten hurt. Nothing made sense anymore. Nothing except her. He had to see her, make sure she was all right.

He yanked open the door to his truck and dove inside. Keys were right where he'd hoped.

As he gunned the engine and shoved the truck in reverse, he prayed Caleb Palmer was dead. Because if he wasn't, James might be the one going to jail tonight.

Cole sent the dart straight into the center of the bull's-eye and grinned. Matty could suck it. Contrary to what his pain-in-the-ass trainer might think, Cole's eyesight and coordination were on point and ready for the ring. Ready to face his first legit opponent, who also happened to be the one and only member of Cole's Shit List Club.

Not ten minutes ago, Matty had texted him with the news that Fred Omega Fontana had signed on to the fight in three weeks. Trying to be coy, the trainer had asked Cole if he knew Omega. If he'd ever fought him before. To which, Cole had laughed, then flipped off the text.

Did he know Fred Fontana? Shit, he knew the arrogant asshole all too well. Used to be an underground fighter just like himself, trying to make his mark aboveground. Cole could just imagine the marketing campaign that was going to be put together for this fight.

The alpha and the omega face off above ground. Cold as ice, Cole Cavanaugh freezes out Fontana.

Cole aimed his dart and let it fly. Another perfect shot. His grin widened. Fontana was the one fighter he'd never been able to beat. In fact, every time they met in the ring, Cole had come out with something: temporary loss of hearing in both ears or a punctured lung. The guy was cunning and massive and evil, and Cole was more than ready to finally make him bleed.

"Can I get you a drink?" a waitress asked, sidling up to him, tray in hand.

"No, thanks."

"On the house," she purred.

"Another time."

She cocked one leather-clad hip and leaned over so he got an eyeful of cleavage. "You sure, honey?"

It didn't take a genius to understand what she was asking, just a guy with two working eyeballs. But he was off everything for the next few weeks. No alcohol, no drugs, and definitely no sex.

"I'm sure, but thanks," he said, giving the woman a wicked smile.

She returned it and sauntered off.

Cole turned and let the final dart fly. But just as he did, his gaze caught on something. This time, the point didn't hit the target at all. It landed on the edge and dropped to the ground with an embarrassing snap. Cole grimaced. Her fault. The vet. She'd stolen his focus. Sitting there in a corner booth by herself sipping a Shirley Temple or whatever pink thing was in front of her.

For a brief moment, he contemplated ignoring

her, grabbing some more darts and going again. That last shot would not stand. But he didn't possess the ignoring gene. He had the confronting gene. The gene that made a man act before he thought things through.

It's what made him a shitty friend, brother, boyfriend . . . but one helluva fighter.

He came up beside the vet's table, all nice and easy. "Evening, Doc."

Her eyes lifted from her pink drink and settled on him. She blanched. "Mr. Cavanaugh."

He glanced around. "You here alone?" Cole wasn't entirely sure why he'd asked. But she answered before he had a chance to examine his motives.

"No. My date will be back soon."

"Date?" he repeated over the din. "Well, how nice. For you, I mean. Taking a break from all that stressful work at the animal hospital and going out with some pretty-faced country boy."

She forced a smile and her chin lifted a few centimeters. "Speaking of faces," she said. "How are your bruises today?"

"The ones on the outside are fine. They'll heal. Always do. The ones on the inside though . . . only time will tell."

Her jaw tightened and she looked away and shook her head. "I need you to stop this. I know you all are pissed, and you have every right to be. But nothing's going to change."

"Because you're more concerned with protecting your daddy."

"Of course I am."

His nostrils flared at her blatant honesty. "Even if what he knows could be protecting a murderer? Someone who's still out there, and may have killed again?"

A muscle in her jaw pulsed as her eyes slammed into his. "He doesn't know anything."

"Hell, woman," Cole said with dark laughter. "Forget about me, you're going to need to work a lot harder on that speech to convince yourself."

Before she could reply, a man came to the table and slid into the booth across from her. Cole was taken aback for a second, as he recognized the guy as Reverend McCarron. Did cloth-types get to date? It felt a little unseemly.

"Evening," the reverend said, eyebrows lifted in silent query. "Nice to see you again, Mr. Cavanaugh. Cole, isn't it?"

Cole snorted. " 'Course it's Cole. You went to school with my brothers, Reverend. Buried my daddy."

"Yes, of course." He turned to the vet. "Everything all right, Grace?" He had that deep thread of concern in his voice that Cole imagined all righteous people possessed.

"Just talking about the past," Dr. Hunter said.

"When her daddy was the sheriff," Cole added.

"Ah, yes," McCarron said. "That's right. I was

just a child when he took on that job, but I remember him. Good man, your father."

"Yes," Grace confirmed with pointed passion. "He is."

"I'd like to hear more about your good father," Cole put in. "What're you doing after confession tonight?"

"Confession is a Catholic ritual, Cole," the reverend said.

"Still good for the soul, I'm bettin'." His eyes were pinned to hers. "And Dr. Hunter here went to a Catholic school—didn't you, Doc?" All that digging for information he and his brothers were doing may not have found the ex-sheriff's whereabouts yet, but it had unearthed a few helpful things.

Grace didn't answer him. She looked nervous. As in, if he knew that, what else did he know? "I'm busy tonight, Mr. Cavanaugh." She gestured to the reverend. "As I told you before. Date."

"Well, you two kids enjoy yourself," Cole said, backing up. He glanced Grace's way one last time. "Another time. Soon."

Before she could answer, he turned and headed back to the game area, back to the dart board. And this time, when he aimed and fired, he hit dead center.

Eleven

His guts twisted up inside his body, James rushed out of the elevator. Down one hall, then the next, he made quick work of locating the waiting area. He just wanted to find her, see her. Know that she was going to be okay.

"What the hell are you doing here?" he called out as he spotted Deacon, all fancy in his three-piece suit and pacing back and forth in front of the nurses' station.

The man was talking on his cell phone, but as soon as he spotted James, he said a few quick words and hung up. James hadn't known his brother was back in River Black. But he didn't have the time or the desire to discuss it. All he wanted to know about was Sheridan.

"What the hell happened?" he demanded, trying to keep his voice low for the sake of the other people littered throughout the waiting area. "Where is she?"

Deacon slipped his cell phone into his pocket. "She's sleeping now. For the first two hours, they kept her up, making sure she didn't have a concussion. They did a shitload of tests—all looks good. There's some bruising on her shoulders, but she's okay."

"Bruising?" James ground out, his hands fisting at his sides.

Deacon looked as if he didn't want to say any more, but knew the man in front of him wasn't going to be satisfied with partial answers. "Seems Palmer pushed her into a wall." He exhaled. "A few times."

James nearly lost his mind. That piece of shit. The dead piece of shit. His hands on Sheridan. He growled, "Where is he? Palmer."

Deacon looked at him like he didn't quite recognize him. Didn't quite get why James was so furious. But he answered anyway. "In custody. They caught him at the bakery. Wife was there too. He was trying to get his daughter to take off with them. I hear he was walking funny when they brought him in. I hope to God that's Sheridan's doing. Hope she took her boot to his crotch a couple of times. That sick fuck."

"He doesn't deserve to be walking anywhere," James uttered blackly. "He deserves to be dying."

Black eyebrows drew up over worried green

eyes. "What's going on with you? That's the kind of talk that lands people in jail, little brother."

"Maybe so," James returned. "Maybe Caleb and I can share a cell."

"Don't," Deacon warned, glancing back at the three other people seated on the chairs behind him. "Don't even think it."

James shoved a finger into his brother's chest. "Imagine for a moment that some bastard put his hands on Mac."

"Something going on between you two?"

James ignored him. "Drove her up against a wall. Gave her bruises. Put her in the fucking hospital."

Emerald fire erupted in Deacon's eyes. "Okay. I get it. Bars wouldn't be enough to keep me out. But," he said quickly, "I'd be no good to Mac in jail. And what if that bastard got out before I did? No matter how much I'd want to pay him back for the pain he'd caused, the true pain would be knowing I couldn't protect my girl."

"That's the trick, brother," James said evenly. "You make sure he never gets out."

"And then Mac finds someone else down the road to warm her bed." His nostrils flared wide as if that idea was the most repulsive thing he could imagine.

Deacon's words were making too much sense to James. He didn't want to hear anything more. "Where's her room?"

"What the hell's going on with you two?" Deacon demanded. "Are you dating my assistant?"

Again, James ignored him. "I want to see her."

A growl exited Deacon's throat and he shook his head. "You can't. Nobody but the docs can. She had me down as an in-case-of-emergency person, but since I'm not family, they won't let me in. Not right now anyway."

"She's got no family?" James asked, realizing how little he knew about Sheridan's history. And how much he wanted to know.

"Mom passed away a few years ago. Dad was never in the picture. She's an only child. I don't know her friends."

"She said that Mac was the first real friend she'd had in a long time."

Deacon smiled a little sadly. "That may be true. She never brought that area of her life into work."

Work. James narrowed his eyes. "This had better not affect her position with you. . . ."

It was as if Deacon had been punched in the gut he looked so damn insulted. "How can you even say that? What the hell do you think I am?"

"I don't know." He sighed and ran a hand through his hair. "I don't know anything."

"Christ, boy. It's why I'm here. Why I jumped in the bird the moment the hospital called." His gaze was all seriousness. "I care about the woman."

The emotions battling inside James were making him unstable. He appreciated what Deacon was saying, but also despised him for it. He was close to Sheridan. Had a history with her. James knew it was irrational to feel jealous over a thing like that at a time like this, but couldn't help it. He didn't want any man saying he cared about Sheridan.

"Which one's her room?" he asked again. "At least I can stand outside. Stare through the glass."

"She's sleeping, brother," Deacon said.

"Doesn't matter."

His brother stared at him for a moment, trying to get a clear understanding as to why he was losing his goddamned mind over Sheridan. Care for a woman in danger? A friend? Lover? Deacon may have seen an attraction between the two of them before he'd left for Dallas, but it was pretty obvious this was something else entirely.

"All right," he said finally, pointing at the first door down the hallway.

Skin tight around his muscles, belly clenching like he'd eaten something foul, James strode over to the thick wooden door and placed a hand on either side of the long strip of glass. All he could see was her arms and hands, and half her body, which was covered by a white sheet. An IV was stuck in one arm and she looked still. So still. His throat felt strange and scratchy. And his mind was jumping all around, refusing to land. He didn't know what was happening to him. What was making him react like a bull seeing red in everything and everyone.

"So you have some feelings for her, do ya?"

For a second, James thought the words had come from his own mind. After all, he'd just been questioning himself. But then Deacon spoke again from just behind him.

"I'm glad," he said. "For her and for you. And don't you worry. We'll take care of this, little brother. Not with violence, but by making sure Palmer doesn't walk out of that jail. Ever."

James didn't reply. His eyes were pinned on Sheridan's hand, her fingers. He'd swear they'd just moved, formed a fist. Was she awake? Was she in pain? Christ! Was it truly his lifelong curse to see the women in his life—the women he cared for—come to harm? He fought the monster inside himself. In one ghoulish breath the thing screamed in one ear to go inside, attach himself to Sheridan's bedside and snarl at anyone who came near. In the other, it mocked him, warned him to get lost, steer clear of her and her brilliant mind, wicked tongue, and addictive sunshine smiles. Because if he didn't—if he pursued her further, kissed her again, held her in his arms—maybe something else would happen to her.

Something worse.

James didn't know how long he stood there, his hands bracketing the thick glass, staring at her hands, the sheet, thinking, questioning, but when he heard Mac behind him, talking to Deacon, he knew it had been a while.

"What do you suggest we do?" she asked him quietly.

"I say just let him be," Deac answered.

"Have you ever seen him like this?"

"Yeah."

"When Cass—"

James flinched.

"Let's go to the Triple C, darlin'," he interrupted her gently. "Get a couple hours of sleep, and come back with some coffee and whatever else Elena can whip up."

James felt his brother's hand on his shoulder, but Deacon didn't say anything. After a quick squeeze, he was gone. James turned and let his gaze move over the waiting room. Quiet, just a few people, either sleeping or reading. No one walking by, and the nurses' station appeared deserted.

Fuck it.

He wasn't going to stand here all night. Behind glass. But only a few feet away.

He wrapped his hand around the door handle and opened it as quietly as he could manage. The monster gave him a growl of warning, but James ignored the bastard and slipped inside Sheridan's room.

*   *   *

The pain was shocking to her system as she came awake. It took several blinks and a slow glance around the sunlit room for her mind to connect to where she was and why. But when it did, and even more so when her gaze settled on the man sitting in the chair to her left, tears welled in her eyes.

"James?" she uttered, feeling a rush of relief that he was in the room with her.

He nodded, his gaze locked on hers. "Everything's okay. It's over."

The events of the night before—or, hell, what she hoped was the night before and not a week ago—blasted through her mind like a trumpet. The initial fear at seeing him in the house, the realization that he was going to hurt her, running, fighting . . . She swiped at the tears in her eyes. "Palmer?"

James's nostrils flared and he said in a deadly whisper, "In jail."

"Oh, thank God," she breathed, then winced when her expression of relief caused pain to shoot through her shoulder blades.

"Please don't move," he said, standing up and pressing a button on the small remote at her side.

"What time is it?" she asked.

"Around seven."

"I was brought in last night, right?"

He nodded.

It was lucky she hadn't fallen into some kind of coma or something. She didn't remember much of the night. Had she been woken up by the nurses? Had she seen James come in? She struggled to focus. "How long have you been here?"

"Not long."

But she wasn't sure she believed him. He looked exhausted. Worried. Furious.

The door opened and a nurse stepped into the room. She was very tall and thin with a pointed face and dark, curious, eyes. "Well, look who's awake." She eyed James with slight irritation, then went to Sheridan and took her vital signs, checked her drip bags. "How you feelin', honey?"

Sheridan nodded. "Okay."

"Any pain?"

"Yes," James answered for her.

The nurse pressed her lips together, but didn't even glance his way. Had James Cavanaugh been here all night? And had he been a pain in the butt to the nursing staff while she was sleeping?

"Only a little," Sheridan told the woman. "And only in my shoulders when I move."

"Well, we'll give you a bit more control of that." She fiddled with the IV. "You hungry or thirsty?"

"Not really," Sheridan said.

The nurse nodded. "All right. Well, if the pain worsens, or anything else is bothering you," she added, pointedly looking over at James, "buzz for me. Or I suppose you can have your brother do it. Again." She sniffed. "I'll be back to check on you in about an hour."

"Thank you." Sheridan could hardly wait for the woman to leave. The door had barely closed, when she turned to stare at James. "Brother?"

He shrugged. "They only let family in."

She nodded, her gaze dropping to the blanket on the bed. "And I don't have any."

"You got me."

Her eyes lifted and a soft, gentle wisp of wonder and hope moved through her.

"Me and Mac," he clarified. "Deacon flew in the moment he heard. And Cole is worried sick about his jogging buddy."

She smiled. It was nice to hear. Comforting. Their care and concern meant so much. But for just that moment, that second, she'd thought James was telling her something. Letting her know that maybe his feelings had changed about relationships. That maybe he'd come to realize that it was time they both risked their hearts, defied their pasts . . .

"Sheridan," he began. He cursed, leaned forward so his elbows rested on his knees and his hands were clasped under his chin. "I'm so sorry."

Her heart seized and she gave him a soft smile. "Don't be. I'll heal."

He shook his head. "That's not what I mean. I should've been there."

A flash of something Sheridan didn't recognize crossed his blue gaze. It reminded her of a wounded animal. A sad, frightened, wounded, yet fierce animal. She didn't understand it. The man was as complicated as a ten-thousand-piece puzzle.

"James, this wasn't your fault," she assured him.

His nostrils flared. "You left my place—"

She cut him off. "I went to work. Doesn't matter, wouldn't have mattered, where I'd started out from. Or what came before." Her eyes implored him. "This would've happened because that maniac wanted it to happen." He looked utterly unconvinced. "It's all right. I'm going to be all right."

He took a deep breath, pulled back from the self-flagellation for a moment and said, "You were incredibly brave, woman. I hear you might've done some permanent damage to that asshole."

Even with the memory of the attack still fresh in her mind, a small smile touched Sheridan's lips. "Took me two times to get him to his knees. Every time he came after me, I went for him too." She inhaled deeply. "Never been so thankful for that month of Krav Maga I got myself for Christmas last year."

She'd meant to make him laugh. Or at the very least, get him to crack a smile. But he remained pensive.

"I'm thankful too," he said, his gaze moving

over her. "But I'll be more thankful when that locksmith Deac hired finishes up today."

"I can't believe Palmer came after me like that. That he was willing to risk his reputation, his career—his freedom. We could've worked it out. I would've fired him, but if he'd have paid back what he'd skimmed, everything would've worked out. Instead . . ." She let her head drop back against the pillow. "Oh, God, I'm so tired."

"Then rest," he said in a firm tone. "Please. No more talking about this. Or thinking about it. Not now. You need to heal up."

A sudden thought had her eyes flying to him. "Are you going?"

"No."

Even though relief moved through her fast and heavy, she still felt the need to say, "You can if you want to."

His eyes softened. "I know. But I don't want to, Sheridan."

Warmth spread through her at his words. She knew she should insist he leave. She had a strong suspicion that he'd been there all night, and he probably needed sleep and food. And yet, the idea of him sitting near, watching over her, made her feel as though she could close her eyes and rest.

He made her feel safe.

And in seconds, she drifted off.

*   *   *

The dream was the same, always the same. And even as he had it, he knew it wasn't real. He was grown and Cass was grown. Nothing had happened to her. Not yet. Not until halfway through the dream. One moment they were walking the land of the Triple C, talking, joking around, the next she was gone from his side. Panicked, he searched the entire property for her. Inside the house, the barns, the outbuildings. But she wasn't there. No one was there, not even the animals. Suddenly, he was pulled from the Triple C and dropped onto Main Street. And out of the misty morning air, Cass came running toward him. She was young, maybe ten years old, and though she was moving in his direction she didn't see him. Terrified, tears running down her cheeks, she screamed his name, begged for him to help her. Then she ran straight through him and disappeared.

James woke with a start, and for several seconds wasn't sure where he was. Cass . . . Why hadn't he gone with her that day? Stood outside the bathroom door, waited for her, and brought her back into the movie theater? She was his sister. His blood. It had been his responsibility—

"Hey. You okay?" It was Sheridan's voice. Soft and gentle. Caring.

He glanced up, his gaze meeting hers in the warm, welcoming light of morning. His hands fisting around the arms of the chair, he forced a nod. "Fine."

"What were you dreaming about?" she asked. She was sitting up in bed, a glass of what looked like apple juice in her hand.

"Can't remember," he lied, pushing himself up, standing.

Why now? Why was that coming back now? He hadn't had that dream in two years. He ran his hand through his hair and glanced at the clock on the wall. Shit. It wasn't morning at all. It was nearly noon.

He turned back to her. Her eyes looked calmer and her cheeks seemed far less pale than they had been earlier that morning. "Sorry. Didn't mean to fall asleep for that long."

"Oh, come on," she replied after taking a sip of her juice. "You needed it. Talk to me. Whatever you were dreaming about seemed pretty intense."

He scrubbed a hand over his jaw. "Was probably about the mustangs. Them getting loose, or me not finding them a place to live." He walked up to the bed and stared down at her, his gaze assessing. "How you doing?"

She nodded and smiled. "Better. My back doesn't hurt nearly as much, and I'm hungry."

James was glad she was all right, but hell, every time he thought about what she'd endured, how that piece of shit had touched her, hurt her, he wanted to head over to the jail and have a little heart-to-heart with Caleb Palmer. Preferably away from the prying eyes of security cameras.

"Hungry's good," he said, his eyes moving over her face. So damn beautiful. "Means your system is getting back on track. Why don't I go get the nurse? See if we can find you something to eat."

"Wait a second." Before he could go anywhere, she reached for him. The instant her hand wrapped around his wrist, heat surged into his skin. He looked down. She had small hands. Pretty fingers.

"Listen," she began in a soft voice. "Before anyone comes in here, I have to say . . . thank you."

He didn't like the way his chest constricted at her words, and he ground out, "For what?"

"Staying here with me," she answered. "You didn't have to do that. I'm grateful."

"Please stop, Sheridan." He despised her thanks. More than she could ever know.

"Why?" she asked, confused. "It's just a thank-you."

"There's no need for it."

"Because that's what friends do for each other?" she asked, a thread of sarcasm in her tone.

His chest tightened. "Sure."

Friends.

He'd tossed that word out all nice and easy that day on the ranch. He'd tossed it out because it was way easier to put a benign and bullshit label on what he was feeling for her instead of dealing with the truth. But now, each time he heard it, he wanted to erase it from the goddamn English language. Friendship wasn't why he'd stayed. Why he continued to stay. Why, right that very moment, with her fingers wrapped around his wrist, he knew he should head out of the room and get the nurse, find her something to eat—not lean down and kiss her.

Her eyes tried to penetrate his thoughts. "James . . ."

He eased his arm away. "Anyone I can call for you?"

The action bothered her, maybe even hurt her, but she hid it fairly well. "Not really. I have one friend from college, but she's in Europe for the next several months. There's really no one else." She laughed, but it was hardly a light, happy sound. "I'm so busy with work I forget to make friends. Even casual ones. The kind you go to lunch with." Her eyes lifted to meet his. "I'll have to remember that when I get back home."

It was James's turn to look hurt. Or feel it. A slow, stabbing pain near his heart. "About that," he said swiftly. "You're gonna need to take a week or two off."

It was the first time James saw a flash of heat cross her gaze since she'd been in the hospital. She even sat up a little straighter against her pillows. "Oh, I don't know."

"I do. And Deacon does too."

Her expression downgraded to panic. "You didn't talk to him about that, did you? He didn't say anything to you?" Her eyes widened. "I appreciate him flying all the way out here, but I hope he knows I can get back to work soon—"

"Stop worrying about this, Sheridan," James cut in. "Deacon was very clear about your job being secure for whenever you want it," he assured her. "But, no more working on the ranch site."

Her eyes widened. "He said that?"

No. I did.

"Relax, please?" he said. He couldn't keep standing there anymore, looking down at her, into those soulful, beautiful, apprehensive gray eyes. Eyes that seemed to tug at his insides and kept him coming back when he should have been giving her a wide, protective berth. "Let me go find the nurse."

Without waiting for a response, he headed out of the room. Once in the hallway, he saw Deacon and Mac sitting in the waiting area. A battle raged inside him. Should he let them take over Sheridan's care so, God forbid, nothing else happened to her? Should he just keep on walking and never come back—hell, never see her again—because . . . ?

Three times.

His gut twisted. Three times bad things had happened to the women he cared about most.

His eyes shifted to Deacon and Mac, who were

sitting so close together no air could get between them. He should let them take over. Let them sit at her bedside and comfort her.

And yet, when he got to moving, he went straight past them and headed for the nurses' station. Sheridan needed to eat.

Diary of Cassandra Cavanaugh

May 3, 2002

Dear Diary,

   Tonight is the worst thing ever. Sweet didn't meet me like he promised. I waited and waited, but he never came. I want to ask Deac if he knows Sweet. But then I'd have to admit I don't know his real name. And Lord, Deac would ask me all kinds of questions.

   Maybe I could ask James?

   Ooooo, that could work all right. James doesn't hover over me nearly as much as Deac and Cole do. Sometimes I think he doesn't care as much about me. Or maybe that's just his way. I don't know. But his way might just help me.

   What if Sweet didn't come because he doesn't like me anymore? What if I said something weird or stupid? Maybe I kissed wrong!! He's probably kissed a lot of girls his own age!! He probably thought I was baby!!

   SOBS!

   I have to make him see me as grown, that is all.

I'm going to see James now. I'll let you know what happens.

Worried,

Cass

P.S. Maybe Sweet not comin' has something to do with what he said last night. I thought he was joking around, trying to make me scared or something. Boys do that to girls they like. I've seen it with Deac and James. He said he thinks we're being followed. I haven't noticed anything. But I guess I'm going to keep my eyes peeled from now on.

Dammit! I wish Sweet would just give me the number where he's staying. It's all just too secretive.

Maybe I should start following him.

Twelve

"Those centerpieces are beautiful!"

From the chair she'd moved and placed directly beside the bed, Mac nodded in agreement. "I think so too, but are you sure you want to be doing this?"

Sitting up in the hospital bed, her legs crossed, feeling rested and nearly pain-free, Sheridan answered the bride-to-be. "I really do. Helping with wedding plans is fun and light, and the eternal happiness factor attached to it appeals to me right now."

Dropping a booted foot across her jean-clad leg, Mac shrugged. "Okay. But if you change your mind . . ."

"I will tell you to pack your bridal magazines and your cake samples and your boutonniere ideas and hit the road," Sheridan finished for her.

Mac's normally tanned face paled. "Boutonniere? What the hell is a boutonniere?"

Sheridan laughed, then winced as the action made her shoulders flare with pain. "Don't panic. It's flowers that the men wear. I believe they're supposed to match your bouquet."

The explanation did little to curb the woman's anxiety. She groaned and grumbled. "Deacon was right. I should've hired somebody to help me. I have a week left to plan this thing, and I have cattle to move for God's sake!"

"I'll help you," Sheridan offered impulsively.

"What? No."

"I'm your maid of honor," Sheridan began. "That is, if you still want me—"

"Are you kidding?" Mac practically cried out. "Please. Of course I want you. It's just . . . I don't want to push you. If you're not feeling up to it—"

"It'd be great for me," Sheridan assured her. "The right kind of rehab, so to speak."

Mac laughed.

"Come on. Let me help you. And not just when you pull me into stores and force-feed me frosting. Or for the rehearsal dinner. For real."

The forewoman sighed. "You know you're sitting in a hospital bed right now."

"I do. But it's not for long. A couple days and I'm going to be back to my old workaholic self." Sheridan chewed her lip thoughtfully. "I have a sneaking suspicion that I'm going to be pulled off the ranch construction. I'm sure there's a little paperwork I could do, but . . . I need to work. I need something to do."

Mac closed the magazine and placed it on her lap. "With what happened, I kind of thought you might want to head back to Dallas for a little while. Maybe until the wedding."

A thread of unease flickered through Sheridan, but she brushed it away. Though she knew she might very well be plagued with flashbacks and nightmares as the days went forward, that hell she'd experienced at Redemption was over. She wouldn't let it run her out of town. She refused to exist in fear. "I don't want to go back to Dallas yet. Mr. Palmer's in jail. And if James has his way, I think the man will be staying there until the end of time."

Mac sniffed. "I think you're right." She shook her head contemplatively. "I've never seen James like this. Granted, he's been away from River Black for a long time, but even Deacon says this ferocity and protectiveness over you is unlike him."

Hearing that was like a warm, healing salve to Sheridan's bruises. Both inside and out. But to Mac, she just said casually, "We're friends."

A touch of amusement lit Mac's eyes. "Right."

"We are," Sheridan insisted.

Though no one else was in the hospital room to hear what she was saying, Mac leaned in and whispered, "He sat in this room for two days. Making sure you got food when you were hungry, medicine when you had even a hint of pain. He wouldn't let any of us take over for him." Her brows lifted. "What does that tell you?"

Sheridan stared at the woman. Oh, how she wished she could confide in Mac. Tell her the truth about her feelings for James. The fears she had about following in her mother's path; loving only to end up losing everything. But she just wasn't ready to let that wall come down—let her true, and oh-so-vulnerable self be revealed. She wondered if she ever would be.

She glanced down at the bridal magazine that was open on her lap. A red rose with a few sprigs of small yellow wildflowers smiled encouragingly up at her. "What about something like this for the boutonniere?" She held it up for Mac to see. "Simple. Masculine."

For a few seconds Mac stared at her, not the glossy page with the flowers on it. She seemed to be wrestling with Sheridan's quick change of discussion. Or her blatant avoidance, depending on how one looked at it. But after a moment or two, the bride-to-be's gaze shifted over to the magazine.

"I was thinking red roses for my bouquet," she said.

"Well, then," Sheridan said quickly, grateful that

Mac hadn't pressed her. "This could work. With two weeks to go, I say we start now."

"Start what?" came a masculine voice.

Sheridan glanced up. Standing in the doorway, in the same shirt he'd worn for the past two days, was her fearsome protector. Her crush. Her friend. Even with two days of no shower, stubbled jaw, and rumpled hair, James Cavanaugh was the best-looking man in the universe. His eyes alone made him swoon-worthy material. But it was his quiet strength, his sensitivity, his passion, and his fierce protectiveness for anything that was seemingly helpless that made her heart beat faster. Made her feel undeniably safe. And Lord, made her want to stay in River Black to get to know him better, even though her instincts warned her to go home.

"Sheridan is going to help me with the rest of the wedding plans," Mac announced, standing up and gathering all her magazines. "An offer that makes me want to weep with happiness and relief."

James didn't say anything, but his gaze grew heavy with concern. A fact Mac picked up on right away. And clearly wanted to avoid.

She cleared her throat. "I'm going to find my fiancé and tell him not to worry about the grave insanity I'd promised him would occur if I didn't have help." She looked from James to Sheridan, gave the latter a quick smile, then swiftly left the room.

"What's wrong?" Sheridan asked as James approached the bed. "You look upset."

"Wedding planning?" he demanded, though his tone lacked heat.

She nodded. "Definitely. I think it would be fun, and light."

A struggle seemed to be going on inside of him. He glanced back over his shoulder at the door. "So, you're staying in River Black?" He turned to face her again. "After what's happened?"

Sheridan flinched. That light mood from a moment ago gone now. She lifted her chin and inquired, "Do you think I should go home, James?"

As he stared down at her, confusion and heat warred in his eyes. "That's not what I'm saying."

"What are you saying?"

He didn't answer, just kept right on staring at her intently. Sheridan's brows drifted together in a frown. Reading James Cavanaugh was a difficult task. Especially when she was feeling insecure. What was he saying? That he was worried about her? That he was worried about his own feelings for her? Or did he truly think it was best that she go home to Dallas?

She reclined back against the pillows and reached for her cup of water. "Listen, you can be honest with me. Like I told you before, I'm good with honesty. I appreciate it." *Maybe my heart will hurt as much as the bruises on my shoulders, but it's better than trying to guess.*

With a soft growl, he sat down on the edge of the bed. "You want honesty? Fine. Here it is, darlin'. I don't like you having to be within a ten-mile radius of that piece of shit, Caleb Palmer. I don't like thinking you feel afraid. And I don't want you to get hurt again."

"Well I don't want that either," she returned.

"Then maybe you need to go."

"Or maybe I need to stay with you," she blurted out.

His eyes jacked up. "What?"

Oh, God. She swallowed at the quick ferocity she saw there. "Nothing," she said with an embarrassed laugh. "I don't know why I said that. Mac's invited me to stay at the main house . . ."

"Do you really *want* to stay with me, Sheridan?" he interrupted, his expression a strange mixture of shock and fascination.

Mortification ran thick in her veins. "Please forget I said that."

"No." His eyes softened. "I can't. I don't want to."

There was nothing Sheridan wanted more in that moment than to rewind the conversation and start over. Maybe with something like, "I'm excited to stay up at the house with my new friend, Mac." But there were no do-overs in life. There was only honesty. Even if it stole your pride.

"Okay," she said, bringing her knees to her

chest and wrapping her arms around them. "If we're telling the truth here . . ." Her eyes lifted to meet his. "I trust you. I feel safe with you."

He looked stunned.

"And let me add," she went on, "I'm not a pain in the ass. I'm a good houseguest. I'm fairly neat. I'm great at boiling water for pasta, and the remote is only mine when *Scandal*'s on."

When he still didn't say anything, she panicked and backtracked hard. "'Course there's something to be said for staying with friends. Girlfriends. Or so I've heard. And Mac says there's a wicked soaking tub in one of the guest rooms." She gave him a tight smile. "A girl ain't nothing without her tub."

"No," he said, a trace of a growl in his tone.

She stilled. "What do you mean, no?"

His eyes darkened to a rich sapphire. "You're staying with me, Sheridan."

Her heart dropped into her belly. "James, I didn't mean to make you feel obligated. I swear. It was a momentary thought—"

"*Game of Thrones.*"

She shook her head, confused by the abrupt segue. "I'm sorry?"

He stood up, the angst in his expression completely gone now. "That's when the remote belongs to me."

"Oh," she said, understanding him.

He gave her a broad, encouraging, and very

knee-weakening smile. "Rest up, Miss O'Neil. I'll be back to get you in the morning."

"What are you doin'?" Cole barked from his position just inside the bedroom door.

James didn't look up. He was too busy. Just muttered a quick, "Packing."

"Hey," Cole exclaimed, coming to stand over him. "That's my gear you're messin' with."

"Yes, it is." James zipped up the massive duffel and stood. "You're moving out."

"What?" Cole exclaimed.

He headed out the door. "You heard me."

Cole followed him. "I heard something. Sounded like bullshit." He stopped when they reached the living room. "Like my brother thinks he's calling all the shots."

"He is," James answered tightly. He didn't have time for nonsense. Not today.

Clearly Cole recognized the impenetrable tone of an older brother and cursed. "Where am I going?"

"Up to the house, in town, to one of the cottages." James dropped the bags right beside the front door, then turned to look at the tatted-up fighter, who was wearing ripped jeans and a white tank top. "Anywhere but here."

"And why's that?" Cole's gaze lifted and, maybe for the first time since he'd walked through the front door a few moments ago, he really looked around the place. "Wait a sec." He inhaled deeply. "It smells good in here. Did you clean up? Is that a new rug on the floor?" His eyes bugged out. "Are those flowers on the table?"

"Well, your eyes and nose seem to be workin' just fine," James remarked dryly. "Guess you weren't hit too hard during training."

Cole's jaw dropped open and he pointed to the bay window. "Tell me you didn't hang those curtains yourself?"

" 'Course I did." Granted, the job had taken a solid hour. The lace he'd picked out hadn't fit on the iron rod. He'd ripped the thing clear apart. He'd had to go back into town to buy a new rod, and have the fabric sewn up.

Cole was staring at him, confused. Maybe even a little wary.

"What?" James demanded.

"Man card's been revoked, brother. Hand it over."

James picked up the bags and thrust them at Cole. "Don't have it on me right now. I'll bring it by tomorrow. Just let me know where you're staying."

A bag in each hand, Cole stood his ground. "I'm not going anywhere until you tell me what this is all about."

Christ almighty. Once an annoying little brother, always an annoying little brother. He shrugged, tossed off a quick, "Just want some privacy."

"Because . . ." Cole nudged.

"Get out of here."

The way Cole was staring at him, like he was trying to drill a hole in his head and get a good look at his thoughts, was unnerving as hell.

"Fine," James ground out. "Sheridan's moving in here with me."

Cole's face scrunched up into a mask of utter bewilderment. "Come again?"

"You heard me."

"Sheridan. As in Deacon's assistant?"

"That's her," James confirmed, opening the front door as wide as possible. *Get the hint, Champ,* he thought.

But Cole was dead-set on being a squatting pain in the ass. "Why?"

Releasing a breath, James leaned back against the open door. The morning air was slowly making its way inside, along with a few beams of sunshine. "You know she was attacked."

"'Course I do," Cole said. His black eyes glinted with menace. "That asshole should be burned at the stake. Putting his hands on a woman. Fucking up people's lives. I heard he even tried to get his wife and daughter to run with him. Poor Natalie. She was always a bit odd when we were kids, but a decent sort. Sure doesn't deserve a piece of shit father like that. But what does it have to do with you?" He shrugged. "I mean I know you and Sheridan are friends. Maybe you have a little crush on her—"

"No," James cut in. It was more than a crush. But he wasn't sharing that with Cole. "It's none of that. She could stay up at the house or in town, but she seems to feel safe with me or something." The words fought against him, yet made his chest fill with heat.

"Safe from what?" Cole pressed. "The asshole's in jail, right?"

"Doesn't stop the fear, Cole."

His brother didn't say anything to that for a minute. Then he nodded his understanding. "All right, but I thought she'd want to go back home to Dallas."

"I thought so too." And had been dreading hearing her say it. "But she doesn't. She wants to be here for Mac and Deac's wedding, wants to stay in River Black. And she asked to stay with me."

"Wait." Once again, Cole looked perplexed. It wasn't a good look for him, and it was really starting to wear on James. "Staying here wasn't *your* idea?"

"No," he ground out. "Shit, I'd never tell someone they're safe with me." The words were bitter on his tongue.

"Why the hell not?" Cole pressed, his gaze intrusive now.

James didn't answer.

"Oh, come on," Cole pushed with the delicacy of a bull through a glass window. "This ain't about Cass, is it?"

A flicker of tension snapped in James's jaw.

"That was a long time ago, J," he continued. "You were a kid."

"Yeah," James agreed. "And if this was just about Cass, I'd agree with you. But it's not."

Coming to stand in the doorway, Cole asked, "What do you mean?"

"Dammit, Cole, why are you pressing me?"

The man didn't say a word. Just stared, waiting. It was irritating as hell.

Finally, James relented in the form of a gruff exhale. "There was a girl in college, okay?"

No confusion this time. Just interest. "Someone you dated?"

Dated? The girl was going to be his wife. But once again, he'd failed in his responsibilities to care for a loved one. He should've been with Tori that night. College parties could get wild. But he hadn't wanted to go and she'd insisted she'd be fine.

She'd been anything but fine . . .

She'd been destroyed.

After the attack, James had lost his mind, went after four of the guys who'd been around that night and had done nothing—said they saw nothing. Battered and bruised and broken, he'd gone to Tori—begged her to forgive him, let him help her—do whatever it took. But she wouldn't even look at him. She didn't want anyone near her, anyone touching her, especially him. A week later, her parents had come to get her, to take her away from school, from the hellish memories—from him. James had tried every which way to see her. Calling, e-mails, letters, traveling to her house, staying close by . . . but she refused any contact. After a few months, she'd written him one cold e-mail saying she wanted him to leave her alone, that she never wanted to see him again. A couple weeks later, he'd left school too.

Two years ago, James had heard she got married. That she had a baby. It had given him some sense of peace. But it never removed the stain of failure and shame on his soul.

Until now, today, he'd never told his brothers anything about Tori or what had happened. When he left school, they'd all thought he'd hated studying and wanted something different for his life. Wanted to go back to ranching. And he'd never corrected them.

"Well, what happened with the girl?" Cole asked in an almost gentle voice.

James shook his head. He didn't want any more of this. Not now. Not today. Sheridan was coming, and he needed to focus on her and what he could do for her. How—God, help him—he could keep making her feel safe.

"I got shit to do, little brother," he said, knocking his chin in the direction of the great outdoors. "Let me know where you end up, okay?"

For a few long seconds, Cole didn't move. His

eyes were filled with worry and curiosity. But he knew James, knew better than to push for an answer he was clearly not going to get at that moment. So he shouldered one of his bags and pushed away from the doorframe.

"Probably stay up at the house," he said. "Elena's cooking will be my new roommate."

"Sounds good," James said, giving the man a quick salute.

Cole was halfway to the porch steps, when he glanced over his shoulder and asked, "You picking her up? Sheridan?"

"Was. But Mac insisted. And you know Mac."

Cole snorted. "Sure do."

"So, she and Deac are bringing Sheridan over."

"You call me if you need anything here."

The words weren't flowery or soft, but they were heartfelt, and James appreciated them more than he ever thought he would.

He gave Cole a clipped nod. "Thanks." Then he headed back into the bunkhouse and straight for his brother's room. He had a lot to finish up before Sheridan got there. The room she was going to be staying in especially. Fresh sheets on the bed, some flowers, soap and towels in the bathroom. He wanted her to feel good as well as safe.

But most of all, he realized as he started stripping the bed, he wanted her to feel at home.

Thirteen

"You sure you want to stay there?" Mac asked, staring at Sheridan in the vanity mirror as Deacon passed through the Triple C's main gates. "Two guys smelling up the joint with their feet and dirty laundry, and all those weird things they eat."

"They eat weird things?" Sheridan asked, deadpan, from her cozy leather bucket seat in the back in Deacon's truck.

"Hell, yeah. Strange sandwiches with condiments that make 'em burp and f—"

"Darlin'." Deacon grabbed her hand and kissed her knuckles. "I'm trying real hard not to take offense at what you're saying."

"Oh, baby," she nearly cooed. "I'm not talking about you."

"I *am* a guy."

"Yes, but you smell amazing, your feet are sexy

as well as clean, and I love when you cook. No weird condiments have ever been introduced."

He laughed, then leaned over and gave her a quick kiss on the lips. "I can't wait to marry you."

"Me either," she agreed. "And you know that if your feet did smell or you had a strange obsession with Sriracha, I wouldn't mind at all."

"If you two would like to be alone, you could drop me here," Sheridan offered, pressing back into the seat with a smile. "A nice walk. A nice chat with a cow or two."

Deacon chuckled. "Apologies, Sheridan. I find it difficult to hold on to my office manners when I'm in River Black and around this beautiful and very infuriating woman."

"Infuriating, huh?" Mac said wryly. "I'll show you infuriating." She leaned in close to his ear and whispered loud enough for all to hear, "Later."

Sheridan cleared her throat. "I understand, sir."

Mac dropped back into her seat and groaned. "Here she goes again. Deacon, I'm beggin' you people, can we please have a moratorium on the *sirs* and *misses* while we're all working on the wedding?"

"I have no problem with it," Deacon said, rounding the drive and coming to a stop in front of the main house. He glanced back. "Sheridan, for now, if you're comfortable with it, I'm Deacon, and Mackenzie is Mac."

"I've already gone there with you on Mac," Sheridan pointed out to the bride-to-be.

"True," Mac agreed. "Now, you'll just have to work doubly hard on Deacon. Or better yet," she grinned and wiggled her eyebrows, "Deac!"

Deacon chuckled, and Sheridan grimaced. She wasn't sure if she would ever feel comfortable calling her boss by his first name. But she appreciated the gesture. Deacon Cavanaugh had been incredibly kind and supportive from the moment he'd heard about what had happened to her. Visiting her in the hospital, making sure she had the best care—making sure she understood that not only did she have a job to return to at Cavanaugh Group whenever she felt up to it, but a raise to go with it. He'd said he felt responsible, as Palmer had been his choice. Sheridan had tried to assure him it wasn't his responsibility, but he wouldn't budge, even going so far as to tell her that he'd not only had extensive background checks done on the new contractor he'd hired, but that every bill and receipt was going through him.

Mac undid her seat belt and turned around to regard Sheridan. "You sure you don't want to stay up at the house with me and Deacon? Dance party every night."

"That's a private thing, darlin'," Deacon said, humor threading his tone.

"Oh, right," she agreed, her blue eyes twinkling. "Fine, then. Movies, popcorn. And Elena's a great cook. You'd love it there."

"She's staying with me," came a gruff voice.

Sheridan's heart pinged and she turned to see James, his head framed by the open window. He hadn't shaved yet today, and his jaw was darkened with stubble. She liked it. She liked it a lot. It made his blue eyes brilliant and sexy. Maybe he'd like to host a private dance party for the two of them.

She smiled at him. "Hi."

His expression warmed as he turned to look at her. "Hi."

"You ready for this?" she asked him.

He nodded, slowly, almost seductively, his eyes pinned to hers, and Sheridan's insides started heating up.

Then he turned back to Deacon and gave him a quizzical look. "Where are her bags?"

"In the back," Deacon said, opening his door and coming around. "Why don't I give you a hand?"

"Not necessary," James said, his tone resolute. He eyed Sheridan. "You all right to walk? I could grab one of the horses and ride you down."

"I'm fine," she assured him. "I'd actually love to walk. I've missed the fresh air and the sun."

"Big mistake, girlfriend," Mac whispered when the men were out of earshot. "You should've held out."

Sheridan leaned into her. "What do you mean?"

"Another minute of that sexual tension, back-and-forth thing you two were doin', and James Cavanaugh would've offered—no, *insisted*—on carrying you." She grinned wickedly. "Frankly, I think the only thing that stopped him was the idea of me or Deacon following you guys down to the bunkhouse with the bags."

Sheridan laughed. She hated to admit it, but Lord, she hoped Mac was right.

"Call me later," Mac said as James opened the back door for Sheridan to get out.

"Will do," she returned warmly. "Just not during private dance-party hours."

Mac's laughter followed her as Sheridan slipped out of the truck and took James's waiting hand. He had her bags over one broad shoulder, and after another quick good-bye, they headed across the drive and past the barn.

The day was exquisite. A blue, cloudless sky and miles and miles of green Triple C Ranch land. Sheridan had been to the bunkhouse a couple days before, but this would be a very different kind of visit. She wasn't staying for an hour or two. She was staying for a few weeks. As they walked down into the lush valley that served as the bunkhouse's backyard on one side, a calming warmth moved through her at the thought. And something else too. A deliciously unsettling kind of heat that hummed inside her every time she looked at James Cavanaugh.

But as they came around the side of the bunk-house and up the porch steps, she remembered that it wasn't going to be just her and James living here. Not that she minded. She liked Cole. But she did feel a little guilty taking some of his space away.

"I hope Cole doesn't feel too put out," she said, realizing, much to her delight, that James was still holding her hand. "I'm great on the couch." *I'm just glad to be here with you. Be close to you. Just for a while.*

Until some of the fear subsides, anyway.

"Cole actually decided to stay up at the house," he said, shoving the door open with his hip.

"Oh, no."

He turned to regard her. "What's wrong?"

"I just feel like a jerk, that's all. This is his home."

James dropped the bags on the porch and ever so gently took her by shoulders. "He was thrilled to get away from me."

"I don't believe that." Seriously, who would want to get away from this man?

He smiled. "It's true. Wanted to be properly fed. Said I was taking weight off him with my burned salmon and dry turkey burgers."

"Well, maybe *he* should've cooked something then," she said defensively.

James's smile broadened. "With the fight coming up he couldn't afford to lose an ounce. Elena

will take care of him. And I think there was something about me snoring too."

She laughed. "You don't snore."

"You'll find out soon enough." She blushed at
the very same time that he added, "Walls are
pretty thin in there."

"Well," she said, clearing her throat. "I think I
snore too. So we'll cancel each other out."

He gently, lightly, moved his hands to the middle of her back. "This hurt?"

She shook her head, almost laughed again because his touch was featherlight. "Not so much
anymore." *And not when you touch me.*

He dropped his hands, glanced past her to the
creek. "I want to kill him," he uttered blackly, his
nostrils flaring.

The loss of his touch and the sudden ferocity
of his statement made Sheridan's belly clench.
"Please don't talk like that."

He turned back to face her, and his eyes were an
amazing combination of stormy and hot as they
moved over her face. "Any man who hurts a
woman should have his life extinguished."

Sheridan didn't know what to say to that. Con-
flicting emotions were swirling through her. She
worried about his anger toward Palmer, but also
reveled in it because it meant he cared about her.
And she'd be lying to herself if she said she didn't
want that. That she didn't want James Cavanaugh
to see her as more than his brother's assistant.

That she didn't want him to change his mind—
and maybe hers right along with it—about love
and marriage.

"Should we go inside?" she asked, trying to
break some of the tension.

He nodded. "It's not much," he warned her,
scooping up the bags. "But you're welcome to it."

"I've been here before, remember?"

"Yeah, but not like this. Not coming home."

Oh, those words. His words . . . they wrapped
around her like a soothing, protective blanket. And
when she did step inside, she allowed herself to
see the bunkhouse with fresh eyes. High beamed
ceilings above and that one lovely, large room below with everything accessible: living area, kitchen,
dining area. She saw the hallway to the right, knew
there was a bathroom down there, and guessed a
couple of bedrooms as well. But her absolute favorite thing was the wall of windows in the living
area that opened out to the backyard and the creek.
It was all so comfortable, so—She gasped suddenly
as her eyes caught on the dining table.

"Is that Indian paintbrush?" she exclaimed,
heading straight for it.

"I found a patch 'bout a half mile down the
creek," he explained. "You like them?"

She didn't turn, just stared at the beautiful red
wildflowers. Her heart pounded inside her chest
and tears pricked behind her eyes. Like them? Did
she like them?

James came up beside her. "What's wrong?" he asked, noting her silence, her expression, which was no doubt worrisome. "Sheridan?"

Her gaze moved covetously over the flowers. She couldn't believe it.

"Shit," he cursed. "Is it the flowers? Are you allergic? I can toss them out. Not a problem."

He reached for the vase, but just as his hand wrapped around the blue glass, Sheridan stopped him.

"No," she said.

He turned to look at her.

She felt like an idiot for getting so worked up. Making him worry. But . . . "I love them," she managed to get out.

Studying her, he shook his head. "Doesn't seem like it. Can you tell me what's gotten you upset?"

"It's stupid."

"Not to me."

Her heart squeezed. James was such a good man, a kind man. Honestly, the fact that he resembled a young Robert Redford, with just a little darker hair, was just a bonus.

She leaned against the table slightly. "When I was a kid I found a bouquet of these on the mat outside our front door."

"Okay." He shook his head. "Doesn't sound stupid to me."

"Every day for a month," she added.

"Oh. Boyfriend?"

She smiled. "Yes. But not mine. I wanted him to be. I was so excited when they showed up and the card was from him." She shrugged. "Seems that they were meant for the girl who lived next door. He'd gotten the house number wrong."

"Ah," James said with understanding.

"The strange part is," she continued. "I've never seen them again, even growing wild, until today." She chewed her lip. "It just kind of startled me."

"Well, if it's any consolation, Miss O'Neil," he said, reaching for her hand, "these flowers were most definitely meant for you."

Air caught and held inside Sheridan's lungs. No one had ever said anything like that to her before. Or looked at her with raw, unchecked honesty. What she hadn't told him was that every night after the bouquets stopped coming, her mother would tuck her into bed and tell her not to fuss. Tell her that romantic gestures were not all they were cracked up to be. She should know. Daddy had brought her flowers all the time, and look where that had gotten her.

Sheridan had held this belief inside her for more years than she cared to count. She hadn't thought it was a big deal. But as her eyes lifted to take in the vase of Indian paintbrush once again, she wondered if the things her mother had said to her under the guise of wisdom and experience and wanting a better future for her daughter were really just symptoms of a bitter heart. A broken heart.

"Come on, Miss O'Neil," James said, snagging her attention and rotating his hand so that their fingers were interlocked. "Let me show you to your room."

The effortless speed of the mustangs never failed to impress him. James rode alongside the herd into the coming sunset, checking fences, checking water, making sure none of them had any medical issues like the one he'd just released back into their group. He did think one of the mares looked pregnant. If so, that was going to be something that might require the good town veterinarian to come out and take a look at before the birth. The mare probably wouldn't even let him get within ten yards of her new baby.

Thorough check complete, James broke off from the herd and headed back to the barn. He just needed to feed, water, and brush out his horse, and then he could get home.

Sheridan was back at the bunkhouse. She'd encouraged him to go out, do what he needed to do. But even so, he didn't like leaving her for long. It wasn't that he believed her unsafe. Hell, he, Deacon, and Deac's lawyer had all been keeping pretty close tabs on Caleb Palmer, making sure the bastard stayed behind bars. But James's concern was more about Sheridan's emotional state. Even though she understood that piece of shit couldn't get to her, it didn't always quiet the fear. Not after what she'd experienced.   •

As he was coming up on the barn, he saw that both of his brothers were hanging out in the doorway, standing side by side talking, their Stetsons hiding their expressions. No doubt they were waiting on him, but for what reason he wasn't sure. Cole had better not be fixing to come back home. James had Sheridan all to himself in the bunkhouse and he was going to make sure it remained that way.

He slipped off his horse and strode up to them. "Did I miss a meeting for the Cavanaugh Brothers Club?" he asked.

Cole snorted. "Shit, brother. You know you were denied entrance into that club a long time ago. That's what happens when you fail the initiation."

"Right," James said, deadpan. "Could never manage to burp the theme song to *Deadwood*."

"I thought it was the theme song to *Gilmore Girls*," Deacon put in, looking from one brother to the other. "That's what I did."

James laughed. "Poor Cole. Couldn't tell the difference."

"Shut up, the two of you," Cole muttered good-naturedly.

"Houseguest settling in okay?" Deacon asked with a touch of seriousness.

"Think so," James said, leading his horse into the barn. "Heading back there after I finish up here. I'll let you know."

Both men followed him, and Deacon helped with getting the mare into a clean stall. Then crossed his arms on the top of the stall door.

"Before you do, we need to talk."

James took off the saddle and lifted it over the door, handing it to Cole. " 'Bout what?"

"The vet," Cole said, placing the saddle on a sawhorse. "And Blue. All that's unsettled 'round here. All that's up in the air and not dealt with for too many damn reasons to count."

The knot that had formed the moment James had heard about his father's death squeezed with tension. "The vet says she made a mistake. That her pop was just ramblin' nonsense."

"You believe that?" Deacon asked, as though he didn't. Not for a minute.

"I don't know what I believe. Shit, I don't know what I want or what I'm doin' here."

Deacon's eyebrows shot up. "And yet you moved my assistant into your house."

James's jaw tightened and he looked Deac straight in the eye. "You want her to feel safe, right?"

" 'Course I do."

"Well, she feels safe with me." *Don't know why. Don't care.* "I won't walk away from that until *she's* ready to walk away."

"I'm not trying to get you to walk away from

Sheridan or anything else," Deacon insisted. "I hate to admit it, but having us all back in River Black right now is a good feeling. I won't say right. But it's good."

"That's 'cause you're feelin' all sentimental," Cole said in an overly sweet voice. "Tenderhearted. It's how all men get when their foot's caught in a trap."

Deacon turned to glare at him. "A trap?"

"Oh, sorry. I mean, loooooove," Cole added, then promptly snorted.

Deacon turned to James. "Punch him for me. I can't get violent this close to my wedding."

Cole tipped his hat back and laughed. "That's right. Don't want to risk getting that pretty face smashed in. Though, if you're fighting me, there's no risk." He grinned wickedly at James. "Just a promise."

Though he enjoyed the shit-tossing between himself and his brothers, maybe even missed it over the years, James steered them back to the present. To the digging that had been put on hold while Sheridan was in the hospital. "Obviously, we can't make the vet talk about something she won't talk about."

"That's right," Cole acknowledged, coming up to the stall door, standing beside Deacon. "So we go around her."

James nodded. "I think that's the only way. I've

looked into seven different care facilities within a hundred-mile radius. Assuming she's keeping him close by."

"I'm sure she is," Deacon put in.

"There's no Peter Hunter registered at any of 'em."

"Damn woman," Cole spit out. "I bet she put him in under a fake name. Maybe even moved him from where he was after we started asking questions."

"I've looked into all of his financial records," Deac said. "They stopped about a year ago." He eyed them both. "I could dig into hers."

"I don't know," James said. "If Dr. Hunter gets wind of any of this and calls the authorities, someone might be going to jail instead of to the altar. Maybe Cole and I should do it."

"Hell, no," Deac said as if he'd just been sucker punched. "We do it together or not at all."

"You could check into this Sweet character," James suggested.

"The boy Cass told Mac about?" Deacon asked. "He was made-up." He looked at Cole. "Had to be. No one could find him. No one even heard about him—or saw him. He was supposedly going to school with us for a time. Did you know him? I didn't. Shit, J, everyone in town was questioned by the police. No one knew this kid."

It wasn't like James hadn't said the very same things to himself. But lately, he'd started to wonder. "If Sheriff Hunter was hiding something or covering up something, then maybe . . . I don't know. Maybe we start asking around. Not just in River Black but the surrounding counties."

Cole nodded. "Yeah, I agree. Cass had a damn good imagination, and she wanted to be like Mac—Mac liked Deac . . . maybe she wanted someone too. But if we're doing this, really doing this, we have to take the case apart."

"What about Mac?" James asked Deacon. "You gonna tell her any of this?"

Deacon seemed to toss this idea around in his mind for a minute before he answered. Then he pushed away from the stall door and said, "Let's see if we can get to the sheriff first. See if there's anything to tell. Maybe the vet's right. Maybe he's out of his mind, rambling about things that never were. Maybe things he'd wished he'd done different."

Cole eyed him, a streak of danger in his black eyes. "So, what? Is that what you're hoping for in all this? That the truth stays hidden?"

"Jesus," James said with a snort. "Talk about seeing shit where there ain't no stink."

Cole shrugged. "Just asking questions."

"Come on, Cole," Deacon said in that older brother to baby brother kind of way. "This is hard on all of us. Scares the shit out of all us. Christ, if we could really, finally, know the truth—"

"Hey, boys."

James glanced past Deac and Cole to see Sam walking into the barn. As usual, the aging cowboy looked bone weary. But there was an appreciative gleam in his eyes when he took in the three of them together.

"Sorry to break up all this brotherly love," he said. "But, James, you got a phone call up at the house."

At the house? Who would be calling him there? "They say who it is?"

"Nope." Sam grinned. "But I asked. Some woman named June Dupree."

James cursed and shouldered the mare's bridle.

"Girlfriend?" Deacon asked with a slight edge to his voice. "If so, you'd better let Sheridan—"

"She's a producer," he said tightly. "Hollywood. Wants me for a show. Some bullshit reality thing. *Horse Whisperer in Hollywood*. She's fucking relentless."

Cole looked impressed. "You thinking of doing it?"

"Not sure I'll have the time, little brother." He motioned for them to step back so he could get out of the stall. "After all, we got an ex-sheriff to stalk, the truth about a boy named Sweet to uncover, a long-lost brother to find and deal with, new land for the mustangs to search out, and a wedding to attend." And then there was Sheridan.

Sheridan. She was the warm, happy light in all of the gray.

"Damn, that sounds daunting," Cole remarked dryly.

"What do you want me to tell her?" Sam asked.

"Tell her I ain't interested," James said. *Not now anyway*. "Tell her if and when I am, I'll get in touch. Right now," he said, grabbing a currycomb, "I've got my family to see to."

Fourteen

"Dammit," Sheridan grumbled as she turned off the burner, grabbed a wad of paper towels, and started mopping up the red sauce that had splattered all over the stove and floor. Hell, maybe it had made it into the hallway, with all that frenzied boiling.

This was so not the way she'd wanted to spend her first night in James's bunkhouse. Seriously, for someone who could multitask, color code, come up with a surefire marketing strategy for just about anything, all while talking a client down off a ledge, she was a total disaster in the kitchen.

But she'd wanted to try. Wanted to prove to James that she could . . . well, it was sappy, but maybe take care of him a little bit too.

She was just spraying cleaner on another patch

of red she'd found over by the dishwasher, when she heard him opening the screen door. She scrambled to her feet, but there was no way to hide the tomato-stained towels in her left hand or the cleaner in her right.

"What's all this?" he asked, walking into the kitchen.

She noticed the flickers of amusement in his eyes. So basically he knew exactly what this was.

She flung her hands—which were still holding the towels and cleaner—up in the air. "I am a terrible houseguest."

"See," he began, coming at her, taking the cleaner and towels out of her hands. "That's the thing." He moved past her to the trash can. "You're a guest, Sheridan."

"I suck."

"My point is you shouldn't be doing anything." After setting down the cleaner, he tried to get the truth out of her. "But for curiosity's sake, what exactly were you trying to do?"

"Oh, the usual. Embarrass myself, start a fire, get kicked out my first night."

His brows lifted. "Wow. Ambitious."

She leaned dramatically against the counter. "Make spaghetti and garlic bread."

"I love garlic bread."

"Dammit!" She hurled herself at the oven and ripped open the door. She felt around at the long loaf covered in foil, then at the interior of the oven. "It's cold. Okay, perfect." She stood up. "Forgot to turn it on."

James laughed and closed the oven door. "Why don't you let me take over here?"

"No, this was my thing."

"I promise I'll make it all better."

She looked at him with what she imagined were supremely pathetic puppy eyes. "Please don't tell me you're a cook as well as a horse genius and a gorgeous . . ." She stopped midsentence, her eyes going wide.

His lips twitched. "A gorgeous what?"

The humiliation factor just kept going up and up. "Girl rescuer," she said with a resigned sigh. "A gorgeous girl rescuer."

"I like that." He laughed and reached past her and took two glasses out of the cupboard. He handed them to her, then grabbed a bottle from the counter and proceeded to uncork it.

"Wine?" she said as he poured the dark red liquid into each glass.

"Beer doesn't sit right with pasta." He pointed the neck of the bottle to the wall of windows, and specifically to the one she'd opened earlier. "Go. Out on the back porch. It's a damn pretty night and I say we enjoy it."

She hesitated, feeling like a jerk. Like a . . . culinary loser.

"I'll be out in a few," he insisted. "Save me a seat?"

"Okay, but I'm convinced that garlic bread will be amazing . . . you know, as soon as it's cooked."

His mouth curved up at the corners. "I'll take care of it."

Glasses in hand, pride shot to shit, Sheridan headed outside. He was right about the night. A gentle breeze was blowing, and the moon was a perfect crescent that illuminated the endless fields and the barn in the distance. She took a seat at the small table on the deck, and thought about how one would have to be crazy to leave here. Crazy or . . . really angry at something or someone. She suspected with James it was the latter.

"Water's boiling, bread is baking," he announced good-naturedly, stepping outside and heading her way.

Under the glow of the moonlight, he looked even more rugged, more handsome than usual. He'd changed into a pair of clean blue jeans and a dark blue button-down shirt. Maybe she should've stayed inside to watch.

She grinned to herself, then handed him a glass of wine when he sat down across from her. When their fingers touched, she felt it all the way down to her toes.

"I thought you said you were a bad cook," she remarked with mock censure.

He looked momentarily confused.

"Or at least that was what was implied," she continued with a wicked smile playing about her lips. "You know, with Cole moving up to the house. Elena's amazing cooking beating your burned fish."

"Oh, right." His eyes regarded her over the top of the wineglass. "So maybe I wasn't being completely honest about that."

"Really?" She sat back, flinched ever so slightly at the bruising she'd momentarily forgotten was there. "Why?"

"I guess I wanted you to feel comfortable here."

"I would've been comfortable with Cole."

His expression darkened, and he took a healthy swallow of wine. When he placed the glass on the tabletop with just a hint more force than necessary, she felt compelled to push him.

"What's wrong?"

"I'm having a boy's reaction, is all." His eyes flipped up to meet hers. "I didn't like hearing you say that."

Her brows lifted. "That I'd be comfortable with Cole? He's your brother. And a seemingly decent guy. Shouldn't I feel comfortable around him?"

"Nah, he's a good guy," he ground out. "And you should feel comfortable around him. When you're out at the Bull's Eye or up at the main house or in town. But sharing living space, a bathroom, shower." His nostrils flared. "Walking around in front of him in a towel or—hell—if he caught sight of something he shouldn't . . ."

"Wouldn't the same go for you, Mr. Cavanaugh?" she observed, her lips twitching.

He took another healthy swallow of wine and avoided answering her question.

"Okay," she began thoughtfully, as though coming up with a solution to this problem was really high on her priority list. When, in fact, realizing that he had some feelings of jealousy and possessiveness where she was concerned made her extraordinarily happy. Granted, those two attributes in most guys could be a big turnoff, but coming from the cowboy sitting across from her, it was totally gratifying.

"How about I never walk around in a towel when you're home?" she suggested.

A flush of red moved up his neck, and she started to laugh. She couldn't help herself.

"Wait a sec," she said, realizing how that sounded. "I don't mean I'll be walking around *without* a towel when you're in the house. Naked. Well, I mean, I'll have to be naked at some points. Showering in clothes is weird."

"Sheridan?"

"Yep?"

His ocean eyes flickered with guarded wickedness. "You can be naked whenever you want."

Momentarily struck dumb, she just stared at him.

He shrugged. "But if you are, I can't promise I won't look." He stood up. "Now, I'm going to go and put the pasta on and check to see if that bread of yours is coming along."

Sheridan's fingers curved around her wineglass as she watched him walk away, her mind abandoning all thoughts about her own nudity around the house for much more intriguing thoughts of his.

"I think I could bathe in this sauce," Sheridan said, her voice threaded with contentment.

And, James mused, as he glanced up from his plate, a tiny hint of ecstasy. "Now, that's something I'd like to see," he said, watching as her cheeks instantly flushed pink in the soft lights of the moon and the lamps from inside the bunkhouse.

"How did you make this?" she asked before sliding a forkful of spaghetti into her mouth.

James watched until the silver utensil slid back out again. It was damn hypnotic. Anything to do with that mouth of hers. "It's a very ancient recipe," he said finally.

"Really?"

He nodded. "Top secret."

She took a sip of wine. "Well, I hope you'll share it with me before I leave."

"Leave?" he said far too quickly and way too fiercely. "Where are you going? You just got here."

She laughed, no doubt thinking he was joking around, being overly dramatic. It was a sexy, throaty, sweet sound that curled around him and squeezed.

"I just mean later," she clarified. "You know, when it's time."

He didn't like talking about this. The idea of her not being around, leaving River Black, bothered him. Probably more than it should. But he wasn't going to let her know that. His job was to make her feel comfortable here, not self-conscious.

Forcing a grin to his face, he leaned in and whispered, "One jar of Ragu, a handful of fresh basil, and some grated pecorino Romano."

Her eyes widened. "The ancient recipe?"

He nodded. "You'll keep my secret?"

She grinned. "My lips are sealed."

His eyes dropped to those lips. And as he was studying them far too provocatively, she placed another forkful of pasta into her mouth and proceeded to suck up the long, curly strands. Good God Almighty, she wasn't making this easy. For the next thirty seconds, he watched, enraptured, waiting for her tongue to swipe at her bottom lip and catch the red sauce waiting there. And when it did, his body groaned in a frustration he knew was only the beginning of what was to come with her living in the same small house as him.

He sat back and forced his eyes to his plate. "How long have you worked with Deacon?" It was actually something he didn't know and had been curious about. He hadn't asked his brother all that much about Sheridan.

"Three and a half years," she said.

"Is he a good boss?"

"I think so. Some might consider him challenging or even arrogant."

"But you don't?"

She shook her head. "He's brilliant."

The complimentary assessment of another man, even if that man happened to be his brother, made James bristle.

"He's what I want to be when I grow up," she continued.

"Head of a company?"

"Doesn't have to be that big, but something of my own, yes. I love investments, marketing. And Deacon has been a great teacher."

"He's taken, Sheridan." The words were out of James's mouth before he could stop them. And hell, he really wished he could've stopped them. What was wrong with him? Jealousy was just not an emotion he practiced. It made him look weak and insecure.

"I think you're misunderstanding me," Sheridan began.

"I know. I'm sorry about that." He stood. He needed to get out of her company for a spell, get his shit together. Hell, he'd probably need to do that every damn day with the way he got worked up around her. Otherwise, their living situation was going to turn into a Shakespearean production. Deep feeling, unchecked action, and maybe intense regret.

"I'm going to take care of all this," he said. "Then hit the hay. I have an early day tomorrow."

"Oh. Well, go to bed then." She stayed seated, but her eyes burned into his with some of that regret he'd just been worrying over. "I'll clean up."

"No." He reached for her plate, but she stopped him. Put a hand over his.

"I love cleaning, James."

Her fingers were too soft, too warm, and they made the blood pop in his veins. He wanted them around his neck. Holding on tight. "No one loves cleaning, darlin', and you just got home from the hospital."

"I'm fine," she assured him. "I actually feel great. I'm just going to sit out here awhile longer, and then I'll take care of it." She cocked her head to the side. "Come on. I want to. Please."

James contemplated putting up a fight and insisting. Hell, it was her first night here. But the look on her face—no, the spark in her eyes—told him she wasn't going to back down from her offer.

He nodded, pulled away from her touch. "All right." Damn, he felt cold. "Good night, Sheridan."

She offered him a shuttered smile, the kind that didn't reach the eyes. "Sleep well, James."

"If you need anything . . ." he started.

But she cut him off. "Thanks. But I'm sure I'll be fine."

He hated her easy manner about as much as he hated his idiotic jealousy. What the hell was he doin'? Moon-soaked, wine-fueled meals with lots of flirting and fantasizing? *Don't pursue this relationship with Sheridan O'Neil any further than you already have, cowboy.*

But see, that was the thing. For years, fear had ruled every choice he'd made, and it had taken away wild, reckless, wonderful abandon. The abandon he'd just tasted for a moment with Sheridan.

As he headed back into the bunkhouse and down the hall toward his room, he felt caged in by that fear. He wanted to be free and reckless. He wanted more abandon. And he wanted it all with Sheridan.

Fifteen

Sheridan immersed her hands in the hot, sudsy water and got to work washing the dishes. There weren't many of them, which was slightly disappointing as she always enjoyed the dishwashing process. Cleaning toilets, doing laundry, cooking? No. But washing dishes she liked. Maybe it was the resemblance to a bubble bath. Or maybe it was because she was just plain weird.

Which could explain why James had taken off.

She took a deep breath, let her hands play with the top of the water, her fingers moving in and out of the bubbles like a couple of dolphins. No, her weirdness had nothing to do with James's quick departure from their very lovely dinner. It was because she'd talked about Deacon, how she admired the man—how she wanted to be him when she grew up. James was jealous. And no doubt as conflicted and confused about his feelings as she was.

"Sheridan . . ."

She jumped at the sound of his voice so near, so unexpected. Then shivered as he came to stand beside her.

"Sorry," he said, his eyes soft as he leaned against the sink. "Didn't mean to startle you."

Her gaze ran over him, and maybe for a second she understood the possessiveness that had perhaps captured him earlier. He was wearing black sweat pants and a black T-shirt and his feet were bare. He looked comfortable, ready for bed, and so sexy she nearly groaned at the sight of him.

He ran his hand through his thick brown hair. "What happened out on the deck . . ." he began in a regretful tone.

She shook her head, went back to the dishes. "It's fine."

"It's not," he insisted. "I pretty much acted like a world-class dick."

She smiled to herself. "Well . . ." Really pretended to think it over. "I don't know about *world-class*." She cut her gaze to his.

His gorgeous eyes remained somber. "Look, I know you're not interested in Deacon."

"No, I'm not," she confirmed.

"And even suggesting that was insulting and childish."

"Yes. Yes, it was."

His grin widened. "You're something else, Sheridan O'Neil."

"You know, I've been told that before." She shrugged. "But no one can seem to figure out what that something might be."

He inhaled deeply, let his gaze roam over her in a way that was proof of his interest. "How about beautiful? Intelligent? Funny?"

"All good, but no."

"One helluva helper in the kitchen?" He dropped his chin and his voice and whispered wickedly, "Excluding the cooking part, of course."

Completely without forethought, Sheridan grabbed the mountain of suds near her right hand and tossed it at him.

Shock enveloped James's face, then a huge grin broke out. "Really?" One eyebrow lifted. "Is that how we're gonna play this?"

Sheridan started laughing. She couldn't believe herself. "Absolutely."

Quick as a breath, James reached into the sink, scooped up a huge handful of suds and water and pummeled her with it.

Sheridan gasped as warm, soapy water hit her neck and chest. "Oh my God. You're going down, Cavanaugh!"

She barely got the words out before another blast of suds hit her belly. Her eyes lifted and she growled playfully. "This. Is. War."

"Bring it on, O'Neil," he challenged, slowly reaching past her to scoop up another handful.

Laughing and getting soaking wet, Sheridan lobbed soap and water at him—in his face, in his hair, on his shirt. And he did the same, wonderfully, unmercifully pelting her with suds.

"You have a good arm, O'Neil!" he called out.

"And one see-through shirt!" she returned merrily, raising her arms.

Just as the words left her mouth, James let another handful of suds fly, nailing her square in the chest. She froze, looked down and doubled over laughing. "Oh my God . . . How do I look? Like a cloud? A cotton ball?"

She glanced up to get his answer. But he wasn't laughing anymore. In fact his smile was fading and morphing into something else entirely. Something hot and hungry. Something predatory.

"You look . . ." he growled low in his throat. "Good enough to—"

"Kiss?" she finished for him.

He shrugged imperceptibly. "For a start."

Sheridan had no time to process that remark before James was on her, before his hands cupped her face and he took her mouth under his. A soft moan escaped her as she wrapped her wet, soapy hands around his waist and pulled him close. He was all impressive muscles and hot skin beneath his soaking wet T-shirt, and she rolled up onto her toes to get closer to him.

"Sheridan," he groaned as he kissed her deeper. He tasted like wine and warmth, and when he slipped his tongue inside her mouth, Sheridan felt her entire body flood with desire.

Her inhibitions long gone—if they had ever been there to begin with—she ran her hands down his back and cupped his butt. He groaned, and she joined him. He was truly glorious muscle everywhere. Lord, all that riding had obviously served a higher purpose. As she squeezed the hard flesh, James ground his hips into hers and kissed her so deeply and so hungrily, she lost her breath. But he didn't let up. His hands fisted in her hair and he eased her head to one side to get closer, deeper, to feast on her lips, on her tongue. Truly he was like a tornado touching down. Fast, furious, and out of control. And Sheridan reveled in every second of it. There was nothing she wanted more in that moment than him. To be utterly and completely lost in him.

Ripping his mouth from hers, he dipped his head and nuzzled her neck. Sheridan shivered as he ran his nose all the way up to her earlobe.

"Oh, God, James," she uttered, her sex going slick with moisture.

"Tell me you want this," he demanded in a husky whisper near the shell of her ear, his teeth grazing gently over the lobe.

"I want this," she nearly cried out. *God, I wanted this*. "I want you."

He dropped his head to her chest, and stunned her by suckling one taut and aching nipple through the wet fabric of her shirt. She gasped, her sex clenching in response, and brought her hands up, threading them in his hair. James growled at her and shifted to take her other nipple into his mouth. Her fingers pressed into his scalp and her breathing turned rushed, rapid. It was the most exquisite feeling. Torture and temptation. She wanted her clothes off, wanted to feel the cool breeze from the open window on her skin as he first suckled and tasted her, then turned her around, kicked her feet apart and drove up into her body like he owned it.

As he eased her wet shirt up to her chin, then pulled her bra cups down, settling them just below her breasts, Sheridan arched her back. She wanted to give him better access, wanted to give him everything. Wanted him to taste her, consume her.

"Goddamn, darlin'," he uttered hoarsely, cupping one of her breasts in his large, callused hand. "You are one achingly beautiful woman."

Sheridan meant to reply with something other than a groan of delight, but she couldn't manage it. His head had dropped once again and he was suckling that breast he held so possessively. Sheridan went brilliantly blind for a moment, let her head fall to one side. What he was doing to her . . . just his hand and his tongue. Squeezing, massaging, pulling, lapping, teasing, twisting.

And then he sent the other hand down to the

button of her jeans. Sheridan held her breath—her crazy, ragged breath—as he worked the zipper. The muscles in her sex clenched in anticipation and she knew her underwear was soaked. Then she heard the metal drop and she moaned. Moaned at just the idea of those callused fingers touching her, invading her heat.

James's palm rested on her lower belly, and he lifted his head. His eyes slammed into hers. His gaze was pained, ravenous. No doubt mirroring her own, she thought, placing her hand over his on her belly. Her eyes pinned to his, she slowly guided his fingers. Down, down, down, until they breached the band of her underwear.

"Oh, Sheridan," he said on a groan as he took it the rest of the way. "Honey . . ."

Sheridan gasped as his fingers moved over the top of her shaved sex, then cried out as one lone digit dipped inside her folds and began circling the tight bud inside.

"Is this for me?" he asked, his deep voice curling around her.

"What?" she breathed, squeezing her internal muscles, wanting, desperate. Every inch of her ached for him, for release. Damn! Why were her clothes still on?

He leaned in past her cheek and whispered into the shell of her ear, "This hot, sweet cream?"

She shivered. *Oh, yes. God, yes!* For him, because of him. All she could do was nod, because in that moment, he thrust two of those thick, callused fingers inside her.

A soft growl of lust escaped her. Or maybe that was him. She couldn't tell. She didn't care. Her mind was seizing up. One moment he was filling her, the next he was gone, drawing back out of her hot sheath.

"No," she groaned. She felt so bereft, so sad, she nearly started raging at him. She needed him— back where he belonged. Inside her. But then his eyes flashed with blue-glass fire, and she watched as he brought those fingers to his lips and sucked the shiny, wet digits into his mouth.

The utterly erotic action made the muscles in her pussy clench so painfully, so hungrily, cream leaked from her sex and trailed down her inner thighs.

His eyes blazed down into hers as he slipped his fingers from his mouth. A growl followed. Then he moved in close and said in a harsh whisper, "You taste like heaven, Sheridan."

Sheridan tried to answer, tried to make any kind of sound. But James didn't give her a chance. He covered her mouth with his and stole her breath completely. As he kissed her, she tasted herself on his tongue and whimpered with the intensity of it. God, this was madness. The perfect kind of madness. The kind you wish for, hope for—never in a million years think you're going to get because of all the disappointments in the past.

The things you're told. The lies you're spoon-fed from those who are supposed to give you hope and encouragement and an open heart.

No more, Sheridan thought through a brain heavy with desire.

James kissed her madly as his fingers found their hot, wet home once again, thrusting into her slow and deep until she moaned and clung to him for support. Her legs wanted to give out, and every inch of her was poised for climax.

"That's right, darlin'," he whispered against her mouth, then nipped the bottom lip. "Come for me. You're right there. Hovering on the edge."

Swinging her hips, grinding herself against his knuckles, squeezing her muscles around his fingers, Sheridan lost herself to the frantic need to come.

And then he brushed the pad of his thumb over her clit. Once, twice . . . Sheridan cried out. Lightning was going off inside her. Lightning and rockets. She was completely lost to the feeling, to him.

"Oh, yeah," he groaned, continuing to circle the tight bud while he thrust inside her. "Milk my fingers, Sheridan. Squeeze me tight, darlin'. Just like you would if my cock was driving into you."

She was gone, crying out, falling down the rabbit hole.

"Oh, fuck," he ground out through tightly clenched teeth. "Your walls are squeezing me so tight, baby. Shaking around me." He drove his fingers deep, then flicked the pads of his fingers against her soft, sensitive flesh.

She came in a rush of whimpers and moans, bucking against him, rubbing her creaming pussy all over his knuckles. But he didn't stop or slow. He remained steady, deep inside her, working her G-spot in tandem with her clit until she cried out and sagged against him. Then he obliged, easing back and gently pumping inside her as her orgasm receded.

It could've been seconds or it could've been hours, but when he finally slipped his fingers from her body and wrapped his arms around her, Sheridan was bone weary. She snuggled into him, and he held her tight, stroking her hair, her neck. Then her back and shoulders. It was only when she winced that he stopped.

No. Not stopped—froze.

Like a statue.

"Oh, Christ," he uttered.

Sheridan instantly looked up, her mind still trying to fully return to reality. She still had *sink, soap fight, wet clothes, wetter Sheridan, want James* running through her brain.

"What's wrong?" she asked.

James released her and stepped back. He looked horrified and guilty, strained and pissed off. None of the ways he should be looking after making her feel the way he had. He ran a hand through his hair. The same hand that just been down her pants, making her sigh and moan. Making her come. "I'm an animal."

Sheridan stared at him. What was going on? "I don't understand. What are you talking about?"

She tried to reach out for him, but he nearly growled at her. "You just got out of the hospital and I'm all over you."

Oh, for goodness' sake. "I'm fine. I told you." She moved toward him. "What you did—"

"Was wrong," he said blackly. "So motherfuck-ing wrong." He turned away, dropped his head into his hands. "What the hell is wrong with me that I can't control myself around you?"

Sheridan's first instinct was to go to him and put her arms around him, try to comfort him in some way, assure him again that she was fine. More than fine. But she didn't think that would help. In fact, she believed it would only perpetu-ate the confused state James Cavanaugh had found himself in. She'd made a decision tonight, when she was in this man's arms, to drop the what ifs—stop letting voices and fears from the past dictate her choices and run her life. It wasn't easy to do, wouldn't be easy going forward. That voice was inside her cells. But the truth was, she wanted what she'd felt with him tonight.

And she wanted it more than she wanted to protect herself.

Her body still reeling from climax, she kept her voice controlled and calm. "I had an incredible time with you tonight. You made me feel amazing. Not hurt. Not in pain. Amazing. Do you get that?"

His jaw tensed, but he didn't answer her.

"I suggest you take a nice cold shower, Cavanaugh, and fix your head. See what's really in front of you before it's not there anymore."

Then she walked past him and headed for her room.

Fix his head?

How did he do that exactly? he wondered, standing beneath the lukewarm spray. Was it this? He leaned down and cranked the ancient handles to cold. Ice mother-fucking cold. He hissed as frigid water pelted his skin. Was shock and pain the way to get him to remove his long-standing beliefs? To see what was really in front of him before it wasn't there anymore, as Sheridan had said?

He didn't know. Shit, he didn't know much of anything anymore. Except that he was done pretending he didn't want Sheridan. It was pointless. He wanted her badly. Desperately, even. Like a starving thing needs food. Like an exhausted thing needs rest. It was all there on a primal level. And how did someone control primal?

He didn't take the woman he's trying to protect in his arms and kiss her, touch her, make her come against a goddamn sink!

He turned and lifted his face to the water, hoping the frigid rain would do something to calm down his body.

Behind him, the shower door opened, and he turned around just in time to see the very reason his cock was hard as a metal pipe walk in.

Naked.

Ridiculously, head-spinningly, gloriously, come-dripping-from-the-head-of-his-dick naked.

"Sheridan," he said, his voice laced with warning.

"You fix your head yet, cowboy?" Her eyes flickered to his erection, then lifted again. "The one on your neck, I mean."

His hands balled into fists at his sides because if they didn't he was going to grab her and lift her up. Place her down on his throbbing cock and tell her to ride him into next week.

"Honey, you gotta go," he ground out. "Get out of here."

"No." She placed her hands on her hips. The action made her breasts jut out. James hadn't seen them as clearly earlier as he could right now. They were a perfect handful, with nipples so tight and pink his mouth watered at the sight of them.

"You're not pushing me away," she said defiantly. "You're not doing that to me again."

He sighed heavily. "I'm not doing anything to you. That's the point. I'm trying to leave you alone."

"Why?" she demanded. "Obviously I don't want you to leave me alone." She lifted her arms, giving him a full view of her spectacular naked body. "How much clearer can I be?"

The cold water at his back felt like spring fucking rain. "Sheridan . . ."

"Please tell me." She moved toward him, her hips swinging gently. Her shaved mound calling to him. "Why are you so afraid of this? Of us?"

If she drew any nearer . . . "I just don't want you to get hurt again."

"Goddammit, James," she said with heartfelt passion. "You're not responsible for what happened to me. Palmer is the only one who's responsible. He hurt me, not you."

And then she was standing before him, the hard tips of her breasts touching his chest, the bones in her hips pressed to his groin.

"All you've ever done is make me feel good," she said. "And free."

As water rained down on them both, James's eyes never left hers. Until she reached between them and took his cock in her hand.

He looked down and groaned at the sight of her smooth, pale hand stroking him.

"The only way I'm going to be hurt is if you reject me right now," she said. "If you ask me not to touch you, not to make you come like you made me come tonight." Her soft, capable hand worked him up and down. "Are you going to hurt me, James?"

His eyes lifted to lock with hers, and his damn broken heart spoke for him. "Never. Fuck. Never, Sheridan." He threaded his fingers into her wet hair and pulled her in for a kiss.

Whimpering, Sheridan kissed him back. So fiercely, he felt precome leak at the head of his dick. She rubbed her nipples across his chest and reached for the spot behind his testicles with her other hand. Despite the cold water blasting him—blasting them—heat raged inside him. He wanted to climax. He wanted to come, then take her against the wall, bury himself inside her and fuck her as he grew hard again.

And he was close. Hell, he'd been close ever since he'd slipped his fingers into his mouth and tasted her sweet pussy juices when they were in the kitchen.

When she quickened her pace, when she ripped her mouth from his and dipped her head to his chest—when she licked and sucked his nipple—he broke. His will, and his need to keep control. His head dropped back and he groaned as he pumped into her furiously, pumped his seed into her hands. But she didn't stop there, didn't still. She kept stroking him, gently, lightly, using his come as lubrication until he was gone, so out of his mind, so over the moon for her that he didn't realize how truly cold the water was until he felt her shiver against him.

He turned away from her and quickly adjusted the temperature, waiting until he heard her sigh to know what level of heat she wanted. Then he came back and wrapped his arms around her. She snuggled against him under the spray and he released a weighty, satisfied breath. Could he? Could he tamp down his fear, his beliefs about himself and what his presence in a woman's life meant? Could he block out the past so maybe, just maybe, he could enjoy the present?

When she dropped her head back and looked up at him and smiled, he knew the answer. It wouldn't be easy. Hell, he'd been carrying the weight of what felt like an unbreakable curse around with him for more years than he wanted to count. But for her, he was going to try.

No. He was going to hope.

"Do you want to sleep alone tonight, James?" she asked over the pounding of the water.

His eyes moved over her beautiful face. "Not tonight." He leaned in and kissed her. "Not tomorrow night."

"Now that's the man who stands in the path of a herd of wild horses, the man who stays by the bedside of a woman in fear for two days straight— the man who took what he wanted by the kitchen sink earlier and made the fearful woman not only fly, but feel incandescently safe."

Her words crashed into him like a wrecking ball.

Before he could say anything back, she lifted one auburn brow and asked in a cheeky tone, "Dry me off?"

A smile playing about his lips, James released her, turned off the water, grabbed a towel from the hook on the shower door, and wrapped it around her shoulders.

"I dunno," he said, rubbing her skin gently. "Sounds pretty counterproductive to me."

"Why's that?" she asked.

"Dry you off only to get you wet again?"

She started to laugh. And the moment she did, James picked her up in his arms and carried her out of the shower, out of the bathroom, and down the hall toward his bedroom.

Sixteen

Cole walked into the veterinary office five minutes before closing time. He knew Dr. Grace Hunter had late hours on Thursday evenings, and he also knew that the place had emptied of patients about twenty minutes before. After the meeting he'd had earlier with his brothers, Cole just wasn't content to hang around anymore and wait for orders or a consensus or a plan from his two big brothers. While they were tending to their women, he was going to get shit done.

Starting with the woman seated behind the reception desk.

All Cole saw was the top of her dark head as she went through a bunch of paperwork. But when he drew closer, that head came up right quick and those pale green eyes narrowed.

"Mr. Cavanaugh?"

"Evenin', ma'am," he drawled, taking off his Stetson.

"Did you lose your way around town?" she asked, standing up. "Or is this a social call?"

"I'm actually here about an animal."

She let her gaze very dramatically move around the room. Then she came back to him and shrugged. "Is he imaginary?"

"Don't think so."

"Do you see him now?"

Cole grinned. He might like this girl if she wasn't purposely keeping secrets from them all. "It's the one you have advertised, Doc."

All sarcasm and humor faded from her features. "The abandoned basset hound?"

"That's right." Just that morning he'd seen a few flyers up around town. "I'd like to see her."

She came around the desk, really interested now. "Why?"

"What do you mean, why? Maybe I have a mind to adopt. I'm a very lonely man."

"I believe you."

He tried to look insulted. "Well, that ain't very neighborly."

She crossed her arms over her chest. "Seriously, Mr. Cavanaugh, what's this about?"

"I just told you, Doc."

She was quiet for a moment, probably thinking he was playing her somehow. Probably wondering why. "You really want to meet her?" she asked him.

"Why the hell else would I be here?"

"Don't make me answer that," she said blackly. Then she gestured for him to follow her. "Come into my office. I'll see what she's doing. See if I can coax her out to sniff at you."

As soon as they were inside the small office, Cole pulled out a plastic sandwich bag. "I came prepared."

Her mouth dropped open. "Is that bacon?"

" 'Course. I know how to speak canine."

"Again, I believe you." Her eyes moved over his face, and then she sighed and gestured to the chair in front of her desk. "I'll be back in five minutes. I'm going to take her for a quick bathroom break so she doesn't try anything in here. Sit tight."

Sit tight? Cole mused as she walked out of the office. Oh, Dr. Hunter, there's no chance of that. As soon as the door closed, he was up and out of the chair. He rounded her desk and started with the drawers, looking up every few seconds. Vet forms, prescriptions, Marabelle's menu, no, no, no. He opened another drawer. Bank accounts. Checkbook. Bingo. Forget Deacon and his Internet detectives. If you wanted to find important shit, all you had to do was look in someone's drawers.

With another quick glance at the door, he fingered quickly through her checkbook until he came to a copy made out to a Barrington Ridge Senior Care. He scribbled the name down on a piece of paper, stuffed it into his pocket and re-turned the checkbook to the drawer. His butt was just landing back in the seat of the chair he'd occu-pied earlier when the door opened and in walked Grace Hunter and the saddest-looking dog Cole had ever seen. She'd been wearing a festive vest and a goofy grin in the pictures around town.

He got down on the floor, patted his lap, and said, "Well, who do we have here?"

"Her name is Belle," Grace informed him.

"Like the princess," Cole remarked, glancing up.

She looked at him strangely. "Uh, yeah. I guess that too. I named her after Marabelle's. It's where she was found. Trying to knock over one of their Dumpsters."

Awww, poor thing. Being alone and hungry. It was something Cole understood. Being all by yourself and trying to figure out where you be-longed—that he got. His gaze connected with the dog. "Come over here, girl," he cooed.

The doctor released Belle from the leash, and the hound lumbered his way. When she stood di-rectly in front of him, Cole reached out and started scratching her ears. As he did, she made this crazy sound, like a cross between a howl and a groan. He laughed. He'd never thought about having a pet. He traveled too much, but the truth of it was that he didn't know if he was capable of being a responsible parent. And he wasn't one of those dopes who thought taking on an animal was anything less.

"You smell the bacon in my pocket, don't ya?" he said, pulling out the bag and opening it.

As soon as Belle got her first whiff, she dropped her head back and offered him a real howl.

Cole laughed again. So did Grace Hunter.

He looked up at her. Her green eyes were bright and her face was lit up with pleasure. Most of the times he'd been around the woman she'd been frowning, nervous, her eyes all clouded with worry or suspicion.

"I'm shocked, but I think she likes you."

"Shocked?" Cole repeated. "Come on, Doc. What's not to like here?"

She rested her hip against the desk and regarded him with serious eyes. "Are you really here to see about adopting? See if Belle's good for you?"

Guilt wasn't an emotion Cole allowed himself to feel. It only made you vulnerable and weak. In the life he'd chosen for himself, there was no room for either.

"She's a special girl," he said, rising to his feet. "And she may very well be good for me. Just not sure if I'd be any good for her."

Sheridan lay on her side in James's bed and gazed out the large picture window. There were no lights on, but the moon's glow filtered into the room, casting everything it touched in pale silver. James was behind her, naked—just like she was— running his fingers so gently across the bruises on her back it almost tickled.

"Tell me what you were like as a kid," he said to her.

They'd been lying like this for a while, their bodies drying from the shower's vigorous assault. At first when James had placed her down on his bed, Sheridan had thought they were going to continue what they'd started in the shower, but then she'd accidentally flinched in pain when her back touched down on the mattress. She'd assured James she was fine, more than fine, but he'd insisted they wait.

He'd been gently stroking her ever since.

Sheridan grinned. Problem was, instead of soothing her, it was only making her more desperate to be touched. It was why she'd rolled to her side. So he couldn't see how tight her nipples were or how wet her sex was.

"Were you always so tough?" he continued, pulling her back to the moment.

She laughed softly. "I don't think of myself as tough."

"You are," he insisted, his fingers snaking down her spine. "You're not afraid to say how you feel or ask for what you want."

"In everything but relationships, that's probably true," she said, unable to control the arch of her back and the jut of her buttocks as he touched her.

"You had no problem telling me what you wanted in the shower, darlin'." This time, his fingers traced the curve of her hip to the indent of her waist.

"No, I didn't. Because tonight I decided I wasn't living in someone else's past anymore."

His hand stilled just above the curve of her ass. "Whose past are you talking about?"

"My mom's." She inhaled deeply, stared out at the moon. "My dad left us when I was little. My mom worked really hard to keep us going. And she did. But I think to keep *her* going she used her anger and her bitterness as fuel."

"Was she angry with you?" James asked.

"No. She loved me—very much. She just wanted to protect me, make sure I never lost myself to anyone the way she did. But in doing that, her cautionary tale became my life's narrative."

For a few seconds, all Sheridan heard was his breathing and her own. And then his hand traveled back up her spine.

"Did you end up losing yourself in anyone, Sheridan?" he asked.

"No," she said, her breasts aching for his touch. Why couldn't he just move closer? Press himself against her? Was he turned on? Hard? She wanted to know, wanted to feel him. "I never allowed myself to get close to anyone," she continued, swallowing the saliva that pooled in her mouth, "Not friends, and definitely nothing serious with guys."

"Do you regret it?"

"I don't believe in regrets," she said in a serious tone despite her heated skin, pulsing sex, and heavy breath. "They're a waste of time. All I can do is something different, you know?"

"Yeah, I do. . . ."

"Have you?" she asked him.

"Have I what?"

"Ever given your heart to anyone?" The moment the words were out of her mouth, she laughed softly. "Oh, Lord, look who I'm asking. Of course you haven't."

"I was engaged, Sheridan."

Though everything south of Sheridan's neck continued to hum and pulse and clench, everything above it—her face, and most definitely her brain— froze. For a good ten seconds. Then she forced out a strangled sounding, "What happened?"

"She called it off."

"Oh." She couldn't believe what she was hearing. He'd said he didn't believe in marriage. Was this why? "I'm sorry."

"Don't be. I was young. College."

Her heart sank into her stomach. "Is that why you didn't finish?"

He took several seconds to answer. "Yes."

She turned over to face him. No longer was she concerned with her blatant arousal. Her eyes blazed into his, so stormy blue in the strained light of the moon streaming in over her shoulder. He'd given her something. Answered her question. It wasn't an entire story, but it was a first chapter.

She draped her leg over his thigh and pulled herself in close. Then she kissed him, slow and soft and hungry. When he growled, and his hand dragged up from her knee to her thigh, then slipped around to cup her ass possessively, Sheridan let all the questions floating around in her mind fade away.

For now, she mused breathlessly. For now.

Seventeen

James dug into his nightstand for a condom. He hadn't expected to use them when he'd grabbed a pack from the drugstore yesterday. But he also wasn't an immature bastard. Sheridan was coming to live with him. He wanted her, and he had been pretty sure she wanted him too. If the time came, and shit, if both of them wanted it, he was going to be prepared. He was going to protect her.

He just hadn't thought that possibility would turn so damn quickly into *let's go*—and *oh, baby, I want you in my bed every night until you decide to leave it*.

Especially after talking about the past. About college. About being engaged. Why he'd left.

Dropping the condom near his pillow, he turned back to Sheridan. She instantly draped her leg over his thigh again and scooted closer. His eyes pinned to hers, he reached down and cupped her.

Heat and moisture surged into his palm and he groaned.

"How long have you been like this?" he asked as he ran his fingers from her clit to the entrance of her sex.

"Hmmm, let's see." One auburn eyebrow lifted. "How long have we known each other?"

He stilled, unsure if he'd heard her right.

She laughed.

"Damn, woman," he ground out good-naturedly, easing his index finger through her folds and finding her swollen clit.

"Okay," she amended with a sharp intake of breath. "The way you were touching my back. Every inch of me was on edge and wanting you and . . . wet."

"You could've said something. I've been ready since we left the shower." His gaze flickered left. "I just didn't want to be a horny asshole. Again, you just got out of the hospital."

She reached up and took his face in her hands, gave him a very serious, very sexy stare. "Listen to me, cowboy. I'm a grown woman."

"Yes, you are," he agreed, flicking her clit gently.

"Don't pull me off my course," she warned with a sharp intake of breath. "I'm a grown woman who knows her body. Knows what it can take and what it can't. I get to make that decision, you hear?"

"I hear," he said. "So what can your body take,

Sheridan?" he asked, dipping his finger inside her pussy.

She gasped and canted her hips. "Oh, that and so much more. Really anything you got, James Cavanaugh."

His body erupted into flame. His cock was so hard it was kissing his belly. "That's way too tempting."

She grinned, her eyes glassy. "Good."

"Well, I won't be putting you on your back—that's for sure," he said, his nostrils flaring, taking in her addictive scent as he pumped a finger gently inside her.

Her grin turned wicked. "Then put me on my front."

His mouth kicked up at the corners. This woman had a way of making a man not only forget his name, but forget he was more comfortable frowning through his life.

With a hungry groan, James scooped her up by the ass cheeks and took her with him as he rolled to his back. The sight that greeted him when his head hit the pillow was like something out of a fantasy. His fantasy. Ever since he'd rescued this woman from the storm and her car, had her in front of him on his horse. That's when it had all started. The dream of having Sheridan O'Neil for himself, laughing with her, making her cry out his name, watching her face, those gray eyes as she told him she wanted him too.

His eyes connected with her spread thighs, and the base of his cock wedged between her glistening pussy lips. Just that had the power to send him howling, send him over the edge, coming like an unskilled teenager. But he wasn't even remotely close to visually appreciating the angel sitting on top of him. Long, lightly muscled legs gave way to lean hips and a plump, biteable ass. Her waist was small, and he could just imagine himself encircling it with his hands, lifting her up and placing her down on his shaft. Her navel was a dime-sized inverted circle that intrigued him, made him think of stopping there to lick and tease her before he ventured lower.

His gaze clicked upward, narrowing on the absolutely mouthwatering sight of her breasts. They were the perfect size and his hands twitched involuntarily as he recalled how well they fit in his palms—how tight and hard her dark pink nipples had become when they were teased. Like precious diamonds.

When she started circling her hips, rubbing herself against his shaft, James reached for the condom he'd tossed next to his pillow. But just as he picked it up, Sheridan stole it from him.

His eyes lifted to hers in question. But she just smiled at him.

"I'm going to do it," she declared. "I've become very familiar with you since the shower."

His breath caught in his lungs; he watched her

unwrap the foil packet, watched her take out the latex and fit it over his cock. Her touch was gentle but firm and James couldn't stop himself from reaching out and touching her as she slid the condom all the way down to the base. His hands ran up her arms, his fingers pressing into her soft, smooth skin. He groaned as he cupped her breasts, then let his thumbs play with her taut nipples.

"I need you, James," she uttered in a pained voice. "I feel like I've been waiting forever to know how you feel."

"Christ, I need you too, darlin'."

Her heart squeezing at his words, Sheridan leaned over and kissed him. Slow, drugged, hungry. And as she did, she dragged the head of his cock back and forth over her clit. Even through the latex, James could feel the bud swell.

His hands gripped her waist and he lifted her up. She released him, but it didn't matter. He was so hard his cock stood at attention, waiting for her. It wanted her so damn bad it swelled even further with anticipation.

His eyes locked with hers, silently demanding that she dare not look away, he slowly placed her down on the head of his cock. His hands continued to grip her waist, easily holding her weight, as he let her sounds and her facial expressions guide him, take him inch by inch until he filled her completely.

Sheridan gasped and smiled at him, then started to circle her hips slowly.

James could've come right there. Being inside Sheridan was the deepest, most incredible pleasure he'd ever known. Her walls were gripping him, bathing him in her hot juices, and he just wanted to fuck her senseless.

But this was her show. For the moment.

He cupped her breasts, letting her lean forward into him as she started to move. Her face turned pink and her breathing grew labored as she set her pace. James kneaded the flesh of her breasts, every so often easing back to pinch or pull her nipples. An action that would make her cry out and ride him frantically for minutes at a time. Then, when she grew tired, she'd lean forward again, and let her hands rest on his shoulders, let her breasts hang right near his face.

He grinned. "I think I just found my heaven on earth," he growled, lifting his chin and swiping at her hard nipple with his tongue.

She gasped and clenched around him.

"My cock deep inside your pussy," he said, blowing gently on the hot, wet bud. "My mouth sucking on your perfect tits."

He felt her walls tremble and he reached around and grabbed her ass. His mouth closed around one of her nipples and as he suckled her into his mouth hard, he thrust up inside her.

"Oh, God, James," she cried out, her head falling back. "I can't hold on."

Then don't, darlin', he wanted to command, but

he wasn't about to break their connection. She was right there and so was he. He just let go. As he fucked her hard, thrusting up inside her, he flicked her nipple with his tongue, quick and fierce. Never stopping, not stopping, not even when she screamed his name, or her legs began to shake against his thighs, or her walls creamed against his shaft.

Not even when he followed her into orgasm.

Not until she collapsed on top of him, spent and breathing hard and whimpering his name. Then he wrapped his arms around her and held her tight, whispering soft, sweet, vulnerable things into her neck until she fell asleep.

Sunlight assaulted Sheridan's eyes as she blinked herself into awareness. Outside the picture window, blue skies and swaying trees told her very clearly that it was morning. She had no idea what time it was, but she did know whose bed she was in. A slow grin touched her lips—her very deliciously swollen lips. Last night had been the most amazing night of her life. She'd never been touched like that, never been treated or talked to or held or taken care of like that.

She turned around to her other side, hoping to wake James up in a very special, very personal way, to show him just how much she'd enjoyed herself last night. But the rest of the bed was empty. Her heart gave a gigantic lurch. That is, until she heard the sound of cupboards closing, pots and pans knocking against burners outside the closed bedroom door.

Jumping out of bed, she bypassed a rumpled sheet that had been tossed to the floor sometime the night before and grabbed James's black T-shirt. Grinning, she slipped it on. No bra or underwear beneath. Maybe she could get him back into bed. Back inside her.

Just the thought of him moving inside her again brought on delicious waves of heat below her navel. James Cavanaugh was seriously the best lover she'd ever had. Not that she'd had all that many. But she didn't need many for comparison purposes. You could tell the man had skills. He was like a wild, hungry creature one second, then a soft, generous lover the next.

And then there was . . . well . . . the incredible size of him.

She giggled stupidly as she opened the door and strolled out of the bedroom, her cheeks flaming with the embarrassing and inappropriate thought. But her laughter dried up quickly enough when a wave of mouthwatering scents rushed her way and enveloped her.

So, he could cook like a dream and fuck like a master.

He really was the perfect man.

"Mornin, darlin'," he said. His voice rolled over and through her.

And then she saw him, and her assessment was

confirmed. Big-time. Sigh. He was wearing only blue jeans, his chest gloriously bare. Oh, yes, she'd had all that tanned muscle wrapped around her last night.

"Sleep okay?" he asked, putting a plate of eggs and bacon on the small kitchen table.

Wait. Her eyes narrowed on the plate. As in one.

"Like a baby," she said, waiting for him to put another plate beside it. When he didn't, she re-marked, "That looks like a very lonely breakfast." She looked up and gave him an amused, curious expression. "Unless of course, we're sharing. Like me sitting on your lap, feeding you."

His eyes darkened and he groaned. "Don't tempt me. I need to meet Cole in fifteen minutes."

He was going? So, no back to bed? She tried to hide her inner pout. "You should've woken me up. We could've eaten together."

"No way." He pulled out the chair for her, then grabbed the white T-shirt that had been draped over it. "I took up enough of your sleep time last night."

"That's true, you did," she said, watching him slip the fabric over his head and cover up her idea of heaven on earth. "And I fully expect the same treatment tonight."

He grinned and came over to her. "Nice shirt, by the way," he said, reaching out and fingering the hem.

"I think I'm going to keep it."

His grin widened and he slipped his hand underneath. When he found that she wasn't wearing underwear, he groaned again. "Okay. I'm blowing off my brother."

She laughed and pulled away. "No, no, no. You can't. Go."

He growled his frustration. "Fine. But don't change until I get back."

"Sorry, cowboy," she said, finally taking her seat at the table. "I am also meeting someone today."

A shadow moved across his handsome face. "Who? Better not be that reverend. I'm hearing he gets around."

"What?" She laughed. "McCarron?"

He shrugged, grabbed his hat. "Women like men of the cloth, I guess."

"Not this woman." She bit off a piece of bacon. "This woman likes horse-whisperin' cowboys who make kickass bacon and really know how to kiss."

His eyes dropped to her mouth. "You got one of those coming over today?"

"Sadly, no. But I'm meeting up with a lovely bride-to-be that we all know and love."

"Mac's coming here?"

"We're going out. Only have four days until this thing."

"You sure you want to go out today?" he asked.

With a forkful of eggs poised near her lips, she gave him a serious look. "Everything is fine."

He nodded. "Yeah. Deac and I both checked on

things this morning. The piece of shit is locked up nice and tight."

"So, there's nothing to worry about."

Shadows crossed his eyes, but he didn't say any more about it. Just leaned in and kissed her. It was the sweetest, sexiest kiss in the world and Sheridan swooned internally.

When he pulled back he touched the brim of his Stetson. "Bye."

"Bye," she said.

She watched him go, watched the hottest jean-clad ass in the country—maybe the world—walk out the door and down the porch steps. Then she picked up another piece of bacon and slipped it into her mouth.

Eighteen

"I don't like being this far away from Sheridan," James grumbled as he pulled off the highway.

"She's fine," Cole answered, staring out the window at the prairie land, which cut off sharply as soon as they reached the bottom of the exit. "You said so yourself. Shitface is in jail and your girl's with Mac."

"Couple hours. That's all I'm giving this," James answered, not correcting Cole's "your girl" comment.

"Turn right here and head into town," Cole instructed. He glanced down at the scrap of paper in his hand. "Should be about six blocks down on the left."

"How'd you get it?" James asked.

"What? Sheriff Hunter's address?"

James shot him an irritated look.

Cole lifted the strip of paper up and waved it arrogantly. "Do you really want to know?"

"Jesus, Cole. What'd you do?"

"Nothing dangerous, harmful, or cruel," he assured him.

"That leaves a lot," James remarked. "Grace Hunter—"

"She knows nothing about it," Cole said quickly and resolutely. "When I was there last night, I just sort of took a look at a few things on her desk. You know, when she stepped out for a second."

The urge to yank his truck off the road, slam on the brakes, and throttle his little brother was strong. "Why the hell were you in her office?"

Cole didn't answer right away.

"Jesus, Cole. You didn't hit on her . . ."

"No. Shit, no." He looked annoyed at the idea, which was curious in and of itself. "I went to look at a dog for adoption."

James didn't say anything for a second. He was too busy replaying what he'd just heard. Then he started laughing.

Leaning back in his seat and kicking his boots up on the dash, Cole ground out, "What?"

"You adopting a dog. And she believed that?"

Cole looked insulted. "I could have a dog."

"When do you head back to training?"

"After the wedding."

"And how often are you at home? And get your dirty-ass boots off my dash."

"I don't have a home where I train," Cole told him, sitting up again. "I live at a hotel."

"So, you get my point, then."

For the next couple of blocks, Cole didn't say a word. It reminded James of when they were little. His younger brother had always been sensitive about what he could and couldn't do. Was always bringing home little critters he'd found around the farm. And Mama and Daddy were always telling him to take them right back outside again.

James sighed. Damn Cole. "Nice dog?" he asked.

"Yup." Cole turned to look at him. "Belle. That's her name."

"Like the princess."

Cole pointed at him. "That's exactly what I said. Vet looked at me like I was crazy." His eyes returned to the road. "Here. Turn in here."

The long-term care facility where Sheriff Hunter was living under the name Peter Green looked just like it had when James had seen it on the Internet a week ago. A very nice, two-story home on a large lot. The sign on the lawn out front read BAR-RINGTON RIDGE SENIOR CARE, and as they pulled in and searched the parking lot for a spot, James felt a giant lump form in his gut. Was this it? Were they going to get some answers here? The truth to what really happened to Cass? Did the ex-sheriff know anything, or was Grace Hunter right?

"You ready?" James asked as he slipped into an empty parking spot and cut the engine.

"I don't know." Cole glanced over at James. "Maybe we should've told Deac."

James shook his head. "He's got enough going on right now. Besides, it's too damn late to consider that." He opened his door. "Come on. Let's get this over with." *Or started*.

Sheridan ran down the list with the eraser end of her pencil. "Cake done, dress done, music done, favors done, caterer hired." She glanced up. "You're sure about the Tex Mex buffet?"

Pacing the floor of the sun porch at the very back of the Triple C's main house, Mac nodded and grinned. "Love it."

"Okay." Sheridan studied the list again. "So, I have dresses to try on."

Mac stopped and clasped her hands together. "I can't wait to see that."

"I think I can," Sheridan returned with a laugh. A bridesmaid fashion show was so not her idea of fun.

"You're going to be gorgeous," Mac insisted. "Red is your color."

Sheridan had no idea if that was true or not. She didn't own anything red. But what the hell. She would wear a potato sack if it would make Mac happy. "I'm sure it'll be lovely," she said. "But remember, it's your day. No one's going to care what I'm wearing."

A slow, secretive smile spread over Mac's face. "I know someone who will care."

Sheridan pointed at her with the pencil. "Stop that."

Mac laughed, then started pacing again.

"Now," Sheridan said returning to her list, though her mind was on James. Him seeing her in the dress. Him dancing with her in the dress. Him unzipping the dress in the backseat of his truck because he had to have her and he couldn't wait until they got home. "What do you think?" she continued, her blood heating up inside her veins. "Do you want any other bridesmaids?"

"No. Deacon will have his brothers standing up there with him, and I'll have you." She stopped pacing for a minute and stood directly in a patch of sunlight, gripping the back of one of the wicker chairs. "I want it to be simple."

"Totally get that," Sheridan said. "Simple, low stress, beautiful . . ."

"Exactly."

"Well, I think that just leaves flowers and your something borrowed and something blue."

Mac looked wistful. "I was hoping the real Blue would be here for that."

"Maybe he will be," Sheridan said, trying to be upbeat and supportive. She didn't know the entire story behind why Blue had left River Black, but she did know that he had been just recently deemed a Cavanaugh brother, which gave him a claim to the ranch. No doubt it was strange and stressful and awkward for them all.

Mac shook her head. "Do you know how many times I've called his cell phone, written him e-mails?"

"And he never answers you?"

"He has, twice. Both times just telling me he's okay. That he needs time and space to figure things out." She pushed away from the chair and started pacing again. "But I need him."

Granted, she didn't have a best friend—yet— but Sheridan could imagine it was close to having a beloved family member not show up for the most important day of your life. And that had to really suck. She wished she could do something to help her.

"I think you should e-mail him one more time," Sheridan suggested. "Tell him you understand why he's doing what he's doing, but that if he could just come for a couple of hours on Sunday, it would mean the world to you." Even as she said the words, she knew it was probably a long shot. But optimism was running around free and happy inside her blood these days. One could always hope.

"I don't think he will," Mac said, echoing Sheridan's thoughts. "I think he's just too angry and confused. He doesn't want to have to make any decisions right now."

"All you can do is try. Be vulnerable."

The word seemed to have some effect on Mac. She inhaled deeply, then nodded. "Yeah. All right. I'll give it a go." She turned back to the one remaining issue. "What to do for the something borrowed?"

"I have a few things," Sheridan suggested. "A pair of earrings, some perfume." An idea struck her suddenly, and she voiced it without thought. "Is there something of Cass's maybe?"

Mac stilled, her face going simultaneously hopeful and ashen. "Wow. I don't know."

Instant regret moved through Sheridan. Sensing she might have opened a can of worms that wasn't ready to be opened, she tried to bite back her idea. "Oh, Mac, I'm sorry. I didn't mean to bring up—"

"No, no," the woman insisted passionately. "Don't be." She was thoughtful for a second, then said, "That's actually a great idea. I can't believe I didn't think of it myself. There are several boxes in the basement. Her things. They were left to me in Everett's will. I was going to go through them with Cole when we had time. But with all the wedding stuff, and him being away training . . ."

Sheridan put her pencil down. "There's time now."

A slow, appreciative smile moved over Mac's face. "Okay. Let's do it. Basement is just off the kitchen."

Nineteen

James was starting to wonder about the life Cole had been living since leaving the Triple C. The man was incredibly gifted at getting people to agree to things they wouldn't normally agree to. Like, for instance, convincing the very protective staff at Barrington Ridge Senior Care that he and James were visiting from Dallas and in some way related to Peter "Green."

"Who are they?" The man seated at a table by the window demanded in a reed-thin voice. He looked James and Cole up and down a few times and sniffed with irritation. "I've never seem 'em before in my life."

The older female caregiver, who had taken an immediate shine to Cole when she'd discovered that he too shared a love of almonds and polka music, turned to James and said in an almost apologetic whisper, "It's the disease. He has a hard time even remembering your cousin sometimes."

"Cousin?" James said without thinking.

"Yes, our cousin, Grace," Cole added helpfully, his eyes narrowing at James with annoyance.

"Grace comes often," the woman said. "She's such a lovely girl."

Cole forced a smile. "She's something else— that's for sure."

"Why don't you two have a seat near Peter, here," the woman suggested, pointing to the vacant chairs around the small table. "I'll just tidy up things while you chat."

As she went to the bed and started fussing over the blankets and some strewn magazines, James glanced over at Cole, brow lifted, and the silent conversation began. They were damn good at it, had spent years reading each other across dinner tables, ranch fence lines, even the playground at school. This woman wasn't going anywhere, and they needed to find a way to speak to Hunter alone.

"Elisabeth," Cole said, heading her way. He'd procured the caregiver's first name about five minutes after they'd arrived, during the almond-and-polka discussion. "I was up all night last night. Couldn't sleep. Found out my girlfriend is seeing someone behind my back."

"Oh dear," Elisabeth said, taking the bait immediately. "That's terrible. The girls today can't commit to a hair color, much less a man."

Cole's grin was predictably devastating. "I'm bettin' you were never that way."

She blushed. "'Course not. Thirty years married to the same man. 'Course, there are times I want to beat him senseless, but I've never strayed."

"I've said it before and I'll say it now," Cole put in. "All the good ones are taken."

James just stood there and watched the treachery with equal parts admiration and disgust.

"Is there somewhere I can get me a cup of coffee, darlin'?" Cole asked. "I think that would pick me right up."

"Of course. I'll take you myself." She hesitated for a moment, looking at James and Sheriff Hunter.

Cole offered her his arm. "James can stay with Uncle Peter. J, why don't you tell him that story about the movie theater, from when we were kids? See if he remembers it?"

The words slammed into James's gut. Granted, he knew why they were there, but hearing Cole talk so damn casually about the theater . . . it just tore him up inside.

Cass . . .

James sat down at the table and let his gaze move about the room. From the now freshly made bed, to the lamp, water cup, and book on the side table. He wondered what the man who might hold the clue to their decades-long mystery—to their torment—was reading. Looked like a biography of some kind. He turned to the framed pictures on one wall. There were five of them, and he recognized Grace in every one. A hundred different emotions rolled through him, but he knew he didn't have time to explore any of them now.

When he looked back, Peter Hunter had turned away from the window and was staring at him. "We're not family, are we?"

Where there had been clouds only a minute ago, now a stark lucidity glistened in the man's eyes. This was Sheriff Hunter talking. Or the closest they were ever going to get. James took his chance and leaned in. "Do you remember a girl named Cass Cavanaugh?"

"No." He didn't even hesitate. Which either meant his daughter was right about his mind going, or he was lying.

"She was abducted when you were sheriff in River Black," he continued.

"Sheriff," he said blissfully, like it was the best word in the world. Then his eyes narrowed. "Cavanaugh, you say?"

Something shifted inside James and he nodded. "Cass Cavanaugh."

"She friends with my Grace?"

"No." Dammit. James inhaled sharply. "Sheriff, she was abducted, killed on your watch. You investigated her murder. But the person who committed the crime was never found."

The man's lips thinned. "That's too bad."

What was he doing here? What the hell was he

doing here? "It's more than that." James turned and glanced at the door. He knew he was losing precious seconds. "Do you have a diary or know of a diary belonging to Cass Cavanaugh?"

"Why are you telling me this?" the man asked, his expression darkening, his eyes growing cloudy again. "Are we playing a game? Detective? Are we solving a murder?"

"The diary, Sheriff," James pressed, his chest tightening. "Do you remember having it? Telling Grace you had it?"

"Grace?" His face brightened. "Is she coming tomorrow to see me? Maybe she wants to play this game of yours."

No, he didn't think she did. Sighing, James sat back in his chair. He was starting to think that Dr. Hunter was telling the truth after all. That her father's memory was long gone, and whatever he had said to her before was bogus ramblings. That is, until the man turned to look out the window and said in an irritated voice, "That boy should've never come to River Black."

Tiny pinpricks of tension erupted inside James. "What boy?"

"He ruined everything. She never would've broke if he hadn't come."

James got to his feet. "Who?" he demanded harshly. "Sheriff Hunter, who are you talking about? Who ruined everything? And who was the girl who broke? Was it Cass?"

The door opened then, cutting off all questions, leaving behind the heavy tension of the unanswered questions. Both Cole and the caregiver looked from Hunter to James, wondering what had just transpired between them, and why James's face was contorted into a mask of fury. He turned to look at Cole, who raised an eyebrow in question.

"Everything all right in here?" Elisabeth asked in a singsong voice as she walked into the room. She went directly to Sheriff Hunter and placed a hand on his shoulder. "Are you having a nice conversation with your nephew, Peter?"

"I don't have any nephews," he replied in a soft monotone.

"Oh, of course you do," she said gently. "How about a little lemonade? Hattie made it fresh this morning."

"I'm tired," he answered, still staring out the window. "I want to rest a bit before my shows come on."

"Of course." She turned to both men and said with a soft, but firm smile, "I think we'll have to cut this short. Another time?" She said the last bit to Cole, her cheeks flushing pink and her eyes sparkling.

"It's a date," Cole said, still standing beside the open door. "Thank you kindly, Elisabeth."

On their way out of the care facility, Cole was so curious and agitated he nearly jumped on James for answers the moment they hit the relative privacy of the parking lot. "So?"

James shook his head, still deep in his frustration. "He was all over the place. Didn't even recognize Cass's name."

"You two looked pretty tense when we walked in."

"He said something about wishing a boy hadn't come to River Black."

Cole stared at him hard. "What boy? That Sweet guy?"

"I don't know. I thought it was something and I pressed him." He shook his head. "But he wouldn't answer. He was barely there."

"Did you mention the abduction? The movie theater?"

"'Course I did," James said, pulling his keys out of his pocket. "I'm telling you he didn't remember a damn thing."

"Fuck," Cole ground out as they headed for the truck. "You should've gone with the nurse, and I should've stayed." His tone darkened. "I would've helped Sheriff Hunter remember."

"Don't talk like that."

"Like what?" Cole said.

James slid into the driver's seat. "Like you don't give a shit who you hurt or what you have to do to get answers."

"Well, maybe I don't," Cole shot back, getting

in and slamming the door. "Maybe knowing the truth once and for all would be worth a few months in jail."

The Triple C's basement was unfinished and full of cobwebs, but somehow Sheridan and Mac made the place feel cozy with lots of blankets and mats to sit on, some cookies, and a little wine. Mac didn't seem to want the experience to feel morbid in any way, and Sheridan was glad for that.

"Did you know there were this many boxes?" Sheridan asked, her gaze running up the tower to her right, five stacked one on top of the other.

"I thought there might be five or six," Mac answered, sounding slightly daunted. "But I hadn't been down to check." Suddenly, her face brightened. "The last time I was down here, Cass and I were hiding from Deacon. I'd taken something from his room."

"What was it?" Sheridan asked, lifting up one of the boxes and placing it on the blanket between them.

"A book on the human body." Mac laughed. "Cass and I, one flashlight, and a whole mess of giggles."

"Sounds right," Sheridan said, nodding. "Nothing can make a preteen girl laugh more than seeing pictures of male anatomy." When Mac laughed again, Sheridan dipped her hand in the box. Then paused. "Are you okay with me going through them with you? Or would you rather do it alone?"

Mac sobered a touch. "Definitely not alone. I'm so glad you're here." She grabbed a cookie and took a bite. As she chewed, she regarded Sheridan. "She would've liked you. Cass."

"Really?"

"She would've thought you were funny. And kickass. She liked kickass girls." She pulled the box she'd grabbed earlier over to her and started riffling through it. "She continually wished she was more kickass."

"I wish I could've met her," Sheridan said.

With a soft smile, Mac returned to the box. "There's so much paperwork here. All her school stuff from kindergarten onward. I bet there're some notes we passed in class, and cootie catchers. Oh my God, the cootie catchers."

"I have no idea what that is."

Mac's mouth dropped open. "Are you serious? They're the paper you fold in all these different ways and you write questions and answers on them. . . . Anyway, it was stellar girlie fun."

"You'll have to teach me to make one," Sheridan said, pulling up something from the box. "Oh, hey. I have photo albums. . . ."

"If you don't mind stacking those," Mac jumped in quickly, "I'd love to bring them upstairs, go through 'em later."

"Of course." She held up another item. "A jewelry box."

Mac gazed at it fondly. "I got her that. She hated jewelry."

Sheridan opened the top and made a little squeal of discovery. "There's something in it."

"What is it?"

Leaning over the plate of cookies, she handed Mac the small diamond ring. "It's pretty."

"It was Lea Cavanaugh's."

"Their mom?"

Mac nodded. "Everett must've put it in here after she passed." She rolled it around on her palm. "Wonder if I should let the boys know about this. See if they want it." Suddenly her face got really pinched and her nostrils flared. Almost as if she were angry. "On second thought"—she placed the ring back in the box and shut it—"let's keep looking."

Sheridan hesitated. Mac obviously knew a lot about the history of the Cavanaugh brothers, as well as the tragedy of losing Cass. But by the expression on her face and how she'd reacted to the ring, misfortune seemed to have befallen other members of the family as well.

As they continued to go through their boxes, Mac asked her, "So, how's it going at the bunkhouse?"

"Pretty good."

"Good."

Sheridan felt her skin warm instantly. Thoughts of James Cavanaugh seemed to bring out that reaction in her. "Very pleasant. James is a good host. Thoughtful."

"Puts the toilet seat down?" Mac tossed in.

"Yes, exactly." Sheridan looked up. Mac was staring at her with a growing grin. "Did I say thoughtful?"

"You did."

"And he is."

Mac stared at her for a moment. Then said, "So you've already had sex."

Sheridan gasped. "What . . . What?"

Mac just shrugged.

"How did you get that from *thoughtful*?"

"Wasn't the *thoughtful*," Mac said on a laugh. "It was the pink-cheeked formality."

Dropping her head to her chest, Sheridan groaned. "Oh, God, okay. Yes. How does that make me look?"

Mac snorted. "A: Do you really care? And B: Like a normal person who, not unlike the girl across from her, can't resist a Cavanaugh brother."

That had Sheridan looking up again. She shook her head woefully, then broke out laughing.

Mac did too.

"I'm so screwed," Sheridan said.

"Yeah, you are."

"Seriously. This is way different from you and Deacon. I'm going back to Dallas, and James is . . ."

"What?" Mac asked, pulling out a couple of folders from the box. "What is he doing? Because I don't even think he knows right now."

For the briefest of seconds, Sheridan contemplated in silence, putting her focus into the massive square box in front of her and finding something borrowed for the bride. But she couldn't stop herself.

"Did you know he was engaged?" she asked Mac. "When he was in college?"

The surprise on Mac's face was enough of an answer, but she still said, "No."

"They broke it off, and whatever happened, he ended up leaving. He won't tell me what happened. But clearly it's affected his life, his outlook, how he views relationships. I think he's terrified of really caring about someone—afraid he's going to lose them."

"That doesn't surprise me," Mac said, placing a folder back in the box and taking out a few ceramic bowls. "Listen, I'll give you a little history on the Cavanaughs because I wished I'd had more to go on when Deacon and I were first spending time together. But everything else is going to need to come from James."

Sheridan nodded. "Of course."

She fingered the painted bowl that had clearly been made by a child's hands. "When Cass was taken, Lea pretty much lost her mind. Understandably so. But she never recovered. I knew things were bad over here, but I had no idea how bad."

A thread of unease moved through Sheridan. "How bad, Mac?"

"Well, that's the part I can't speak to. I only know Deacon's history, not James's or Cole's. But if it was anything like Deac's . . ." Her eyes connected with Sheridan's and they were more grave than she'd ever seen them. "Our conversation can't leave the basement—"

"Never," Sheridan assured her. God, what had happened to James? Had his mother blamed him for Cass's disappearance?

"The Cavanaugh brothers are great men," Mac said, setting the pottery aside and continuing to dig inside the box. Sheridan followed her lead. "But sometimes, a great man needs an even greater woman to remind him of that."

Sheridan nodded. Problem was, what if the man refused to listen? Refused to share his emotional history? Granted, James had opened up to her a little last night in bed. But would he continue to do so? She didn't know. Her hand brushed over something soft, and at first she got slightly creeped out thinking it might be an animal who had crawled into the box and died. But it wasn't anything like that.

"Hey, look at this," she said in wonder.

"What is it?" Mac glanced up.

Sheridan pulled out a red Stetson. Going by the size, it was a child's.

A bright, happy smile touched both Mac's mouth and her eyes. "Cass's hat. She loved that hat."

"It's gorgeous," Sheridan said inspecting the inside, the stitching and leather. But when she turned it over again something dropped out and landed in her lap. "A piece of paper."

"What?" Mac asked.

"It was stuck in the sweatband." She picked it up. "It's a note."

An instant hum of tension filled the dank space.

"Go ahead, read it," Mac urged. "What does it say?"

Sheridan unfolded the paper, her eyes scanning its contents. "'Meet me at our spot at midnight. I can't wait to see you. Be careful. I think someone might know about us.'"

"Is it signed?" Mac asked, her voice the tightest Sheridan had ever heard it.

She shook her head. "No. Just an *S*."

"*S?*" Mac said on a gasp.

Sheridan looked up. Mac was on her knees, her eyes huge and her face pale.

"What's wrong?" she asked.

"Oh my God, that's him. Can I see it?"

She handed the note over immediately. "Who?"

"The boy she liked. The boy she'd been seeing

in secret." Mac stared at the paper, her eyes moving back and forth over the words. Then she glanced up at Sheridan looking utterly bereft. "The boy we could never find after she was killed. The boy everyone believed didn't exist."

Diary of Cassandra Cavanaugh

May 4, 2002

Dear Diary,

I have to hurry. I'm late for school. I'm late because I tried talking to James about Sweet last night.

It didn't go well.

At. All.

I was trying to see if I could find out if he knew Sweet by asking about all the boys in his class. What they looked like and who he thought was the cutest and who might look like a surfer.

He thought I was crazy, and he told me to get out of his room. He's so mean.

I'm just going to have to find out a different way.

For now, maybe I'll talk to Mac. I can't keep this in anymore. I need advice. I'm scared of sneaking out at night, cuz I know my parents

are going to catch me. Or Deac or James or Cole
will. But I want to see Sweet.
     I have to.
     I love him.

                         Crazy in love, but worried,

                                        Cass

Twenty

After the day he'd had, James couldn't think of anyone he wanted to see more than Sheridan. As he opened the door to the bunkhouse and walked inside, he hoped she was back from her afternoon with Mac. But if she wasn't, maybe he'd make her dinner. Serve it to her in bed.

Hell, he grinned, heading down the hall, feed it to her while he whispered in her ear all the things he wanted to do to her. But the moment he entered his bedroom, all thoughts of cooking disintegrated.

"Wow," was all he could manage as he took in the woman before him.

He'd seen Sheridan O'Neil in jeans and tanks, shirts and skirts—and she was as hot as blue fire in every last one of them. But this . . . What was turning in a slow circle in front of the free-standing mirror his great-grandmother had brought over from Ireland moons ago was out-of-control forest-fire territory.

She turned to face him. "Like *wow*, pretty? *Wow*, hideous? *Wow*, sexy?"

"Hideous?" he fairly growled, his gaze running the length of her. From bare feet to long, lean legs, to a cherry-red dress that fell just above her knees and curved upward, adhering to the shape of her spectacular body. It was sexy, but elegant. Strapless, and, Good God Almighty, the way it made her top half look. His fingers twitched and his mouth watered, and when he spoke, it sounded like something was caught in his throat.

"Honey, you look gorgeous," he stated firmly. Hell, was he panting?

She beamed. "Thank you."

"That said, you could wear a flour sack and be the hottest goddamn woman in the room."

"Oh, go on." She made the accompanying gesture with her hand, then turned back to face the mirror. "I'm trying on bridesmaid's dresses."

"I think you found the one." He came up behind her, brushed her hair off her right shoulder and kissed her warm, soft skin. "Problem is, beautiful girl, you're going to upstage the bride in this."

She looked at his reflection in the mirror. "You're sweet-talking me, right? That's what that is?"

He wrapped his arms around her waist and grinned. "Maybe."

"But for what purpose, Mr. Cavanaugh? Getting me naked?"

He shook his head slowly, his eyes pinned to hers. "Don't you dare take that off."

"Well, I'm insulted," she said, turning in his embrace and looking up at him with defiant eyes. "One night together and you no longer want to see me naked."

His lips twitched. "That's probably the most insane thing I've heard all day." And he'd heard some pretty insane things today. "No, darlin'. I'm taking you out. For dinner."

Her ruby-red lips curved up into a smile.

He leaned in and whispered into the curve of her ear, "But just so we're clear, I'll always want to see you naked. And when we get back here, I'll prove it." His eyes flickered in the direction of the mirror. Or more specifically to the red heels on the floor beside it. "However, if you end up wearing those shoes, we may not make it home before I do."

She backed away from him, her eyes flashing with flirtatious heat. Then with a quick grin, she walked right up to the very shoes to which he was referring and slipped her pretty feet inside.

In Dallas, wearing a fancy red dress with matching heels to dinner was nothing to gape at. But in River Black, it might just make the front page of the morning newspaper.

Seated in Marabelle's best booth—the one without the patched seat—Sheridan glanced up and gave her date a very seductive smile. "Anything I want?"

James's aqua eyes flashed with amusement. "Anything." He'd changed too. Not into a suit. Though Sheridan couldn't help but wonder if he had one. But into a nice long-sleeved white shirt, black jeans, and black boots. He looked ridiculously sexy, and eating dinner across from him had been torture. More than a few times she'd had to stop herself from slipping off her shoe and tucking her toes into certain unmentionable areas.

"Well," she said, licking her lips. "What if I want two things?"

"Hell, baby," he exclaimed. "Have three."

She grinned at him, then looked up at the waitress who had been standing there for close to a minute. "I'll just have the chocolate cake, please, Stevie."

The woman slipped her pencil into her bun. "I knew you two would end up back here."

"Can't stay away," James said, but his eyes were on Sheridan. "When something's that good, you keep coming back."

"Good Lord," the woman said with an exaggerated eye roll. And as she walked off, Sheridan distinctly heard her add, "Get a room already."

"Did you hear her?" Sheridan asked him, laughing.

He nodded. "Yes, I did, and she has a point."

Sheridan laughed. "Chocolate cake to go?"

"No way." His eyes dropped to her mouth. "I want to watch you eat it."

Heat swirled in Sheridan's belly and she slipped off her shoe. "So, you didn't mention anything about today. How was your time with Cole?"

It was as if a bucket of ice water had been tossed on the table, the majority of it hitting James Cavanaugh in the face. Every shred of relaxed, flirtatious, sexual man fell away, to be replaced with the calm, cool, and very controlled rider who'd found her near her broken-down car weeks ago. She didn't understand it, but damn, it hurt her heart to see.

"Pretty boring, actually," he said, his gaze flickering past her.

She studied him. "That's a bummer. What did you do?"

"Went for a drive." His eyes were now on her water glass.

"How romantic."

He looked up and sighed. "Sheridan—"

The door to the restaurant burst open, cutting off their conversation, and Deacon stormed in. He looked pissed and formidable in black jeans, a gray shirt, and a black leather jacket. He spotted them quickly and had barely reached their table when he started barking at James.

"What the hell did you do?" he demanded.

James didn't even flinch. He was still wearing that suit of emotional armor. "Cole talk to you?"

"No. Grace Hunter."

"Shit."

"Yeah. Seems her daddy was paid a visit today by a couple of nephews he doesn't have." His eyebrow lifted. "Care to shed some light on that?"

James's gaze flickered in Sheridan's direction.

Deacon's did too, then widened as if he'd just realized his brother had company. He grimaced. "Sorry about this, Sheridan."

"It's okay." But that was the last thing she felt. Was what going on? What had happened today?

"You look real nice, by the way."

"Thanks." She gave him a tight-lipped smile.

James drew his attention back. "I'll meet you at the Bull's Eye in thirty minutes."

This didn't look like it set well with Deacon. Knowing him as she did, Sheridan was pretty sure he wanted James to stand up and follow him out the door. But he didn't make a fuss. After a quick nod to the both of them, he turned and walked out.

When James found her gaze again, she saw the weariness in his eyes. "I'm sorry to cut this short."

"Everything okay?" she asked. *Please talk to me.*

"It's complicated."

"Your romantic drive with Cole was complicated?"

He sniffed with dark humor. "There was nothing romantic about it, Sheridan, I assure you."

She nodded, growing weary herself. "Okay." She shrugged. "Maybe at some point, you'll feel like you can talk to me. Share what's going on in your life. The hard stuff that's so obviously weighing on you. Because it breaks my heart that you don't feel like you can."

Stevie took that exact moment to place her dessert in front of her. "Here you go, hon."

Her appetite gone, Sheridan barely glanced at the chocolate cake. Until she realized it wasn't chocolate cake at all.

"It's Reese's Peanut Butter Cup cake," Stevie announced with a bit of a squeal. "Your boyfriend here ordered it special from Dallas. Trying to impress you or something. Frankly, Natalie's apple pie from Hot Buns is way more impressive—"

"Thanks, Stevie," James interrupted her.

She pursed her lips at the shutdown. "Fine. Enjoy."

As the seconds ticked by and Sheridan didn't even make a move to pick up her fork, James asked, "Aren't you going to try it?"

The confusion that battled within her was shockingly heavy. Clearly James Cavanaugh wanted her, was attracted to her, had cake brought in from Dallas for her. He was letting her stay at his bunkhouse, but not before redecorating it to make her feel at home. He even told her how he felt about her, how she made him feel. And yet, he couldn't tell her the truth about his life, his past. All the things that made up who he was.

She was no expert on relationships, but she didn't see how something could grow with sunshine, but no rain.

"I think I'm going to take it to go," she said finally.

"You sure?"

She nodded. "I'm still pretty full from dinner, and you need to meet Deacon."

"This was not how I wanted our night to go," he said, turning to flag down Stevie for the check.

" 'Can one desire too much of a good thing?' "

As she expected, quoting Shakespeare brought his head around, and his eyes locked with hers.

"Oh, Sheridan," he said, his tone pained as Stevie placed the check in front of him. " 'Tempt not a desperate man.' "

Twenty-one

"Bull's-eye!" Cole exclaimed as the dart he'd just sent toward the board hit dead center. He turned and headed back to their table. "I need to get me one of those for the road."

Deacon ignored the comment. He was far too pissed off. "I can't believe you two jackasses did that without me. We're supposed to be in this together."

"Are we?" Cole said, pulling out a chair.

"Fuck you," Deacon returned flatly.

"I'm serious." He dropped down and grabbed his half-full beer. "It's been a long time since we were in anything together."

"Maybe so," Deacon acknowledged. "But that has nothing to do with the here and now. With Cass. With finding out the truth."

Up until that moment, James had just been watching the two fire blanks at each other. Yes, he wanted the truth about what had happened to Cass. But listening to Deacon bitch over dollar beers wasn't going to get them there. Frankly, he just wanted to get back to the bunkhouse, back to Sheridan. He knew she was upset, knew all she wanted from him was the truth. About his past and what had fed these demons inside him. But every time he meant to lay it all out on the table for her, his gut yanked him back.

"James, you got something to say about this?" Deacon asked, breaking into his thoughts.

"Look, we weren't trying to piss you off," he said with a slight edge to his voice. He was still angry at his brother for interrupting his dinner with Sheridan. "We were trying to do you a favor. With the wedding a few days away, we thought it was better not to involve you in case shit went south."

Over the neck of his beer, Deacon asked, "Did shit go south?"

"Depends what you mean by that," James said, then brought his own bottle to his lips and took a drink. "Cole hitting on the ancient nurse was pretty far south if you ask me."

Deacon looked from one man to the other. "What?"

"I did not hit on her, asshole," Cole jumped in caustically. "I was trying to keep her out of your hair so you could question Hunter." He sniffed. "For all the good it did."

"You questioned Hunter?" Deacon asked him, his eyes flashing with heat. "What did you find out?"

"Nothing," Cole said, giving James a pointed glare.

James flipped him off, then turned to Deacon. "Not exactly nothing."

Pushing back his chair, but still remaining in it, Cole cursed. "What the hell, J? You said the sheriff was just talking nonsense."

Finishing off his beer, James placed it on the table. "It very well could be just nonsense. Thing is, my gut tells me different."

"What did he say?" Deacon asked, his own beer completely forgotten.

"Shit like 'That boy should've never come to River Black' and 'He ruined everything. She never would've broke if he hadn't come.'"

The two men were staring hard at him; then Deac piped in, "You think he was talking about Sweet and Cass?"

James nodded. "I do."

Cole had stopped listening when James revealed what the sheriff had said. "I say we go to the vet right now and tell her what he said. Find out if she knows what it could mean."

"Can't," Deacon said, his jaw set. "Because of how you two handled this, she's getting a court order. Keeping all of us away."

James cursed.

"She was that pissed?" Cole asked, mystified.

"You mean for going into her office under the pretense of wanting to adopt a dog and looking up her father's address?" Deacon said.

The fighter shrugged casually. "I liked the dog."

Deacon shook his head. "You're still an infant, you know that?"

"I get things done," Cole fired back.

"I'd watch your back, Cole," James said. "And maybe your front too. She does know how to neuter shit."

"So what now?" Cole asked them. "We just give up?"

"Hell no," Deacon said. "We're going to find that boy."

"That's right," James agreed. "I got all the newspaper articles from that time already loaded on my laptop. We'll see who had talked. We'll see how Sheriff Hunter handled things. We'll question everyone again. But first . . ." James stood up. "We take a breath. We clean up, make ourselves pretty—Cole, in your case that's gonna take both days—and give our brother away to a great girl on Sunday."

Cole was quiet for a moment. Then he reached over and gave Deacon a hard rap on the back. "Can't wait to get rid of you, buddy." Then he eyed James. "And two days to look pretty? Please. That's only a worry if I get into a fight." He hesitated for a moment. "You think Grace Hunter knows how to throw a punch?"

"Definitely," James and Deacon answered together.

Beneath the covers in the guest room, Sheridan heard James walk through the bunkhouse door. She glanced at the clock. It was just before eleven. Her entire body relaxed. She hated it, but she hadn't been able to fall asleep without knowing he was there. She was really going to need to work on that. Or go back to Dallas.

She heard him walk past her room and go into his own. She wondered what he thought when he saw the bed empty. It wasn't as though she hadn't wanted to slip under his cool sheets again. But she'd felt odd about it. They weren't at that stage where it was definitively her bed too. And after the way dinner had ended, she was feeling unsure about a lot of things.

Just when her body started to relax and she was thinking he'd bunked down for the night, her door opened. Instantly, her heart leapt into her throat. But she didn't move, didn't say anything. But then again, neither did he. With gentle hands, he eased back her covers, then slipped his hands beneath her back and knees.

"James?" she whispered.

But still he didn't say anything. Just lifted her

into his arms and carried her out of her room. When they entered his, he oh-so-gently placed her on the bed, on top of the cool sheets. Then he left the room.

Sheridan stared around the moonlit room, listened, trying to gauge what was happening. She heard him in the bathroom. The water running in the sink. What was she supposed to make of this? Was this him being upset or sad? Or just wanting to be close to her? And why wasn't he talking?

When he came back in, she watched him take off his shirt and boots, but leave his jeans on. He looked amazing like that, chiseled and lean in the moonlight, and she ached for him. Not just for the comfort of his presence, but to connect with him. His eyes met hers then and locked. Behind those incredible blue-green orbs she saw a question—or was it many questions? God, why couldn't he talk to her? Just let her in a little bit.

The mattress dipped with his weight, and his gaze left hers as his hands wrapped lightly around her ankles, then started raking upward. Over her calves, knees, thighs. Sheridan released the breath she'd been holding. Then drew another in sharp and quick as he moved up her hips and eased down her underwear.

Oh, God, she inwardly groaned as he slipped her panties off and tossed them to the ground. Her skin tingled and her breathing grew erratic. All she was wearing now was her pale blue tank top, and she wanted that off too.

She stared down her body at him, her heart slamming against her ribs, waiting for him to say something. Anything. But he didn't. His gaze was locked on her sex, which was glistening with arousal, and when he placed his hands on her knees and spread her thighs apart, thinking became virtually impossible.

She just wanted to feel.

James's hands were moving up her inner thighs, slowly, slowly . . . so incredibly slowly. Sheridan tensed, waiting, wanting him to knead her flesh, then slip his fingers inside of her again. She loved him inside her—any way she could have him. But instead of touching her, he slid his hands under her buttocks.

Heat slammed into Sheridan as she realized what he was going to do to her. And as his head dropped and his face disappeared between her splayed thighs, as his mouth closed over her pussy and his tongue flickered over her tight clit, she knew the sweetest, most amazing sensation in the world. She never wanted it to end. Ever. She just wanted to live her life in James's bed, writhing beneath him, coming with him.

As his fingers pressed into the flesh of her ass, he licked her. Soft swipes of his tongue one moment, then suckling her clit deep into his mouth the next. Sheridan bit her lip, her hands fisting in the sheets at her sides. She didn't want to come. Not yet. But James was unrelenting in his pursuit of her climax. She could feel it in him. Hungry, needing, consuming, primal. He wanted every drop of her juices, commanded every cant of her hips, drew on every pulse of her clit.

And then he lifted her ass up another inch and pushed his tongue inside her.

Sheridan cried out at the sweet invasion, her hands leaving the sheets and plunging into James's thick hair. Her fingers burrowed, gripping his skull, and like the madwoman she had now become, she held him tightly against her and started pumping his tongue in and out of her pussy.

She was hot, shaking. She wasn't going to last long but she didn't care anymore. Lost to the incredible feeling, she opened her legs even wider for him.

A groan escaped James's throat, and he drew out of her and took her aching clit into his mouth. Sheridan cursed and writhed, and hardly noticed that James had released one of her ass cheeks until his fingers were up inside her, teasing her G-spot. She bucked against his mouth, rolled her hips. Anything and everything to keep the feeling—follow the feeling.

Sensing her impending climax, James pressed his tongue flat over her clit, and as he pumped inside of her, he circled her pussy. It was the perfect pressure, and the perfect pleasure, inside and out. Sheridan was lost, gone. Try as she might, she couldn't hold on. A volcano erupted within her and she screamed his name, her hips bucking wildly, her mind splintering. It was perfect. So perfect she wanted to weep.

And maybe she did. Just a little. All while he licked her softly and gently. Brought her back down to earth.

When she sagged against the mattress, spent, sweaty, and exhausted, James crawled in after her and pulled her into his arms. She fell asleep that way, half of her body draped over him, her heart calling out to his, and her mind forgetting that he had yet to say a word.

Twenty-two

"You need to understand," James said, his tone calm as he stood in the center of the Triple C's riding ring. "In his mind he's still wild. And that needs to be respected."

"He won't even let me get near him," Kerry Murphy said, standing just outside the arena.

"So don't get near him."

She looked confused and worried. "Then how—"

"Not at first. It's our body language they respond to. You keep going in and he keeps backing away." Though he spoke to Kerry, he kept his eyes on her horse, Derby. "Just stand still for a moment."

Hands to his sides, no rope, no nothing, James did just that in the middle of the arena. The flea-bitten gray stallion had run around him hard and fierce for a good ten minutes after being led out of the trailer. And James had let him. He wasn't looking to break him. Not yet. He just wanted to forge some trust.

"Look at him," he said to the woman who'd called him early this morning and begged him to meet her—meet her horse, who would do just about anything to get away from her when she approached, including jumping fences. Wood or wire, it didn't make a difference. He'd been injured four times in the past month, and she was at her wit's end.

The woman who had pulled him from his bed and the half-naked woman in his arms—the woman he could still taste on his tongue, still scent in his nostrils. For most of the night, he'd lain there with the hard-on of a lifetime, watching her, refusing to wake her up so he could touch her again. Because she'd needed her rest. And maybe because he was punishing himself for what an ass he'd been to her. For what he couldn't seem to give her no matter how much he wanted to.

In his mind, he could see her face as she woke up. Looking around for him, her eyes hitting on the note he'd written her.

Seeing about a horse.
Be back around nine.

Nothing about the night before. How he'd loved being close to her, making her cry out. How he wanted to do it again. Especially after he'd seen her in the gray light of dawn, naked from the waist down. A hint of arousal still glistening on her shaved pussy. His eyes closed for a moment. He'd wanted to. He'd sat there with the pen in his hand. . . .

"He's watching you so closely," Kerry observed, pulling him back to the moment.

"He's thinking," James said. "He's wondering why he should stop running. Because, truly, runnin's all he knows. It's what's kept him safe."

"Former owner got him when he wasn't even a year," she explained in a bitter tone. "The bastard left him in a field by himself. He barely saw humans." She exhaled heavily. "I was hoping I could help him."

"And you will." James started to walk. He took the half circle on the other side of the area. Kept his body calm, his voice calm. "It's just that he feels your frustration, Kerry. Your impatience with him. He knows you want him to put aside how he was livin' and survivin', and just be your boy. But they're like us. Fear and loneliness and distrust can run thick. It takes time to break that down."

"Okay," she said. "I'll do whatever it takes."

James continued to walk his half of the arena, real slowly, stopping every so often to let Derby get a look at him. After about half a dozen times, with the sun overhead turning dawn to morning,

Derby walked in his direction. Not all the way, but close enough that James could see into his eyes.

I hear you, friend. I'm trying to let go of my past too.

Slowly, James turned around and started walking. He didn't know right away if Derby was following him. But when he caught sight of Kerry's face, he smiled.

For the next hour, he just walked and let the stallion follow him. "Start like this," he told Kerry. "Only this for a week maybe. Don't talk to him. And don't even think of trying to get him under saddle."

"No," she said as James started walking over to her. "Of course not."

"And you need to learn to control your emotions. You think you can do that?"

She nodded just as his phone vibrated against his hip.

"I'm going to take this." *Could be Sheridan*, he thought with a kick to the heart. He slipped through the fence and called back to Kerry, "You might as well start now. Get in there and give it a try."

Nerves glittered in the girl's expression, but she did as he instructed. It would take some time—a damn good amount of it—but the horse would heal its insides and fall in love with her.

James pulled out his phone as he walked a ways off so the stallion wouldn't be spooked. He grinned. Maybe Sheridan had tried to cook breakfast.

But it wasn't Sheridan. Wasn't even close.

"Finally," the woman said. "You are very diffi-cult to get ahold of."

California accent, pushy, Hollywood all the way. He knew exactly who was calling. "You're very stubborn, Miss Dupree."

"I just go after what I want," she replied evenly. Then amended, "No, what the people want."

"Frankly, I don't care about the people."

"That's fine."

"And I'm not interested in money."

That gave her pause. Maybe she'd never met anyone who'd said that to her before. "What *are* you interested in?"

"Finding a ranch for my mustangs," he said dryly. "Can you do that, Miss Dupree?" He chuck-led. Of course he hadn't meant to say something so ridiculous to her. He should just be saying no, thanks and hanging up.

But she wasn't finished yet.

"Yes, Mr. Cavanaugh. I can find a ranch for your mustangs."

"I don't think you understand. I'm not talking about fancy cars here."

"Oh, I know that. You have several hundred wild mustangs on your late father's ranch prop-erty," she said matter-of-factly. "And you want to move them."

What the hell? "How could you possibly know that?"

"It's my job," she answered simply.

This was nuts. He couldn't even believe he'd been on the phone with her this long. He didn't want to be on television. Hell, he didn't know what he wanted at the moment. "Listen, I got work to do."

"And I wouldn't dream of keeping you from it," she said quickly as though she was used to dealing with people who tried to evade her. "But just think about it. No reality show. No Hollywood. It would be ten to twelve episodes taking on difficult cases. You'd be helping horses and people who would never normally be able to afford your services. We can film it in Texas if you'd like. Frankly, that would even be better. We'll purchase the ranch property of your choice. The mustangs can live there forever. You could even bring on more if you'd like."

James stood there blankly. No reality show. No crazy bullshit. Just what he already did. And the mustangs get off Triple C land. His eyes narrowed. "Why?"

He could practically hear her smile. "It's good television, Mr. Cavanaugh. Plain and simple. Think about it. I know you have your brother's wedding tomorrow. I'll get in touch in a few days."

Wedding! How did she know— "How the hell—"

"Again," she cut in. "It's my job. Good-bye."

She disconnected quickly, and James was left staring into space. Ever since he'd come back to this godforsaken ranch, his life was just up and down and sideways. Maybe he needed to get away from it for a while so he could think clearly.

He was stuffing the phone back into his pocket, when he heard someone coming up behind him. He turned to see Sheridan walking his way.

"Morning," she called out.

Lord in heaven, he thought, drinking in the sight of her. Was there ever a moment when this woman didn't look stunning? She was wearing faded jeans, what he believed to be an old pair of Mac's boots, and a gray tank top. Her face was rosy and makeup free, and her hair was pulled back in a ponytail. She made his goddamn heart race.

"You're up early," he said, wanting to remedy that by taking her right back to bed.

She came to stand beside him at the fence. "Got your note."

"Found it on my pillow, did ya?" he asked, trying to sound light and teasing.

The stallion in the ring twenty feet away nickered.

Sheridan didn't even glance his way. Her eyes were fixed on James. And they were serious. Too serious. "So the waking up alone in your bed thing is starting to freak me out. No, wait," she corrected. "Not freak me out. Insult me."

"Oh, honey," he began apologetically. "That's the last thing I want you to feel. I got a call from Kerry here. Her horse needed some help."

"I understand. I just would've loved to watch you help him."

He was such an idiot. The woman was trying here. Trying to be a part of his goddamned life. "I'm sorry, Sheridan. Christ, I would've liked that too."

"I'm not looking to be the overbearing chick here. It's just confusing. One moment we're together—like really together—and the next you treat me like a stranger. Like someone you don't think you can trust." Her gray eyes searched his face. "Can we talk about last night?"

Thunder and heat rumbled through him. "Last night was amazing. You were amazing. I love making you feel like that."

Her cheeks turned pink, but she shook her head at him. "I don't mean that. I'm talking about what happened at dinner. After dinner."

It was like a window closing in front of him. And he was the one shutting it in her face. He couldn't stop himself. "I had to talk with my brothers about the ranch, about—"

"Cass's death?" she said.

A breeze blew across the land and James felt himself grow cold. "Yeah. Maybe some of that too."

Her eyes implored him. "You could tell me about it."

"I don't want to," he returned quickly. "I don't like talking about it."

"With me?"

"With anyone."

"But maybe you need to."

He narrowed his eyes. "What are you doing, Sheridan?"

"Trying to get you to open up to me," she said passionately. "This is what it looks like, James. A relationship. I'm not all that experienced or anything, but I'm pretty sure the people in them share scary, hard shit with each other. Are you going to let me in?"

"I have let you in. We're living together, sleeping together—"

"No," she said fiercely. "Into here." She put her hand on his chest. "I need to know if this is it. If this is as deep as we go."

James felt the heat of her palm through his T-shirt.

"I need to know," she said as her breath caught, "because I think I'm falling in love with you."

James felt the blood drain from his face. *Love.* Holy fuck. Love was how things went from wonderful to destroyed.

She backed up an inch or two. "Look. I'm not trolling for an *I think I might love you too.* I'm just trying to be honest. If you aren't capable of something real, please tell me. I want us to be able to stay friends." She gave him a sad smile. "I just don't want to get hurt. And I know you don't want to hurt me."

"Of course I don't." The word *friends* gnawed the shit out of his gut, piranha-style. The word *love* was battering his blood.

"Well, pretending this is something more than a fling will do that." She glanced at her watch. "I got to get going. I'm working on flowers with Mac, then checking on a few things for tonight's dinner."

Shit, tonight's dinner. He'd forgotten. "I can meet you later," he suggested. "Help."

She shook her head. "I'll handle it. Can you just hang here and make sure the caterer, the rentals, and the band all have what they need?"

"Of course."

"Great." She started to walk away, then stopped and glanced over her shoulder. "Hey. I didn't thank you for the Reese's cake. That was really sweet." She gave him a quick smile before heading on her way.

James turned to face the arena and the miles and miles of Triple C land beyond, wishing he'd been born somewhere else, and into another family, another life. Then he might be the kind of man who deserved Sheridan. The kind of man who grabbed and kissed a woman when she told him she might be in love with him.

But the Triple C had broken his heart.

And God only knew if he'd ever be able to heal.

"Ouch," Sheridan said with a hiss.

Mac glanced up from the pile of flowers in the center of the table they'd taken over at Marabelle's. "What?"

"Thorn," she said, sucking the tiny drop of blood off the pad of her pointer finger.

Mac sat back in her chair. "I appreciate you risking your life for me and my wedding."

Laughing, Sheridan placed the three boutonnieres into the box. "I can't believe we made these happen. The Internet is an amazing thing. Hey, Stevie," she called out. "Could you put this into the fridge?"

The waitress appeared from the back of the diner. "Sure thing, hon." She scooped up the box but not before taking a look. "Very nice."

Sheridan beamed proudly. "Thank you." When she turned back to face Mac, the woman was staring at her with a silly look on her face.

"What?" she asked.

Gesturing at her with a red rose, Mac said, "Look at you."

Instantly, Sheridan glanced down and did a quick personal inventory. No obvious stains. Did she have food on her face? In her teeth? Wait, they hadn't eaten yet.

"All comfortable around River Black," Mac continued. "Knowing everybody's name." Her brows drifted up. "You'd better be careful or you're never going to want to leave."

That took the wind right out of her sails. "Right," Sheridan said, gathering up some flowers to start the small table vases.

"Which would be great for me, is what I mean," Mac continued. "Okay, what did I say?"

"It's fine," Sheridan insisted. "Just interesting timing is all."

"Why?"

"Well, I've been thinking about going back to Dallas. I have work and my apartment. And frankly, my life there."

"Ah, crap," Mac said on a groan. "What happened?"

"I don't know what you mean," Sheridan said, though her heart was squeezing with just the idea of walking away from him.

"Don't make me stab you with this thorn, O'Neil."

Sheridan looked up and laughed, but not with any true humor. "I told James I think I'm falling in love with him."

"Wow."

"Well, you wanted to know," she said dryly.

"No, I mean you're amazing. Damn, woman,"

she exclaimed, waving her long-stemmed rose around. "What did he say?"

"Not much. But there was definitely a look of panic in his eyes."

"Well, sure."

"But the thing is I didn't say it to get him to say it back. I said it because I needed him to know where I stand. Where my head's at." Sheridan picked up the scissors and clipped off a few inches of stem. "That I can't get any more serious with a man who refuses to open up to me." If she was truly going to leave her past fears behind, she couldn't get involved with someone who refused to allow her into his life. She didn't mind the risk of her heart as long as they were both going to put themselves out there.

Mac's eyes were sympathetic. "You need to give him time."

"I have," she assured her. "And it's about to run out. I'm going to get a serious broken heart if I continue this."

The bell over the door jangled.

"I understand," Mac said. She made a face. "Is it selfish of me to want you to stay here forever?"

She smiled at her friend. The woman who would continue to be her friend no matter what. "I work for Deacon, remember? You're going to see me."

Mac's attention wavered as she caught sight of someone behind Sheridan. "Hi, there. Grace, isn't it?"

Sheridan turned around to see Dr. Grace Hunter nearing their table. She looked tired and a little pale, but she forced a pretty decent smile.

"Hi, Mackenzie," she said.

"I'm Sheridan," Sheridan said with a little wave of hello.

"Join us," Mac said.

"Oh, no. I'm just going to grab some coffee."

"Have it with us," Mac insisted.

"No Cavanaugh brothers allowed," Sheridan tossed in for good measure, knowing that was why the woman was acting standoffish and weird.

"Deacon and James are really fine actually. It's Cole," Grace said, taking the chair next to Mac. "He has serious problems. Not to mention boundary issues."

"He can act without thinking," Mac agreed.

Grace stared at her. "He went through my desk at my office and found out where my dad is living so he could go and question him."

Sheridan's mouth dropped open. "No, he didn't."

"Oh, yes, he did."

"You should have him arrested," Sheridan said.

"No, no, no," Mac said quickly, holding up a small, but incredibly beautiful bouquet. "He's in my wedding tomorrow. I need him there." She shrugged at Grace. "The day after he's all yours."

"Okay, I think we need something," Sheridan announced. "Something to toast the bride-to-be. Stevie?" she called.

The waitress came over. "What'll it be, ladies?"

"Three coffees?" Sheridan said and asked at the same time. When both Mac and Grace nodded, she added, "And something sweet. What do you have?"

The woman put a hand on her hip. "More of that cake James had sent in from Dallas for you."

Heat rushed into her cheeks. Oh this was going to be fun. "We'll take it," Sheridan said. "Three pieces please." When she turned to face the ladies again, Grace's brows were a half inch higher and Mac was staring at her like she'd just announced she'd had nude photos taken of herself.

"I'm sorry, what?" Mac said, hand to her ear. "Cake sent in from Dallas?"

"I love Reese's Peanut Butter Cups and James knew that, and he also knew that River Black didn't have any desserts that used—" She stopped and groaned. "Okay, it was incredibly sweet and thoughtful, and it made me want to jump him and kiss him. But then he became Mr. No Share again, and there we are."

"I feel as though I've missed something important," Grace said with a smile as Stevie placed three coffees on the table.

"Me too," Sheridan said, smiling at her. "Okay." She held up her coffee cup. "A toast. To my new bestie—"

"Awww," Mac said with a couple of sniffs. "Love it."

"May your marriage be long lasting. May you love each other always. May he open up and tell you things that are hard to say, but are important in a relationship . . ."

The bell over the door jangled again, interrupting her. Good thing too.

"All right," Mac said. "I think you might be going off track."

"I think so too," Sheridan said with a giggle.

Once again, Mac looked past her to the door. But this time, instead of smiling, she turned white as the baby's breath they'd refused to use in the bouquets, but stuck in their ponytails.

"What's wrong?" Sheridan asked.

"I did what you told me to do," Mac said, still staring. "The e-mail."

Sheridan turned around just in time to see a shockingly good-looking man coming their way. He was tall, lean, and had the most piercing dark blue eyes, which were accentuated by his shock of black hair.

"Hey, Mac."

Tears sprang to Mac's eyes. "Sheridan, Grace, this is my beloved long-lost friend. Who I want to punch in the face, but after I hug him senseless. Blue, this is Sheridan and Grace."

Blue turned those eyes on her and Grace, granting them the whitest smile since a toothpaste commercial.

"Can I join you, ladies?" he asked. "I can help with whatever you're doing here, but mostly I want to celebrate my girl here." He gave Mac a wink. "Before she does too much damage to my face."

Twenty-three

He had to give her credit. The two long, sanded-wood tables draped with flowers and food, candles, and wine and beer out in the pasture looked beautiful. Especially with the light from the heaters and the moon overhead. What had once been just trampled land with a few wildflowers dotted here and there had been transformed into a rustic, magical, and highly romantic scene. And everyone seemed to be having a great time.

Everyone except James.

Sheridan had gone ahead and sat them at two different tables. Sure, she'd been nice to him. Real cordial. But it was all formality and it sucked. James was starting to wonder if she was even planning to come home with him afterward or stay with Mac at the main house. The two of them were real buddy buddy now.

About ten feet away, the band was warming up.

The sound filled the air around them, comingling with the bustle of servers clearing away plates and silverware. The speeches were coming up. James hadn't prepared anything, really. Was just going to go off the cuff. He glanced over at Sheridan. She was looking his way, too, no doubt thinking the same thing.

She looked like an angel. She was wearing a pale gray dress that clung to every inch of her spectacular body. Her hair was piled on top of her head, and tiny threads had escaped and were blowing about her face. That beautiful face. She nodded at him, and James tore his gaze away and grabbed his spoon. It took only five clinks against his water glass before everyone quieted down.

Grabbing his beer, James stood up and faced Deac and Mac, who were seated at the head of the table on a bench for two. It was strange. Something jerked through him at that moment, as he looked at his brother, and he tried to push it away.

"Deacon, Mac," he began. "I'm honored to be the best man. Especially over Cole here." Everyone laughed. Even Cole. "I'm honored to watch the two of you finally get your happy ending. You deserve it." He felt something hard in his throat and pushed it away. "This love business isn't easy. You've got to work and trust and forgive. But it's also the greatest gift there is. I'm so happy for you both."

Even as he sat down to the hoots and hollers and applause, the lump in his throat hadn't gone away. Then Sheridan stood up, and he relaxed, every muscle in his body going warm and tight.

"Mac, Deacon," she said, her eyes pinned to the couple. "I never thought I'd be standing here toasting you, wishing you the very best in your life together. But I'm so happy and honored that I am. Deacon, don't worry. The moment I get back to the office next week I will return to calling you Mr. Cavanaugh."

A few people laughed, and Deacon called out, "Not necessary, Sheridan."

"Mac," Sheridan started. She touched her heart. "Thank you for asking me to stand up with you. And for being my friend. I've had the best time with you, getting to know you. I wish you every happiness in the world, tomorrow and all the days to come." She raised her glass. "See you both at the altar."

After another round of applause, everyone raised their glasses and drank deep. The music began and the party got under way, with lots of merry conversation and dancing. But James only had eyes for Sheridan. She was over by Deac and Mac, giving them both a hug. Then she turned and looked around, spotted him, then pointed at the dance floor.

James met her in the very center of the floor, not saying anything as he eased her into his arms and started swaying to the music. Fuck, he hated how good she felt against him. How right.

"I think we did a fantastic job, don't you?" she said.

"Looks like."

She pulled back a touch so she could see his face. "Are you angry about something?"

Hell, yes, he was. Angry at himself. Angry that he couldn't have her. "Why'd you put us at two separate tables, Sheridan?"

Her eyes shuttered. "We're both hosts. We shouldn't be at the same table."

"That's bullshit and you know it," he returned hotly. "You're trying to avoid me. No. You're trying to push me away."

Her expression went utterly blank for a moment. Kind of like she was in shock. But after a moment, she broke into a peal of laughter. Not the kind that comes from happiness, mind you. More along the lines of bitter-ass scorn.

"Me pushing you away," she repeated after she'd sobered. "You've got to be kidding."

His jaw clenched. "I heard what you said in your speech. About going back to work."

"It has to happen sometime."

"Why now?"

She glanced around and lowered her voice. "You know why now."

James took her hand and led her off the dance floor and over near the fence. "Listen to me, Sheridan. I can't just change myself like that. It doesn't happen in an instant."

"You're right," she agreed so calmly and coolly it scared him. "It doesn't happen in an instant. It happens when you want it to."

"So, what? You leave and go back to Dallas and we never see each other again?"

"I'm sure we'll see each other," she said.

"This is bullshit," he ground out. His head was spinning, his gut aching. He was losing this woman, and it was all his own fault.

"These people," she continued. "Your people, are my friends now. I want that for us too, James. I want to be your friend."

"I don't want you as my fucking friend, Sheridan!" he shouted.

The air crackled between them. Sheridan looked as if she was struggling with what to say, what to do. Then she released a heavy breath.

"I'm going to stay at the main house tonight," she said.

"Sheridan, wait—"

But she was already walking away from him. "I'll see you tomorrow."

Mac and Deacon's wedding day dawned foggy and cold, but by ten a.m. the sky cleared. And by the time the crowd was assembled near the lake on Redemption Ranch, bright, yellow sun was warming the world.

Sheridan had never seen a more beautiful bride than Mackenzie soon-to-be Cavanaugh. She'd helped her get ready that morning, and had deemed her amazing looking. But this was different. There was something magical, otherworldly about seeing her in her dress, her dark hair loose about her shoulders and flowers in her hair as she made her way up the aisle to Deacon.

And Deacon.

For years, her boss had been this brilliant-minded, incredible business mogul whom she admired. Now, he was her friend's husband. Or almost. And so obviously head over heels for her that it brought on true pangs of gratefulness from Sheridan. She wanted the best for the both of them.

As they said their vows under a billowing white awning, Sheridan's eyes lifted to find James. He stood directly across from her, and was looking at her too. They hadn't said much before the wedding, but she was hoping they could have a little time later.

A smile touched his lips then, and she returned it. Even though he was conflicted about so many things, he was happy for his brother and Mac.

"I now pronounce you husband and wife," Reverend McCarron intoned. "You may kiss your bride, Deacon."

Oh, hell, Deacon didn't need permission. Grinning, he took Mac into his arms and kissed her so thoroughly and for so long that everyone starting laughing and clapping. Sheridan felt tears behind her eyes. She'd grown so fond of her friend. Of

River Black. Of James. It was going to be hard to say good-bye. But it was looking like that was going to be her best choice. Her only choice.

After the ceremony, guests milled about, eating hors d'oeuvres and talking, listening to the Dixieland band Deacon had hired. It was all very festive, and Sheridan thought about joining in. She didn't see James anywhere. Maybe he'd ducked out early. She hoped not. She wanted to say good-bye to him face-to-face.

She took a few shrimp puffs from the tray and went in search of him. There were a lot of trees on the property and it was easy to hide yourself if you wanted to. But he was nowhere to be found. She was just heading back when she felt the hairs on the back of her neck lift. Then a hand reached out and grabbed her, and she was being pulled back into the trees.

For long seconds, she did nothing. Maybe because of the trauma of the last time. But she had her back to a tree trunk and a very disturbing face in front of her before she found her courage again.

"Hello, sweetheart," Caleb Palmer hissed, his breath vile.

"How . . . ?"

"My lawyer found a technicality." He grinned. "The asshole owed me."

Sheridan didn't wait to ask him anything more. She brought her knee up, ready to do some damage to his balls. But he was ready this time. He slammed her back against the tree and pressed his body against her. So tight it was hard to breathe.

His eyes flooded her own. "I should've killed you when I had the chance."

Sheridan turned her head and bit down on his hand. Hard. He released her for only a second, but it was enough to scream her head off. She stomped on his foot and was about to elbow him in the stomach when he whirled her around and put his hands around her neck.

"You're not going to testify against me, you uppity bitch."

One moment, she had no breath and the next, air rushed into her hungry lungs, and Palmer was being pulled off her. Her eyes fought to clear. And when they did, she saw that James had the man on the ground, his eyes murderous.

Twenty-four

"How the hell did you get out, you piece of shit?" James shouted, pressing right up against the man's face.

Rage unlike anything he'd ever experienced before blasted through him. He squeezed harder. Leaned closer. He swore he heard Sheridan behind him. She was saying something. Or was she yelling something?

He couldn't tell. All he wanted to hear was the breath leave this man's body in a rush, and for good. But he kept on talking.

"If you . . . kill me," Caleb Palmer wheezed.

James pressed his thumbs into the man's throat. "Oh, I'm going to kill you."

"Then . . ." He dragged in air. Or tried to. "You'll never know the truth . . ."

"The truth I know is that you're not getting out of jail again."

"The truth . . . about your sister," he rasped.

James's hands stilled, and his heart changed rhythm inside his ribs.

"What do you know?" he demanded. But when the man said nothing, James cuffed him across the face.

Palmer gasped and blood spilled from his lower lip.

"Speak, you miserable, cocksucking—"

"The truth about . . . who took Cass," Palmer managed to push out. "Who killed her."

Before he could say anything more, before he could force the bastard to continue, James felt Cole's hands on him. His younger brother pulled him up and off Palmer.

"Holy shit, man," Cole said as several male guests from the wedding came running into the clearing, heading straight for Caleb Palmer. "Maybe you should be the one fighting in the ring."

"Are you all right?" James asked her, his narrowed eyes running all over her as they stood near the steps, outside the bunkhouse. Checking, assessing.

"I'm fine," she assured him for the hundredth time.

"Again," he uttered through gritted teeth. "He went after you again."

The demons were back. In his eyes, in his soul.

"Yes," she agreed. "And you saved me."

For one blissful moment, she thought her words had penetrated that thick layer of self-doubt. But then he looked away. "Today," he muttered. "Right now."

"What does that mean?" she asked.

Around them, afternoon was coming to a close in several shades of orange and yellow. "What about tomorrow, Sheridan? Next month? Five years from now?"

She fought to understand him, but it wasn't easy. It was like he was trying to convince himself of something.

"I can't always be there," he said.

"For what?" she asked.

"To protect you."

Oh, Christ. "Of course you can't."

He turned back to her, took her face in his hands. His eyes implored her. "I love you."

Oh my God. Sheridan's heart dropped into her feet. Hell, maybe it dropped farther. Into the ground. It was the last thing she'd expected.

"Not just I 'think,' I do," he continued. "I do. When I found you after the storm . . ." He smiled a little. "I was caught. You held me, captivated me. I'd never in my life felt that kind of connection to a person. And every day those feelings have gotten stronger and more intense. That night at Marabelle's I knew I was in love with you."

"James . . ."

"But I also knew I couldn't keep putting you at risk."

"That is crazy!" she cried. "You're not making any sense. You're not putting me at risk by being with me. Why the hell do you think that?"

"It's me," he exploded. "Okay? It's fucking me!"

"What's you?"

He held her tightly. "Every woman I've ever loved, who's loved me, has either gotten hurt or died. Cass. My mother. Tori. I've failed to protect them all."

Sheridan's breath had stalled inside her lungs. "You can't believe this."

He looked utterly convinced.

"What about me? You love me. You didn't fail me."

He released her. "Yet."

For several seconds, Sheridan just stared at him, this broken man. "James, life is a risk. Doesn't matter who you're with or what you're doing. All of it is a risk."

"I'm not risking you." His nostrils flared and she swore she saw tears in his eyes. "You're going back to Dallas tomorrow."

Shock barreled through her. Hurt too. She bit her lip. "Why wait for tomorrow?" she uttered, turning away. "I'll have someone get my stuff tonight."

She left him there, in the patch of moonlight and his own misery, and headed up the hill to the main house. Yes, it was time to go home and stop fighting a losing battle. River Black and the first man she'd ever allowed herself to love had just broken her heart.

Twenty-five

"How the hell did he get out?" James demanded the second Deacon and Cole walked through the bunkhouse door. His eyes pierced Deacon. "I thought you'd had this taken care of."

"I thought so too," Deacon said, his expression grim. "But he's in for good now. Too many witnesses. He's been denied bail."

"I thought James was going to take him out," Cole remarked. "Palmer said something that shocked his system. What was it, J? Something about Sheridan?"

James eyed his big brother. "You should get back to your wife."

Deacon wasn't having it. Not this time. "Tell me," he commanded.

"One of us needs to get in to see Palmer."

"Why?" Deacon asked.

"It's not going to be you," Cole said to James.

"You'll kill the bastard. And then we'll be visiting you through bars."

"I won't kill him," James declared. "What he said to me"—he looked at both men—"was about Cass."

Both men looked startled.

"He claimed to know the truth about what happened."

"Fuck, I'm going to the jail right now," Cole announced, heading for the door. "That bastard will spill, or I'll spill."

"Stop," James said. "What we need to know first is if Hunter knows Palmer. If he ever questioned him back then. If he was ever a suspect."

Cole thought about this, then nodded. "I'll find out."

"Restraining order," Deacon reminded him.

"I remember."

James blew out a breath, faced Deacon. "Go now. You belong with Mac tonight."

He nodded, then paused and glanced around. "Where's Sheridan?"

Pain slashed through James, but he answered. "Heading back to Dallas."

Cole made an exasperated sound. "What a moron."

"I'm protecting her."

"You already did that."

"Not from Palmer, from myself."

Deacon and Cole exchanged a look. And after a

moment, both men dropped down on the couch, making it very obvious that they planned to stay awhile—or at least until James explained himself.

"Sheridan, you want to go to lunch today? There's a new sushi place that just opened up."

Sheridan glanced up from her computer, slightly disoriented. Valerie, one of the executive assistants from marketing who Sheridan knew was as ambitious as she was—and had been the one woman in the Cavanaugh Group to have asked her to go to lunch—stood over her. She glanced at her watch. Was it lunchtime already? She'd been working straight through since six a.m. She'd been doing that a lot in the past week. Anything to keep her mind off River Black and its occupants.

She gave Val an encouraging smile. "I'd love to."

The answer seemed to surprise the woman, since Sheridan rarely left the office for lunch—and never with coworkers. She just hadn't wanted the distraction. But things were different now. She was different. Having Mac in her life, realizing what it felt like to have true friendship—well, it had changed her. She wanted friendship. Maybe even love. Again.

Pain lashed at her insides. That bit would take a lot longer. If she could ever erase James from her mind, her soul. He was a tattoo on her heart now. And how did one erase that?

She grabbed her purse and headed out of the office to the elevators with Val.

"So, how was ranch country?" Val asked.

"Beautiful," Sheridan replied, hitting the button for the lobby.

"Can you imagine living there? No sushi restaurants close by, no Starbucks on the corner. How did you manage?"

Her mind filled with places and faces, all ones she had come to adore. "It has other things going for it."

"Like what?" Val's eyes glittered with interest. "Hot cowboys?"

Sheridan laughed. *Oh, God, yes.*

"You know, you seem different since you got back," Val observed. "You even look different. Maybe it's all that fresh air and cows."

"Horses," Sheridan corrected without thinking.

Val looked perplexed. "Pardon?"

"Fresh air and horses." Then she realized what she was saying and amended, "And of course there are cows too. It's a cattle ranch, after all."

"But you liked the horses, huh?" Val smiled knowingly as they exited the elevator and headed for the double doors.

Yes, she had liked the horses. But she'd loved the man who worked with them. Someday she'd be strong enough to go back there and visit. Who knew if James would still be around, but it would be worth—

Her thoughts, her breath, everything, it seemed, came to an abrupt halt the moment she stepped out onto the sidewalk. It wasn't possible. He wasn't there. It was her mind, her imagination running wild. She'd thought she'd seen him a hundred different times in a hundred different places around Dallas. And of course it was never him.

Sheridan's heart kicked inside her chest as she stared. Waiting on the street outside the Cavanaugh Group building were a horse and carriage. And who was sitting on top, reins in hand?

James Cavanaugh.

"Do you see him?" Sheridan asked Val.

The woman laughed. "I'd have to be blind not to. He's probably one of the hottest guys I've ever seen." She leaned in. "Next time you go back to that River Black, can I come along?"

Sheridan turned to look at her. "You knew about this?"

Val winked. "Have fun."

"How . . . ?"

"Our boss wants his brother happy. Even from his honeymoon in Madrid. I'm so glad you didn't say no this time." She smiled. "Lunch tomorrow?"

Sheridan nodded. "Yes, I'd like that."

James jumped down from the buggy and had his hand outstretched. "Can I take you for a ride, Miss O'Neil?"

Nerves working through her, Sheridan went to

him and allowed him to help her into the buggy and up onto the platform with him.

As they moved down the street, James glanced her way every couple of seconds. "When Cass was taken, we were at a movie theater. She asked each of us to go with her to the bathroom, but we were way too interested in the movie." His jaw tightened. "My mama understandably fell apart. She was angry and sick and she blamed us boys for what happened to her baby girl."

Sheridan held her breath as she listened. She didn't want anything to interrupt him.

"She told me that I was worthless, that I should've died instead of Cass. That what happened to her was my fault. I didn't know she was saying the same things to all of us. Hell, not until much later. I remember telling my young self it wasn't true. But obviously it got in there and did some damage. In college my fiancée, Tori, she was attacked. I wasn't there to protect her. I felt that pain and shame all over again. I felt I wasn't safe to be around."

Understanding moved over and through her. "I'm so sorry, James," she said.

"No, I'm the one who's sorry." He took her hand. "I love you so much, Sheridan. I was afraid of that. Of what it would do to me if I lost you. But then I realized the reality was a thousand times worse than the fear."

"Love is a risk," Sheridan said, her heart so full it was near bursting. "For all of us."

"Best risk ever."

She smiled, her eyes filling with tears.

"We could do what Mac and Deac are planning," he said. "Some time in River Black, some time here. I'm thinking more and more about that offer to shoot a series. *Horse Whisperer*."

"I think that sounds amazing. I'd love to see you in action."

"Maybe it could happen at the Triple C," he said.

She leaned in and kissed him. "I think at this point, anything can happen at the Triple C. Even a few small miracles."

"Don't want to marry you there, though," he said with a wide grin. "That's been done."

Fireworks were going off inside Sheridan, but she held back her squeal. "Where, then?"

"I don't know. First you have to tell me you will, then we can get to planning."

"Oh, I will, Mr. Cavanaugh," she said. "I most definitely will."

As James clucked the horse forward, he put his arm around Sheridan and pulled her close. Was it truly possible that in the city where she'd felt her most lonely, she now felt her most loved?

Twenty-six

Tossing the poop bag into a trash can, Grace Hunter headed back to her office. The night was a gorgeous one. A full moon, lots of stars, and a light breeze. Belle liked it too. The dog was prancing as she walked across the parking lot. And that was a very hard thing for a basset hound to accomplish. But just as they passed a clump of bushes, she stopped.

Grace's heart leapt in fear, then promptly flared in anger as she spied Cole Cavanaugh stepping out of the shadows.

"I can have you arrested, you know." she said.

He gave her a charming smile. "You'd do that to Belle's future papa?"

"You're never getting your hands on this dog."

He shrugged as he walked toward her. "I don't know. She's already smitten. It's what I do with the ladies."

She made a face. "You're gross and arrogant, and just a . . ."

"What, Doc?" he asked. "What am I?"

"Well, you're a criminal now."

He took a deep breath. "Does any part of you understand why this is so important to me? She was my twin, Grace."

Two heat spots erupted on her cheeks. "It doesn't give you the right to do what you did."

Her words hit their mark, and he nodded. "You're right. But I was desperate."

"And what did your desperation do for you? You went there, you saw him, you learned nothing. I told you he was losing his grip on reality, but you—"

"Not nothing," he interrupted.

Her eyes narrowed. "What do you mean?"

"'That boy should've never come to River Black.'" Cole's brow lifted. "Does that mean anything to you? Do you know who that boy was that he was talking about?"

"I have to go. Don't follow me."

"Grace, please. He said this to James right after my brother asked him about Cass's murder. We think it might be a boy my sister called 'Sweet.'"

She kept walking, her face tense. So was her grip on Belle's leash.

"Please just ask him if he knows that name!" Cole called out, desperate once again. "Ask him if he knows Caleb Palmer."

This time, she stopped, frozen in place. "Caleb Palmer's in jail," she said.

"He got out. Attacked Sheridan O'Neil again."

She turned, her expression horror-struck. "Oh my God. I hadn't heard. I was out on a call. Is she okay?"

Cole nodded. "But when he and James were wrestling, he said something. Said that if James killed him, he'd never know the truth about Cass's murder."

Shaking her head, Grace looked away, then back at him.

"What is it?" Cole asked.

"Caleb Palmer was my dad's best friend."

Acknowledgments

Thank you to my wonderful family for their love and support.

And to my New American Library family, as well. Especially my editor, Danielle Perez. Keep kicking my butt, darlin'. ☺

Maria Carvainis, you rock!

And to my first and most beloved dog, Bud. Thank you for fifteen amazing years. I miss you every day.

Don't miss the next novel in
the Cavanaugh Brothers series
by Laura Wright,

BRASH

On sale from Signet Eclipse in March 2015.

Diary of Cassandra Cavanaugh

May 5, 2002

Dear Diary,

I think Sweet's right. Someone is following us. This is what happened. I was at the drugstore today after school. I was hoping maybe Sweet would come in because I haven't seen or heard from him in three days. And it is where we first locked eyes and all. I really wanted to know why he didn't meet me the other night like he said he was going to. I wanted to know if it was because of the kiss. I practiced it on my hand a couple of times, and I didn't think it was all that bad. Well, he did come in. He was buying all sorts of strange things like headache medicine and soap. He looked surprised to see me. But when I went up to him, he smiled his amazing smile and told me he'd meet me behind the diner in ten minutes.

Diary, I waited for a half hour, and he didn't come. Why would he do that? Did something happen to him? Does he just not like me anymore?

My brain tells me to hate him, but my heart tells my brain to shut up. Who do I listen to?

Stupid boys.

Okay, here's the weird part. When I was walking over to the diner, I felt someone's eyes on me. I looked all around and didn't see no one. But I swear they were there! What if it's one of my brothers?

Maybe they discovered what we've been doing.

I could ask 'em? Or talk to Mac? Waaaaaa! I'm so confused. I hate how my heart feels right now. Heavy and broken.

Cass

Cole Cavanaugh watched as Johnny Blair dropped his needle into the red ink, then resumed his special brand of torture.

"You going to tell me what this stands for, man?" Johnny asked, working the final curve of a C on Cole's shoulder. "Or do I need to guess?"

Cole smirked at the Austin-based artist who had inked nearly every one of his tats. "Guess away, brother."

Black brows lifted over pale green eyes. "Woman's initials?"

Cole snorted. "Hell no."

The guy chuckled, the two small studs in his lower lip flattening against his teeth. "Your next victim in the ring?"

"Nah, man. That joker's blood on my knuckles is all the stain I need." He glanced down at the finished artwork. "These three Cs are for the ranch where I grew up."

Johnny placed the tat gun on the metal side table beside Cole's chair. "I didn't know you were a ranch boy, Cavanaugh."

"Born and bred."

"And now branded," the man said as he cleaned Cole's skin, then slathered some A&D ointment on it.

"Let's get to bandaging," Cole said, not wanting to get any further into discussions about the Triple C, and how he had grown up, and why he'd left. Some shit needed to stay private outside River Black. "I have training in an hour."

Johnny shook his head, but grabbed the bandages and tape. "Will it do any good if I tell you to wait until tomorrow? Give this some time to heal?"

"Thirteen tats and I've never had a problem."

"Fine," Johnny said. "I'm gonna wrap it up extra good, but if someone knocks you there, it's going to hurt like a motherfucker."

"I'm counting on it," Cole said without thinking.

"Damn," Johnny said, fitting the bandage. "Had no idea you were such a masochist, man."

He wasn't. Not really. Well, maybe in the beginning right after he'd left home—gone underground. Maybe then he'd wanted to feel the pain. Hell, maybe he'd thought he deserved it. But now . . . He eyed the tattoo artist. "Just makes my adrenaline rush. Heightens my awareness. Fuels the fight."

"When is your match?" Johnny asked him.

"Next week."

"Who you beatin' down?"

"Fred Fontana."

The man's head came up fast. "Oh, shit."

Oh, shit, indeed. Fred Omega Fontana had a rep for nearly killing anything that stepped into the ring with him. He was the one bastard Cole had yet to beat. But Cole fully intended to end that streak next week.

"You ready?" Johnny asked him as he pushed back in his chair and stripped off his gloves. "Physically? Mentally? All that shit?"

"Hell yeah," Cole said convincingly.

But it was all show. And, boy, did he need to put on a show. The fire and fury that normally pulsed in his blood this close to a fight weren't there. Maybe too much had happened at the Triple C—too much up in the air. Too many damn memories assaulting him at every turn. It was why he'd gotten the Triple C brand inked into his skin. He was hoping it would put that wicked heat back into his gut and heart. Because, fuck him, if he didn't, not only was he going to lose hope that he'd ever discover the truth about his sister's death, but he might very well lose his life in the ring next week.

"You have issues, Belle," Grace Hunter told her passenger, an aging basset hound who had just howled her damn head off as they drove past the Triple C ranch.

And it wasn't the first time.

Any time Belle was within spitting distance of where Cole Cavanaugh hung his hat, the dog howled.

Grace glanced over at the pup sitting on her cute rump, buckled in, staring out the open window. "He's not interested in you, Miss Girl. He was only out for information."

Belle ignored the reminder that Cole Cavanaugh's visit to the vet clinic a few days ago—under the pretense that he wanted to adopt the basset hound—was a lie. As soon as Grace had slipped out of the office, that rat bastard had gone through her drawers and found out where her father was living.

"He hasn't been back in days," she told Belle as she got onto the highway. "Probably off practicing for that bloodbath he calls a job." She grimaced at the thought. "You don't want that kind of guy buying your kibble, now, do you?"

This time, Belle turned to look at her.

"Someone who beats people up for a livin'?" Grace asked.

The basset hound barked.

"Yeah, yeah, I know he's good-looking and unpredictable, and charming in an overbearing way." Grace continued. "But let me tell you from experience: that combination is nothing but trouble."

Belle seemed unconvinced, and once again turned to look out the window.

"Fine. Don't say I didn't warn you. And when he breaks your heart, don't come crying to me." Oh, who was she kidding? Sweet Belle could come crying to her, and Grace would take her in her arms and let her know it was okay. Then later, when they were sharing a pint of ice cream, she would gently tell the canine that if she wanted a real future with someone who would be there for her through thick and thin, she needed to look for stable instead of stunning, reliable instead of reactive. And instead of inked-up skin and hard waves of muscles, a balanced, tender, soulful heart.

She pulled off the highway and headed toward the center of town. Speaking of tender hearts, she was going to see her dad today. See if she could get him to clear up this mess with Caleb Palmer. Her father's best friend had claimed he knew something about Cass Cavanaugh's abduction and murder. What was he thinking? she mused darkly as she turned into the Barrington Ridge Senior Care parking lot and found a space. And God, could that actually be true? Granted, the man was not the same one she'd known as a child. In fact, he'd turned into a monster. He'd hurt Sheridan O'Neil, and Grace prayed he would never get out of the jail cell he was in now. But what she was really interested in was clearing her father's name. Making sure everyone knew that he wasn't connected to Caleb's actions. Hell, she didn't want him connected to Caleb in any way, if she could help it. No visits, no phone calls. Maybe then she could finally get the Cavanaughs off her back.

With Belle leashed and walking beside her, Grace entered the front door of the care facility. Gentle piano music played from the speakers overhead, and she could smell the combination of cleaning products and breakfast foods. The care facility had cleared her request to bring Belle along. Her dad had owned a dog for many years—one that had been at his side nearly day and night—and Grace was hopeful that the canine would stir his memory. Or at the very least keep him calm and lucid.

"Awww, ain't she sweet?" called one of the nurses as they passed by.

"Hiya, Grace," another called out.

"Morning, Bev," Grace returned cheerfully. She pointed to her father's door. "He awake?"

Beverly nodded. "Just finished his breakfast 'bout ten minutes ago."

"Thanks," Grace said, moving down the corridor as Belle tried to sniff every inch of the floor, wall, and desks.

Bright sunlight welcomed Grace as she entered the room. As usual, her father was seated at the small table near the window. He liked the light and the breeze, just as he had at home. His nose was in a magazine, and he was flipping through the pages at lightning speed.

"What are we reading today, Dad?" she asked, coming over and slipping into one of the chairs beside him. "Fishing or dirt bike racing?"

Peter Hunter glanced up and smiled. "Gracie?"

Grace's heart ballooned inside her chest. Every time she walked into his room, she wondered if his eyes would flash with warm recognition or cool disinterest.

"Hi, Dad," she said with gentle warmth. This was the man who had tucked her into bed at night. Told her stories about his adventures as sheriff. Protected her, loved her, treated her like she was the most special thing in the world. Made her believe she could be anything she wanted to be. She reached for his hand and gave it a squeeze.

"Who's the mongrel?"

She grinned. "This is Belle. She's a friend of mine."

Her father reached down and gave the basset hound a pat on the head. Suddenly his face fell. "She looks about as miserable as I feel."

A fist squeezed her heart. "Why are you miserable, Dad?"

He looked up at her. His eyes were no longer crystal clear. "I have a job to do, Gracie," he explained, his chin lifting in that way it always did when he talked about his work as a sheriff. "People out there who need me."

God, it hurt her so much to hear him talk about the past as though it was the present. There was nothing she could do. Nothing except protect his good name.

"Dad, I need you to tell me about Mr. Palmer," she began gently.

His dark brows rose. "Caleb?"

She nodded.

"Well, he is my very best friend, honey." A hint of a smile played about his lips. "Good man. Right good man. Always there for me. That's how friends should be. Don't you forget that."

Grace reached down and started stroking Belle's head. "He's done something very bad."

Her father didn't even hesitate before answering, "No, no, baby. Not him."

"Yes, Dad," she insisted. "He hurt a woman."

That snagged his attention. He sat back in his chair, looking utterly dumbstruck for a moment. Then he gasped. "Lord Almighty, he takin' the blame for that, is he?"

"He admitted it, Dad. There were witnesses and a police report. And the woman's going to testify against him."

A sad smile touched the man's mouth. "How can she, baby? She's dead."

A boulder the size of Texas rolled through Grace at his words. She wasn't exactly sure why, but she wanted, more than anything, to get up and walk out. Not ask him anything and not hear anything.

But she had to, didn't she? "Who are you talking about, Dad?"

"That girl, Gracie dear." His gaze dropped to his magazine, and he started thumbing through the pages once again. "Cass Cavanaugh."

Also available from
New York Times bestselling author

LAURA WRIGHT

Branded
The Cavanaugh Brothers

When the Cavanaugh brothers return home to River Black, Texas, for their father's funeral, they discover unexpected evidence of the old man's surprising double life—a son named Blue, who wants the Triple C Ranch as much as they do. The eldest son, Deacon, a wealthy businessman, is looking to use his powerful connections to stop Blue at any cost. He never expected the ranch's forewoman, Mackenzie Byrd, to get in his way.

Mac knows Deacon means to destroy the ranch and therefore destroy her livelihood. But as the two battle for control, their attraction to each other builds. Now Deacon is faced with the choice of a lifetime: Take down the Triple C to feed his need for revenge, or embrace the love of the one person who has broken down every barrier to his heart.

"A sexy hero, a sassy heroine, and a compelling storyline...I loved it!"
—*New York Times* bestselling author Lorelei James

Available wherever books are sold or at
penguin.com